Tales of the Were ~ Redstone Clan

Bobcat

BIANCA D'ARC

DEDICATION

To my family, who continue to support my crazy dream of being a published author. It's been a wild ride and I couldn't have done it without you.

A special thank you to Peggy McChesney and Anna-Marie Chaconas Buchner, two incredibly supportive friends I have met though this wonderful journey of writing. I've really met some nice people through writing and going to conventions. You guys are great!

CHAPTER ONE

Bob wasn't usually sent on important away missions for the family, but in recent months all his older brothers had gotten hitched and they were sticking close to home. Or at least, close to their mates. They were all in the blissful honeymoon phase of their relationships and frankly, it was getting a little annoying. Everybody at home was all lovey-dovey all the time. It made a single guy want to puke.

Okay. Maybe not puke. Bob was really happy for his brothers. Nobody deserved happiness more than they did, but it was getting a little hard to watch. Mostly because Bob was feeling kind of lonely.

Before, he'd be able to call one of his brothers to go out on the prowl and get a few beers any night of the week. Now, of course, they were all busy with their new mates. The eldest, Grif, had always been busier than anyone else because of his role as Alpha. He led one of the biggest shifter Clans in the States. Redstone Construction wasn't just the family business. It was a collection of many different kinds of shifters, all working together under the banner of the Redstone family and Clan.

The second-oldest, Steve, was the badass head of security. He'd been mated for a few months now. He'd met his half-water sprite mate only a little after Grif had come home from a trip to Wyoming with his own cougar shifter mate. Both of them were busy with Clan affairs all the time, and now they had mates to consider. Sure, the middle brother, Magnus, was still available to hang out during the day when his new mate, who was a vampiress, was asleep. But it just wasn't the same.

The youngest brother, Matt, was still single, but he was usually off in California, running a few critical construction jobs for the company, and hanging out with his vampire buddies in the Napa Valley. Bob felt like the odd man out. The only single guy who stayed close to home.

But that had changed suddenly when Grif asked him to go north to act as the Clan's liaison with the Lords. It was just what he needed—a little break from all the happy domestication of home. Maybe he'd get a chance to have a little fun and make new friends among the shifters that gathered around the Lords—the two most powerful werewolves in North America.

Every shifter in the States answered to those two guys. They were identical twins who had been designated from birth to be this generation's leaders. Twin births were rare among shifters. Identical twins were almost unheard of. But once in each generation, a pair of identical twins was born who were destined to be that generation's Lords.

The current Lords were Rafe and Tim. Bob had met them for the first time yesterday when he'd arrived in their territory. He'd been nervous about it. It wasn't everyday he met shifter royalty.

The Lords were wolves this time around. It varied. Bob got along well with the werewolf Packs in the Redstone Clan. In fact, he was probably on better terms with most of them than any of his brothers because a lot of them worked directly for him on the work crews he managed. He'd gotten to know a bit more about wolf habits than his brothers, and it was easy to apply that knowledge when he met the Lords.

But he shouldn't have worried. The Lords were great guys from everything he'd seen so far. Their people were happy and well organized. That spoke well for the men who ruled over them all. And the shifters here were welcoming, though they seemed to want to get to know Bob better before they trusted him with the keys to the kingdom.

That was cool with Bob. He'd have felt the same if one of them had come to his territory. It took a while to build trust between shifters. They had to sniff each other out a bit first before they could extend more than a basic welcome. Bob hadn't expected anything different.

The fact that they'd given him a cabin of his own, and permission to prowl a decent section of forest on their mountain, spoke well for them. They obviously wanted the representative from Redstone to feel welcome. Bob could have done a lot worse. As it was, he had a nice log cabin to call home for the next few weeks and a new forest to explore.

It was cold out there, which he looked forward to. Las Vegas was great, and the desert did get cold at night, but up here in the mountains…this was the kind of terrain Bob really liked. Lots of cover. Trees, rocks, fresh running streams filled with fish. Bob couldn't wait to shift into his fur and do a little claw fishing.

A grizzly shifter had shown Bob to the cabin right after he'd finished his initial meeting with the Lords. It was late in the day and the bear—an affable guy named Rocky—showed him the path to the cabin, which was lower down the mountain from the bear's home. Strategically, it was placed at a much lower elevation than the Lords' place, up near the peak, and the bear made it known that he and his mate, not to mention his bear-shifter parents inhabited the two closest homes to the cabin. No doubt, it was a not-so-subtle message that a bunch of grizzlies stood between Bob and the Lords. His actions would be watched by some of the most powerful shifters in the woods.

That was okay with Bob. He didn't have any intention of doing anything wrong. Far from it. He would work hard for his Clan while he was here and enjoy the wilderness. It had been far too long since he'd had time to prowl new grounds and his inner cat couldn't wait to discover what he might find just outside the cabin's door.

The place was wired for internet, phone and cable television. All the modern conveniences, including a small kitchen and comfortable looking king sized bed. It may be just a cabin, but it had all the amenities a bachelor could want. Especially a bachelor who craved the wilderness just beyond his front door.

Bob stowed his gear, then stripped quickly. It was time to check the perimeter and make himself acquainted with his animal neighbors. The local wildlife was about to learn there was a new cougar in town and though it was only temporary, the cat inside him had a need to check things out and scratch some trees, maybe mark them in other ways that humans didn't like to hear about. This was Bob's territory for the next few weeks. It was time to let the wild cousins know it.

Bob opened the front door, placing his clothes in a neat pile just inside. He'd shift on the porch when he came back, though the handles on the doors were the type that a cat's paw could easily push down and open. That was pretty standard for shifter accommodations. All the homes in the Clan's neighborhood had them.

He closed the door and turned to survey the area. Not a soul in sight. His sensitive ears didn't pick up any sounds except the rustle of leaves and normal forest sounds. Bob shifted, feeling his muscles stretch and reform, his bones slide into the new configuration with a blur of magic. A moment later, he was the cat. A full-grown, adult male cougar. Although Bob had always liked the name *mountain lion* a bit better. It made him feel sort of majestic. And he was now in the mountains, after all.

Bob nosed around the area by the porch steps. There were two simple wooden steps up onto the low porch. The cabin was dark wood. No paint marred the natural look of the place, and it blended beautifully into its surroundings—as did most of the buildings he'd seen so far. Whoever the architect was, he or she was a genius with blending the shapes and colors of the homes into their environments.

Bob's sensitive nose picked up traces of the bear shifter who'd walked with him to the cabin. He could also smell old trails left by passersby. The faint scent of a human female had been in the cabin as well. Probably the person who'd prepared the place for his arrival. He'd have to remember that scent and if he ran across her, he'd thank her.

He moved out a bit from the steps and picked up other scents. Most of them were old, but one was tantalizingly fresh. And cat. Not cougar, but something similar. Wild. Furry. Feline. And very, very female.

Hmm. This would bear further investigation. He wanted to know more about this female who had pranced right across his new territory in the last fifteen minutes. He set off to follow the trail, enjoying the hunt. Bob, both in his cat form and in his human form, liked to play, and this might prove to be a fun game. If nothing else, it would help him learn the territory a bit and maybe he'd meet a pretty woman. She smelled young, but definitely adult. Ripe. Delicious. Like salted caramel and honey—two of his favorites.

Bob felt a strange imperative inside himself to find her. Such a heavenly-smelling female shouldn't be out wandering alone. Especially not when there were strangers in town— meaning himself. Though Bob didn't know for sure. There could be other visitors to the area besides him.

Unless that's what she wanted. Maybe the feline female was looking for a little excitement with a new guy? Bob quickened his pace. Never let it be said he turned down a willing, playmate. Even if she wasn't exactly a cougar.

When he found her a few minutes later by the stream that wound around the back of the cabin, he realized exactly what she was. He laughed, but in his cat form it came out more like a huffing sound. If he wasn't much mistaken, the lovely, spotted lady with the tufted ears was a bobcat.

Serena's head swiveled when she heard the sound of another cat. Scratch that. A *big* cat. The feline watching her was a full-sized—and then some—adult male mountain lion.

A shiver of fear passed over her skin and made her back arch as she hissed involuntarily. The cougar, standing about ten yards behind her on the crest of a rise took a step back in what looked like surprise.

Yeah, so, she'd overreacted. She was in the Lords' territory. She was safe from any shifter found prowling here. Or at least, they'd promised her she would be. She shouldn't still be so skittish.

But she was. She couldn't help it. Fear was something that had been learned over time. It wouldn't dissipate overnight.

She tried to take deep breaths and consciously loosen her stiff muscles and arched back. Making her fur lie flat was a little harder, but when the mountain lion didn't come any closer and didn't seem angry, she was able to master her reaction. Little by little, she calmed.

The mountain lion just sat there, on his haunches, his head tilted quizzically to the side as he watched her. After a few minutes of just looking at each other, he stood up and took a tentative step toward her. Serena stood her ground. She was safe. She was on the Lords' lands. If she wasn't safe here, then she wasn't safe anywhere. Right?

She consciously kept her breathing as even as possible as the big cat slowly approached. His head was still tilted, his long tail waggling a little behind him. His paws were massive compared to hers, his size at least double hers. His coat was shiny and looked soft, his fur not quite the length and depth of hers. And he didn't have spots. He was the tawny color of his kind. Like burnished gold. Very pretty.

But he was huge and she felt very vulnerable. She sniffed as he drew closer, but she didn't recognize anything about his scent. He smelled a little of sand, which was odd. Unless…maybe he was the visitor she had been told might be arriving today. A shifter from Nevada, the wolves at the Pack house had said, though she didn't know what kind of shifter.

Well, if this cat was the visitor, Serena knew now what creature shared his soul.

And having figured out the most logical answer for who he might be, she was able to gain a little more calm. She stood her ground as he got closer and was able to remain stationary when he stretched out a big paw toward her.

He didn't touch. In fact, he stopped coming closer and sat quietly on his haunches, waiting for her response. Taking a deep breath, Serena allowed the cat in her soul to respond to the bigger feline. She reached out with her smaller paw and batted at his.

He allowed it, batting back gently. Allowing her to set the pace for their encounter.

Next, he lowered his head and sniffed at her, coming very close. She allowed it, sniffing him as well. He smelled deliciously dangerous to her feline instincts. Not the same as the male bobcats she had known, but still feline and very male. His scent didn't remind her of bad times, as the scent of her own kind did now. Instead, the decidedly cougar aroma was just foreign enough to not trigger bad memories, but the feline edge of his musk made her feel surprisingly comfortable around him.

Serena didn't think she'd ever feel comfortable around a male cat again, but this big, gentle giant seemed to be proving her wrong. And she didn't even know his name. In fact, she'd never even seen his man form. But his cat was impressive. She'd bet his human form was the same.

Not that she'd go out of her way to find out. She had been through a lot in the past few months. She'd come here to heal and didn't intend to get involved with any males while she was here—or any time in the foreseeable future, for that matter. She'd had enough of men for a while.

But she admitted to being a little lonely. Sure, she liked to prowl alone, but not all the time. Sometimes it was fun to have a fellow cat to share the wilderness with. Just to play. Cats loved to play and it was hard to play by yourself all the time. Eventually, even loners wanted someone to share a few moments of innocent fun with.

So she stood still while the bigger cat sniffed at her and

then butted his head against her. It was a feline thing she understood well. Working up her nerve, she did the same to him, and then raised her paw to boop him on the nose.

He batted at her smaller paw, but he wasn't fast enough. She scooted backward and nearly landed in the small stream. Twisting and yowling a bit, she scooted away to avoid getting wet. The mountain stream was *cold*. Fine for lapping at with a thirsty tongue, but her human side preferred to bathe in a nice, hot shower.

The cougar seemed to laugh at her antics as she settled on her haunches about three feet from her previous position. Even she had to admit, she'd probably looked funny. She reached up with her paw and waggled her stubby tail.

The cougar stopped to nose around the stream a bit before taking a drink. The waters here were clear and fresh. The Lords made sure they were kept that way so the shifters and their wild cousins could enjoy the streams and pools in their territory without fear of becoming ill. There were also a lot of fish in this waterway, but Serena hadn't done much fishing. She had made it a point to take her meals in her human form since she had been here, eating at the communal tables in the wolves' Pack house.

She had taken her turn cooking for those same tables too. Everyone in the Pack chipped in on the labor to keep the Pack house up and running. It was a vital resource for their little community and they'd been amazing to her since allowing her to stay there.

The cougar twitched his tail and jerked his head in invitation to walk with him. She was confident in her own speed and knew she could always outrun him if he turned out to be just another male on the make, so she followed along. They walked through the woods behind the old cabin at a leisurely pace. He stopped once in a while to stretch, rub his fur along the bark of trees and scratch his long claws into them, making deep gouges.

He was marking his new territory, she realized belatedly. He had to be a high-level visitor if they gave him the best guest cabin to stay in. When Serena had arrived, there had been a visiting Alpha from one of the big wolf Packs in the northeastern part of the country staying there. He had left, and then a few days ago her new friend Maggie, Rocky's human mate, had cleaned the place and prepared it for its next occupant.

Serena hadn't realized the shifter from Nevada would be staying there, but it seemed logical based on the cougar's actions. They walked companionably up and down the little hills and valleys created by the stream. He rubbed against her once or twice and she allowed it after an initial moment of unease. She batted at him when he tried to get closer and he seemed to take the rebuke with easy amusement.

And then they came up on one of the deeper holes fed by the stream. The cougar seemed to perk up as he examined the water from the very edge of the pond. There were plenty of fish in there and they seemed to have caught his attention.

When he pounced, landing in the water with a joyful, deadly splash, she could tell he was enjoying himself. His head dipped below the water line for a moment and then came up with a big fish in his mouth. He paddled for a while, then reached an area near the bank where he could stand on his hind legs, the rest of him buoyant in the murky water. His front paws lifted out of the water and he had another, slightly smaller fish in them. He lobbed it toward the bank and it landed at her feet, wriggling. She put one paw on it to prevent it from sliding back down the bank as he trotted out of the pond, tail swishing.

He dropped the fish in his mouth alongside the other one and then walked a few feet away to shake out his coat. Considerate of him, though she still felt a tiny bit of the water spray as he shook himself. She watched the fish, wondering if he was going to chomp on them raw.

Her bobcat didn't turn its nose up at raw food. In fact, there were times when she preferred to hunt her meals in the forest, but lately she'd been trying to overcome her more primitive desires. She'd been trying very hard to reconnect with her human half. Eating cooked food was one step on that path. She'd been careful not to eat raw meat since coming here and she thought it was helping her on her road to recovery.

But the fish looked good. Really good. Still, she didn't know if this big male would share his catch with her. His actions seemed to indicate he was offering the smaller fish to her, but she didn't want to presume.

She was looking at the fish when she felt the unmistakable tingle of shifter magic. The cougar had transformed.

Serena raised her chin and got her first good look at the man who had worn the cougar's fur. He was a knockout. Hands down. Hot, hot, hot. Even her cat could appreciate his male perfection.

Blond hair on his head and around the part that seemed to perk up under her scrutiny. Oh yeah, he was *definitely* male. In a very emphatic way.

His body was beautifully honed. Like a sculptor had gone nuts creating the perfect male specimen—a specimen that had muscles in all the right places, including the most impressive six-pack she'd ever seen.

As a shifter, Serena was used to seeing nicely shaped, muscular bodies. Most shifters benefitted from the active lifestyles of their animal halves. Most were in good shape and good looking due to a blessing of genetics. This man, though… He was way beyond her experience.

"Hey there." His voice was gentle, as if he was aware of her skittishness now that he'd shifted shape. "Do you want to eat this raw or shall I cook it up for us back at the cabin?"

Neither option appealed to her sense of self-preservation. There was a third option though he hadn't mentioned it. She stared at him, blinking slowly. He'd get the message that she didn't want to talk when she stayed in her fur.

"I'm Robert Redstone, by the way. You can call me Bob." He sighed. "I guess you don't want to talk, eh? That's all right. I just wanted you to know I enjoyed prowling with you. I've never actually met a bobcat before, though people have

10

called me that for years. It started as a joke because my name is Bob and well…I'm a cat." He shrugged and she couldn't help but be a little affected by his natural charm. She was getting the idea that this powerful shifter was about as far from the strong, silent type as you could get. That was fine with her. It made him somehow less of a threat, even though he was still way bigger than her. "If you want to stick around and maybe take your human form later," he went on with a gentle tone of hope in his voice, "I'll cook up these fish for us."

She was tempted, but she really couldn't take the chance. This man was very appealing but it was too soon. She'd only just started to be able to stay in her human form for more than a few days at a time. She'd come here to heal. She hadn't come here to get involved with the first pretty cat-man that strolled across her path. That could only lead to trouble. And she'd had enough of that for a lifetime.

Serena bent down and took the slightly smaller fish in her teeth, then stood on all four feet. It was a clear sign of refusal he should understand. She looked at him once more.

He shook his head slowly, just once, his expression a bit deflated, but not quite defeated. "Okay then. But the offer stands as long as I'm here. I'd like to see you again, kitten." His final words were said in a low voice that sent tingles down her spine, but she refused to allow this smooth-tongued devil to make her stray from her chosen course.

With a surge of his magic and a blur of energy, he resumed his cougar shape, taking the larger fish between his teeth once again. Together, they walked back toward the cabin at a leisurely pace. It was as if he didn't really want their encounter to end, and she had to admit—if only in the privacy of her own mind—neither did she. Not really.

He was the most handsome man she'd ever seen up close and his feline form was impressive, to say the least. His presence impacted her on many levels and made her feel the cold shiver of excitement along with the warm impractical belief that somehow, even though she didn't really know him at all, she was safe with this man. He exuded confidence and a calming power that made her feel comfortable with him in a way she hadn't felt comfortable with any male in a very long time. It was something to ponder.

When they reached the short path that led to the front door of his cabin, Bob tossed his fish onto the slightly raised front porch with a quick jerk of his head. His jaws were larger than hers and rather impressive, and he'd already proven he was a good hunter—at least in the water.

Bob paused for a moment to rub his head against hers in a sort of feline farewell that she allowed. She even returned the gesture with somewhat shyer motions. She didn't want to give him the wrong idea, but she also didn't want him to think she was either stuck up or angry with him. So she stood and allowed the touch for a moment or two, trying not to skitter away or respond too enthusiastically. Either was a possibility with her unstable emotions in play.

She was rather proud of herself for standing her ground, and when he finally stepped away from her, she was able to leave him with her head held high. Serena scampered away from the cabin and headed toward the building that had become her refuge and salvation, the fish still held in her mouth. She would drop it in the kitchen, then go to her room to dress and then go back down to the kitchen, to fry up the fresh fish that had been the first gift a man had given her in too many years to count.

A spontaneous gift that expected nothing in return. It was a beautiful concept. And though a fish wasn't exactly chocolate or roses, it appealed to the predator in her soul. The strong male had gifted her with the means to survive. Sustenance. It was a basic survival instinct that impressed her inner bobcat with the skill of the male who had been able to provide for her.

Her bobcat liked the cougar, even if he was a different species. Goddess knew, she'd had enough grief and terror from bobcat males to turn her off them permanently. Serena had thought any feline male would be a problem for her going forward, but apparently cougars were just different enough. And this particular cougar male had impressed her both in his fur and with his friendly words and accepting nature when he'd shifted and spoken to her.

Serena padded into the kitchen of the Pack house and dropped her fish on a low platter left out for just such instances. Many within the wolf Pack hunted and delivered their excess to the Pack house, to provide for those that needed the help of their community. The concept of the Pack house was something unique to wolves, but the Lords had welcomed Serena to stay there while she recovered, extending the hospitality of their Pack as well as the wider community of shifters that surrounded them. It was an honor she didn't take lightly.

Going up the stairs on paws she'd been careful to wipe off on the doormat, Serena stayed in her fur until she entered the room she'd been assigned. It was a suite, really. There was an attached bathroom that was fully stocked with necessities, and even a few frivolous things like bubble bath. Serena had discovered she really loved bubble baths. She took one almost every night, finding they helped her relax enough to sleep in her human form.

With a quick burst of her magic, she shifted to her two-legged version and went into the bathroom. A quick shower was in order. She'd been prowling around in the woods all day and would present herself clean and tidy in the kitchen. It was her turn to help cook anyway. She would be able to prepare her fish just the way she liked it, as well as pitch in with the communal meal. Win-win.

Serena smiled as she dressed a few minutes later, having finished her quick dousing. She paused a moment to savor the feeling. She hadn't had much to smile about in recent years. It was definitely a nice sensation. She had to believe that the encounter with Bob the cougar had a lot to do with her suddenly positive mood.

It was sort of shocking. A male feline was responsible for her smile. It was something she wouldn't have believed before meeting the cougar.

A cougar who had admitted, somewhat sheepishly, that his nickname was Bobcat.

CHAPTER TWO

Bob really tried to keep his curiosity to himself the next day when he interacted with one of the Lords' top lieutenants, but he couldn't help himself. He was working with the grizzly bear shifter, Rocco Garibaldi. Everyone called him Rocky, he'd said, as Bob started to work on filling in some of the tiny details left out of written reports. All of the recent encounters with *Venifucus* agents in Las Vegas had been reported up the chain of command to the Lords.

Basically, Bob was here to fill in the blanks that were inevitable in a written account. He was allowing himself to be questioned in minute detail about recent events, starting with his mother's murder and leading up to the time he'd been dispatched to meet with the Lords.

Bob knew what he'd been in for. His brothers had warned him. He had expected to be grilled, and knew it was for the good of everyone. The Lords and their people needed every little detail—no matter how inconsequential it might seem—to be fully understood and recorded by one of their people. Rocky and several other trusted lieutenants, along with the Lords themselves, were analyzing every shred of data from around the world, piecing together every small clue. They were trying to figure out where the *Venifucus* might strike next. They were also trying to stop any attacks before more shifters were hurt or killed.

It was a worthy goal and one Bob could really get behind. That's why he'd agreed to be the one sent here when Grif had asked. His oldest brother and the Alpha of their Clan had given him the choice. Grif had *asked* Bob to go. He hadn't ordered him to do it, which he easily could have.

But all three of his older brothers were newly mated and he hadn't wanted any of them to have to travel, worrying about the safety of their women—all of whom had faced danger of one kind or another in recent months. Those newlyweds deserved a little peace, if at all possible.

Their youngest brother, Matt, could have gone, but he was in the midst of some tricky details on a project he had been supervising since its inception in California. At this particular time, it would have been especially tough to take Matt away from it. The company that was the lifeblood of their Clan needed Matt where he was for now. Others could have been sent, but Bob knew it was important to show proper respect to the Lords. Sending an actual Redstone—one of the brothers and not merely a cousin or something—was a show of good faith.

So Bob had agreed. He'd liked the idea of travel. Cats, in general, liked to roam and he was no exception. He had outfitted his favorite SUV with all sorts of gadgetry and driven the distance from Nevada to Montana, enjoying seeing the sights along the way.

Now that he was there, in Montana, he was glad he'd been the one available for Grif to appoint. The Lords' domain was like nothing Bob had ever seen. They had an entire mountain to themselves and their people roamed at will through the forest. It was a place like no other, where shifters could just *be*. No worries about being seen by humans. No hassles of everyday life—at least not that he'd seen.

For Bob, the place was like a holiday camp. He was pretty sure it wasn't that way for the folks who lived here full-time, but the snug little cabin and idyllic woodland setting sure made Bob feel like he was on vacation. Until the questioning started in earnest.

The first day, Bob worked exclusively with Rocky. They went through half of the older reports the Clan had sent from Las Vegas in the morning, then paused for lunch. Oddly, Rocky escorted Bob to the wolf Pack house, a short distance around the mountain from his home office, to have lunch in the communal dining hall. The gathering was made up mostly of wolves, as Bob had expected, but there were a few other kinds of shifters as well. Rocky introduced him to a couple of the men, but Bob and the bear shifter ate their meal at a small table in the back of the room, away from everyone else.

He realized then that the otherwise friendly grizzly was being cautious, and Bob didn't blame him. Bob was an unknown—and a strong Alpha in his own right. Sure, he would probably have trouble besting a grizzly of Rocky's size in a fight, but Bob was experienced enough to be able to do some damage if he had bad intent.

Nobody here really knew him. They didn't know he was as affable as he seemed. It took a lot to anger Bob, and he didn't fly off the handle easily. Still, he understood the bear's caution. Rocky struck him as a very protective sort, which confused Bob for a moment. Why had the bear taken him into the heart of the wolf Pack—the Pack house where the weak and vulnerable were taken in and given places to live while they got back on their feet?

Why had the bear exposed the wolves to a potential threat? He could've sent Bob to his cabin to make his own meal. But then Bob would've been out of sight. So that meant the bear wanted to keep an eye on him. Why then had they come here to the Pack house, when they could've eaten lunch at Rocky's place? Bob realized Rocky would only have done that if he had something even more precious to guard at home.

A child, most likely. They had been working in Rocky's office, which was set apart from the rest of the house, but the place was plenty big, with a fenced-off backyard. A young child, then. Still able to be contained by a simple fence. The bear cub probably hadn't learned to climb yet and wasn't strong enough to push the fence over. If Bob guessed right and it was Rocky's child though, it wouldn't be long before it was a force to be reckoned with, even as a cub. The man was huge, and very, very powerful. His kid would probably be just as formidable.

Bob did his best to talk of lighthearted things when they weren't working on the reports. Rocky wasn't much of a conversationalist, but that was okay with Bob. He could talk enough for both of them and felt comfortable telling the bear shifter things about the Redstone family and Clan that would help set Rocky more at ease. Grif had cleared Bob to be as open as he wanted with the Lords' people. It was important to Grif as the Redstone Clan Alpha, to show unmitigated support for the Goddess-blessed Lords.

The Clan had taken a stand, along with the local Vampire Master in Las Vegas, to declare themselves firmly on the side of Light in what they feared was an upcoming show-down with the evil *Venifucus*. It was important to show the seriousness of their vow to the Lords and let them know that the Redstone Clan and its allies could be counted on if the worst should come to pass.

Bob knew gaining the full trust of these people wouldn't happen overnight. He'd have to build trust slowly. That's why he was here for the duration. Grif had told him to stay as long as it took.

When Rocky asked why Grif had chosen to send Bob on this mission during their lunch conversation, it was easy to answer. He used the opportunity to tell the bear shifter a bit about his family.

"My three older brothers are newly mated. Not just Grif, but Steve and Mag too. And the priestess of our Clan mated with your friend Slade," Bob said between bites of rare roast beef. "There's a glut of marital bliss in our area right now," Bob joked. "I'm single and was able to rearrange my work schedule, so it made sense for me to come. The other guys are very protective of their ladies. None of them had what you'd call an easy path to finding their mates."

"Magnus is the one who mated the vampire, right?" Rocky seemed to be making conversation but Bob was experienced enough to realize the bear knew the answer to his question already. Mag's unconventional mating was the subject of much conjecture, Bob was sure.

He nodded anyway. "Miranda is pretty amazing. I wasn't sure about the whole arrangement at first, but when you see them together...well, you realize it's the real thing. Goddess-blessed." Bob paused, thinking about the truth of his words. "It's sort of cool to realize my brother might outlive all of us by centuries. Probably will suck for him though, when the rest of us start aging and his immortal mate keeps him young indefinitely. It was hard for us all when our mother died. I can't imagine it will be easy for Mag to watch his brothers follow her." Bob realized he'd gone a little too far with the introspection.

These were thoughts that had been bothering him since Mag had mated with Miranda, but he hadn't voiced them to anyone. He probably shouldn't have said anything now either, but there was something about the quiet bear that invited confidences. Not that Bob had anything to hide. He was pretty much an open book with the Lords and their most trusted lieutenants, but the grizzly probably didn't want to hear every little thought in Bob's head.

"Sorry, man." Bob wiped his mouth with his napkin and threw it on the tray that held his now-empty plate. "Didn't mean to get so serious."

Rocky merely nodded as he finished his sandwich. The grizzly was good at saying a lot with just a look or a gesture. Definitely a man of few words.

They bussed their trays and headed outside to walk back toward the bear's den.

"I've been meaning to ask..." Bob started, uncertain for once about his words. "Yesterday when I got here, I took a little walk around the cabin in my fur." Rocky nodded, unsurprised. Bob knew he'd probably been watched since the moment he set foot on the Lords' land, but he didn't mind. "I crossed paths with a female bobcat and we prowled around for a bit together. She seemed really shy and wouldn't shift. I sensed..." Bob let the silence drag while he thought about his next words. Rocky didn't interrupt. "She seemed kind of fragile in some way. Like she'd been hurt recently or something."

Rocky nodded, but didn't say anything. Bob was getting annoyed with the lack of words coming out of the grizzly shifter's mouth. He wanted to know more about the bobcat woman, but he didn't know what questions to ask. He started with the most basic one.

"Is she okay?" Bob felt a weird kind of desperation to know more about her, to make sure she was all right.

Rocky seemed to consider a moment, then shrugged as they walked under the trees, dappled sunlight lighting their path back toward the bear's house in the distance. "Depends on what you mean by okay, I guess."

When he didn't say anything more, Bob had to suppress a growl. "Physically, she seemed fit, but a little fragile, like I said. But what about her mind, her emotions? She was fine when we were letting our cats roam, but she shied away when I shifted and didn't want to take her skin. What's up with that?"

Rocky stopped in the middle of the path and faced him, his expression grim. "Your instincts are right. She's been having a hard time being human. Not a physical problem shifting. She does that just fine. It's more that she doesn't like being in her skin that much, and has come here to help overcome that. She was almost lost to her animal side when she got here, but she's making progress. She's staying two-legged more and more, though she still does like to prowl in her fur a lot. Give her space, Bob. She's had a rough time of it."

Bob regarded the other man for a moment, considering his words. It was a warning, but it seemed to come from the right place. Rocky was sympathetic and concerned for the female, which felt right to Bob. Still, he didn't like being warned off. It rankled. But this was the Lords' mountain and Rocky was one of their top people. Bob was only a visitor. He had to at least make the effort at being compliant.

"Understood," Bob answered finally. They began walking again and for once, Bob didn't have anything to say.

They reentered the office and set back to work. Rocky pushed and pushed for more information, and by the end of the day, Bob was beat. They hadn't gotten through all the reports. Not by a long shot. They were maybe halfway through dissecting the information that had been sent to the Lords over the past year or so, but tomorrow was another day. They'd start bright and early and do more then.

He ate dinner alone in his small cabin. It wasn't much. A grilled steak and a can of hastily opened baked beans. He wanted more—he was an Alpha male, after all, with big appetites in all things—but he didn't want to spend a lot of time cooking. After replenishing his energy somewhat, he decided to take a relaxing prowl down to that watering hole. He could swim a bit in his fur, and maybe catch another fat fish or three to supplement his paltry meal.

He might even run into a certain little bobcat again, though he wasn't holding out much hope in that direction. Rocky had seemed very protective of her and the thought of the bear's reaction to Bob's questions still made him frown. Rocky had hinted at some dark trauma that had sent the little female into the protection of her bobcat form. Bob didn't like the idea that she had been hurt in any way. He wanted to know more, but he also recognized that it was her right to tell him...or not.

Bob bristled as he stripped before leaving the cabin. He didn't like the idea that she might never tell him about the problems in her past. He also didn't like the knowledge that he might never see her again if she chose to avoid him. This wasn't his territory. He couldn't force the issue. It would be up to her—and all the wolves and Others around here who had agreed to protect her when she'd been accepted among them—if she ever crossed his path again.

Bob growled as he shifted shape into that of his cougar. He padded down the two small steps from the low porch and went to sniff around his perimeter. He was always on alert for scents of prey and other predators, but tonight he was looking specifically for a sweet honey scent he'd caught only once before. Last night. The scent of the pretty bobcat who had fit so neatly at his side.

There.

Faintly, there it was. The caramel-honey scent that told him she had come this way recently. Bob's pace increased, though he was careful to not make a sound. He didn't want to scare off his prey.

He followed her scrumptious scent over the path they had taken the night before. He thought about that and almost purred at the implications. Retracing their steps from the night before meant maybe she was looking for him. Maybe she was hoping to run into him. Maybe she'd been as attracted to him as he'd been to her.

Bob's blood ran just a little bit faster as excitement built within him. He'd thought about her all night and most of the day—when Rocky hadn't been verbally pummeling him with his questions. Bob had known this would be a tough assignment when he'd left Las Vegas. Nobody here really knew him. The Lords had dealt with his brother Grif, of course, but Bob was new to them. Building trust was the hardest part. These initial few days had always been destined to be rough on whoever got sent here. Only Grif, as Clan Alpha, could have avoided some of it, but Grif was needed at home.

It had made sense to send Bob and he hadn't been naive to the challenge ahead of him. He'd been willing to take one for the team and do his part to earn the trust of the Lords and their people. But now that he was here, something had changed. He was starting to believe that he'd been sent here. Not just by his brother, but possibly by the Mother Goddess

Herself.

Since meeting the female bobcat, something had come over him. Some kind of *knowing*. Along with an attraction that wouldn't be denied. He didn't know much about her at all, but something inside him was saying he'd found his destiny.

Sometimes it happened like that for shifters. Very often, they knew their mate at first sight or *scent*, in the case of cougars. Bob admitted he had been confused by the fact that the woman he'd met hadn't been a cougar shifter. The whole bobcat thing had thrown him a bit. But interspecies mating wasn't unheard of. Sure, it didn't happen a lot, but sometimes…well…the call of the wild just had to be answered whether it was with a human, a vampire—as in the case of his brother Mag's new mate—a mage, or even another shifter species.

At least they were both felines. She might be a little smaller and a lot fluffier around the ears, but they had similar predatory natures. They were both cats at heart. He was just a lot bigger and physically stronger than her.

But she had been hurt somehow in the recent past, Bob reminded himself. He would have to temper his strength with gentleness. He would do his best to subdue his demanding Alpha nature with easy words. And he would do it happily, for the chance of having a mate that would bless his life with her presence.

Eagerness in every silent step of his paws, Bob moved through the undergrowth without making a sound. When he pushed through the final barrier of trees and brush, and had the pond in sight, a woman was waiting there for him. Not a cat. The female had chosen her human form and she looked for all the world as if she'd been expecting him.

She wore a floaty dress of what looked like soft cotton. The fabric had been dyed in brown and gold colors that complemented her lovely topaz eyes. He noticed a knapsack of some kind beside her. Had she prowled down in her fur, carrying the pack in her teeth? Had she come prepared with clothing so she wouldn't have to face him in her birthday suit? Seemed odd for a shifter.

Bob slowed, unsure of his footing. Not physically, but mentally. Had she chosen to face him now because she wanted to tell him to leave her alone? Or had she overcome her fears and decided to meet him in her human form—something she'd balked at the night before? This could go either way. Bob approached cautiously.

Serena was sitting on a flat rock that bordered the pond, trailing her hand in the water when she first scented the cougar's approach. Her sense of smell was only slightly less acute in her human form than in her fur, and she'd been expecting—no, make that a strange mixture of hoping and dreading—that the cougar would again prowl the path they'd taken last night.

His scent was like what she imagined a desert wind must smell like. Slightly dusty, but not in a bad way, with subtle hints of cactus and mesquite. Intoxicating. Unfamiliar, yet absolutely delicious in the most invigorating way possible.

She had enjoyed roaming with him through the dark woods. It had made her feel free in a way she hadn't felt in years. The only problem came when he'd wanted her to shift into her human form. She'd spent all day thinking about how she had chickened out when push came to shove. She might as well have been born a werechicken rather than a werecat—if there were such things.

The thought made her smile, even as anger at her own failing made her want to do something about it. This time in the Lords' territory was supposed to be about healing. About overcoming the fears that had defined her for so long. About taking small steps each day to rejoin the world of the living and reclaiming her future.

It had taken all her courage, but she had come here tonight, hoping to take another small step on that path. A small step that might actually turn into a giant leap forward…if her senses weren't playing her false.

If she could trust her instincts—though past performance

indicated she might be wise to be cautious—this strange cougar could become very important to her. She wasn't completely sure, but she knew after last night, she needed to find out more about him. She had to give him a chance.

It had been so long since any male had caught her attention. None of the cats back home had appealed to her. In fact, even though the bobcats she had lived among were much smaller than the cougar, each and every one of them brought out her defensive instincts. She was afraid of them. She would rather fight and claw the male bobcats than talk to them. Not after the complicity. Not after the way they'd ignored how she was being treated by those who were supposed to care for her.

Serena shook her head, banishing the bad memories. Tonight was for making new memories. Perhaps taking another step forward in her recovery. Maybe making a new friend. Or maybe more. Only the Goddess knew for sure.

She turned her head, unsurprised to see the cougar's glowing, topaz eyes prowling steadily toward her.

"I was hoping you'd come. I'm sorry about last night. I wasn't ready to…" her voice trailed off.

It was hard for her to speak her mind, but she had promised herself she was going to give it her damndest. She was already so much stronger than she had been when she'd come to the Lords' territory. She still had a way to go, but she was improving faster now that she had overcome the initial issues that had sent her running here for sanctuary.

The cougar halted a few feet from her and sat on his haunches in an unexpected show of patience. Maybe he understood, on some level, how hard this was for her? It seemed unbelievable, but perhaps he sensed what she needed most right now was time and space to regain her footing. The way he held his body seemed to say he understood and was willing to wait until she found the right words.

When had a male cat ever been willing to wait for her? Not in recent memory. This cougar was one in a million as far as she was concerned. Everyone she had met here since

25

her escape, had been gracious and kind, but there weren't a lot of cats on this part of the mountain, and she had been careful to keep clear of any that happened to cross her path…until this cougar last night.

"I'm sorry," she repeated, trying to start over. "My name is Serena Wicklow. I should have told you that last night, but I…" She looked at the water and then back again at the cougar. "I've had a hard time dealing with anyone in my human form for the past few months. I just wanted to thank you for the fish, and say I enjoyed prowling with you last night too. I made these to thank you."

She picked up the cardboard box she had put beside her on the rock. It was still in the knapsack she'd brought with her, in an effort to keep bugs away from it. She opened the pack and then lifted the lid on the box so he could see the pastries she had spent part of her afternoon baking for him. It had done her good to work alongside the other women in the Pack house's kitchen. It had also felt right to save a few of the choicest pastries to give to the cougar who had been so nice to her.

He made a soft sound, almost like a purr and stepped closer. The werecougar shimmered before her eyes and took his human form. She watched as he became the man she'd seen the night before, his gaze on the pastries, his lips curled into a grin.

"I'd say you shouldn't have, but it'd be a lie," he joked, even as he reached for a pastry. In a flash of sharp, pearly white teeth, half the pastry was gone. He groaned as he chewed, clearly enjoying himself.

She reached into the sack again while he polished off the rest of the treat. She had brought more than just the pastry box. She'd thought a lot about how tonight might go and had tried to prepare for all contingencies.

"I hope you don't mind, or think I'm crazy, but I brought these for you." She held out a pair of baggy swim shorts to him, unable to meet his gaze or even look at him. "I'm sorry," she said again, though she knew it was a sign of weakness. "It would just make me a little more comfortable so we could talk. I haven't always lived among shifters."

When he didn't answer or move for a few moments, she dared a quick look up at his face. His head was cocked to one side as his eyes narrowed in concern. He didn't look angry, which allowed her heart to start beating again, but he definitely looked confused and somewhat uneasy about her request.

Nevertheless, he reached out and took the swim trunks from her trembling hand. Moving efficiently, he slipped them on while she averted her gaze.

"It's okay, sweetheart," he said softly as he stilled, his crotch covered by the fabric. "I'm decent now. Well…" he chuckled, his tone inviting her to laugh as well. "About as close as I'll ever get, anyway."

She smiled and looked up at him again, more at ease now that he had complied with her rather odd wishes. She knew nudity shouldn't be a big deal among shifters but she'd been raised differently. The fact that the cougar Alpha was willing to humor her meant a lot. A whole lot.

"Thank you for the pastries," he continued, snagging another from the box as he moved slowly closer. "How'd you know I had a sweet tooth?"

"Most men do," she answered quickly, feeling almost comfortable in his presence. She hadn't felt the least bit comfortable around a male shifter in a long time.

"Ah, yes. Sadly, most of us are simple creatures," he agreed in a wistful tone that made her smile deepen. She had never known an Alpha to take himself so *un*-seriously.

He polished off the second pastry with one more bite. While he chewed, she felt his gaze upon her, but she couldn't meet his eyes again. Her shyness was something she was working on, though she'd never been a truly dominant female.

Every shifter Pack, Clan and Tribe had its dominants and its submissives. They needed both to survive. Dominants were protective of the weaker members of the group. In fact, without weaker Clan mates to protect, the dominants usually ended up tearing each other apart. Protecting the weaker members of the Clan was something they could unite behind and it made for a stronger Clan all around.

"You said last night…" she began, wanting to find something to talk about that might help set her on more steady footing. "You said you'd never met a bobcat shifter before. There's a relatively large community of us in the Cascade Mountains."

"My Clan is headquartered in Las Vegas," he replied, sitting down near her, though not on the same rock. She was glad. She wanted to talk to him, but close proximity in human form would probably still be difficult for her—at least for a while. All of the beatings had been administered while she was in human form, which was why she'd spent so long as a bobcat after escaping. She had yet to overcome the fear of being overpowered and abused while on two legs, but she was getting better day by day.

"You're Alpha, right?"

"One of them," he confirmed. "Actually, I'm the fourth of five brothers. We're all Alphas. The eldest is our Clan Alpha, my brother Grif."

She was perplexed by the concept. "How can there be five Alphas in one Clan?"

Bob actually smiled, confusing her further. "Oh, there's a lot more than just the five of us. We're all cougars, but there are Alphas for every group of shifters under our banner. The Redstone Clan is probably the largest in North America. It takes all five of us just to keep the business running and the Clan matters sorted out. The four younger brothers act as Grif's deputies in different aspects of running both the Clan and the business."

"You're one of *those* Redstones?" Serena's eyes widened. She'd just realized the kind cougar she was unaccountably attracted to was in essence, shifter royalty. Or the next thing to it.

She was totally out of her depth. Panicked, she stood.

Fight or flight had set in, and she'd never been one to fight back much. She wanted to run away, but the man who'd been so relaxed a moment ago was now standing in front of her, his hands on her shoulders.

"It's okay, Serena. I've got you. You're all right."

How did he know to say those things? How had he guessed she needed comfort and reassurance?

She looked up at him, knowing he'd see the confused fear in her gaze. "Why are you being so nice to me? I'm nothing. Not worthy of an Alpha's notice. Especially not an Alpha of your standing. This is a mistake. I have to go." The whispered words were torn from her heart as she tried again to flee, but he held her still with just a simple pressure on her shoulders. Not hurting. Not really holding. Just asking wordlessly for her to stay. Overriding the fear to some extent. At least enough to allow her to stay for a few more minutes.

"You are the most worthy female I have ever met. The most worthy of my respect and regard. The most worthy of my concern and protection. The Mother of All wasn't making a mistake when She allowed our paths to cross, kitten. I believe that with all my heart. I hope someday soon, you will too."

CHAPTER THREE

The fear in her eyes brought out all of Bob's protective instincts, and they were considerable. Being Alpha meant protecting the weak and helping those who needed help. It was important to him to get to the bottom of her problem and put an end to it, but he sensed he'd have to tread carefully with the skittish female.

The fact that she had wanted him to put on the swim trunks was odd. Most shifters were comfortable with nudity. It was a fact of life when you had to get naked to shapeshift.

Something had made this little female uncomfortable with skin. What he didn't know was the extent of her problem. Was it just males that she objected to seeing in the buff? Just Alpha males? Someone who might pose a physical threat?

The thought made his blood run cold. If some sick bastard had hurt this little wildcat, he was going to answer to Bob sooner rather than later.

But she'd also refused to shapeshift in front of him and chosen to meet him tonight in her human form, fully dressed. Maybe it wasn't just male nudity she was uncomfortable with. Still, it was damned odd and very worrying. Bob did his best not to let his anger show.

She had said something about not having always lived

among shifters. He needed to know more about that, but he sensed she would run if he started to interrogate her about her past. He had to tread lightly and figure out why a beautiful little bobcat was so uncomfortable in her own human skin.

"Why don't you sit back down and we'll talk. We can eat the rest of those delicious pastries. My Clan is far away and I'm a guest here, just like you. We're equal, here in this forest, next to this pond. Just two cats, enjoying the evening breeze." He tried his best to sweet talk her into calming down and sticking around. He'd stopped her headlong flight away from him, but he had to coax her to choose to stay.

She looked like she was softening as some of the panic left her gaze. He cupped her shoulders, stroking gently. He wasn't holding her. Not really. His touch wasn't meant to confine or restrict, but rather to comfort. She seemed to understand the difference, which was definitely a step in the right direction.

"You're an Alpha. You're a Redstone Alpha. Even my Clan up in the mountains knew about the Redstones," she whispered.

"I'm a Redstone and I'm an Alpha, but that doesn't mean much here." He looked around the dark forest. "All I see here is you and me. A girl and a guy. A box of pastries. A moonlit night. And a pond full of tasty fish."

He lifted his hands off her shoulders, taking the chance she would flee, but she remained stationary, looking up at him. He started to breathe again. He still had a chance.

"Why don't we sit down," he invited again, gently. "Of all my brothers, I'm the most talkative. Ask anyone. Being cooped up alone in that little cabin is hard on me. I'm a very social cat who feels very much the outsider here in the Lords' territory."

She took a deep breath and nodded, resuming her seat with slow, deliberate movements. He sat a short distance away, not wanting to crowd her. He felt like they were making progress.

"It gets better, once they get to know you a bit," she

offered. "When I first got here, I wasn't sure of my welcome, but everyone here is really nice. The ladies at the Pack house have sort of taken me under their wing—or paw, might be more accurate." She smiled a little at her own pun and the simple gesture enchanted him.

"I had lunch at the Pack house with Rocky today," he said, keeping the conversation light and innocuous.

"I know," she surprised him by saying. "I was baking these…" she offered him the box of pastries again, "…in the kitchen while you were there. The ladies were speculating about who you were and why Rocky had chosen to bring you to the Pack house. He usually takes his meals with his family."

"I suspect it was to protect his cubs from me—the big, bad stranger." Bob scowled in a humorous way that made her laugh. He was fast learning he'd do just about anything to hear that sound of joy fall from her too-serious lips.

"I don't think he meant anything by it. He's just super protective of his mate. I've heard she's human," Serena added.

"The giant grizzly fell for a human girl? Well now, that's interesting. Of course, I'm no one to talk. Three of my brothers have gotten hitched recently and each one found an exceptional woman who wasn't quite what we expected."

"Really?" She seemed curious, so he elaborated, hoping to set her more at ease.

"Grif's mate, Lindsey, was the granddaughter of a Native shaman. She was raised among humans but through some pretty intense magic and a little divine intervention, she became a cougar. According to Grif it surprised the heck out of them both. She's been learning how to handle her claws for a while now. She's getting the hang of it, but it's still kind of fun to watch. She's like a full-grown kitten, just learning how to walk sometimes." He chuckled remembering.

He liked Lindsey a lot. Nobody could fill his dead mother's shoes, of course, but Lindsey was carving out her own place as a new kind of matriarch for the Clan. She had a kind heart and she made Grif happy, which was the main thing. Bob liked seeing his family in good spirits—something that had become difficult for the brothers to achieve since the murder of their mother.

Little by little though, as the older ones found mates, the debilitating sadness was beginning to lift. They'd already gotten justice for their mother. They'd tracked down the killers and made them pay. Now it was just a matter of healing the holes in their hearts where their beloved mother had been. Three of them had found mates in the last year, which Bob counted as a blessing.

"Then Steve managed to find a mate with some pretty amazing powers. She's part water sprite, though she was raised mostly in the human world. She was unaware of shifters until she met Steve, actually. It's been fun to see her becoming comfortable with all the magic in our Clan, and in the world in general. She's a very powerful woman who has no airs about her amazing abilities. And she loves my brother a lot. It's good to see that kind of bond between them. Gives the rest of us hope." Bob smiled and he knew he probably looked wistful. He meant every word.

"And then there's Mag," Bob went on. "He just brought a whole new weirdness into the family by mating with a vampiress. It's not generally known, but it's not quite the secret it had been. Still, their mating was Goddess-blessed. The priestess and her mate said so. I believe it. I've never seen Mag like that with any woman, and it's obvious Miranda would do anything for him. They have a really strong bond."

"That sounds both strange and wonderful. I thought cougars as highly ranked as you and your brothers would only mate with other cougars," Serena said in a quiet voice.

"Apparently the Mother of All has other ideas." Bob made a respectful sign toward the heavens. "I've been thinking about it a lot, actually. Maybe it's because our Clan is so diverse. Or maybe it's because Grif is the Clan Alpha. He mated a cougar—albeit a newly minted one—and the rest of us are more or less free to go where the wind takes us. Or maybe I'm full of it. I have no idea why things have worked out the way they have, but I can't complain. My brothers are happy. Their mates are happy. The Clan is happy. That's the important thing." He shrugged.

"And what would make you happy?" she asked unexpectedly. He looked at her, his eyes narrowing in thought.

"I suppose the same things that make most men happy. A good job—which I already have. A purpose in life. Again, something I've got thanks to my family. A loving home life. A mate. That's something that's eluded me up 'til now, but I have high hopes." He winked at her and loved the way she blushed in response. His little wildcat was shy, but not unresponsive to him. That was a step in the right direction as far as he was concerned. "What about you?"

She paused, seeming to think before she answered. "I just want peace."

"The peace-of-mind kind of peace, or the world peace kind?" he pushed.

She looked at him, her gaze direct and sincere. "Peace of mind," she replied with no hesitation, though her voice was soft.

They talked softly there by the small pond, long into the night. Bob had a gentle spirit despite his Alpha nature. Or maybe it was because of his strong nature that he recognized the need to be gentle with her. Whatever it was, the big cougar put her bobcat at ease over the hours that followed.

They talked of inconsequential things as well as important things, in a general way. She told him a little bit about the places she'd lived and where she'd grown up. Bob opened up to her a little more about his family and it was clear to her that he loved his brothers and surviving sister deeply.

"Our mother was murdered not too long ago, so it's good to see my older brothers overcoming that and finding joy again in their lives, and their new mates."

He sounded so wistful, the look in his eyes so faraway, she

felt the need to reach out to him. She touched his hand where it rested on the rock a foot away from her. He hadn't moved too much closer over the time they'd talked and she'd liked that he'd respected her unspoken boundaries. But now she wanted the small contact. She wanted him to know she felt for him.

"I lost my parents when I was very young," she admitted in a quiet voice. She seldom shared this painful part of her past with anyone, but she recognized the same loss in his eyes as she still felt in her heart when she thought about the loving bobcat shifters she remembered from her early childhood— so different from what had come after.

Bob accepted her sympathy with a sad smile and turned his hand around, grasping hers lightly. They held hands and watched the water ripple in the pond as fish nibbled at leafy plants near the surface.

"I'm sorry," he said after a time, and she felt the real meaning behind his simple words. "Losing a parent is an especially difficult pain. It changes you and your life is never quite the same. We lost our dad a long time before our mother was taken from us. That was really hard, but mom was there. We were strong for her and she was always there for us as we took over the running of the Clan and the family business. Grif took the brunt of the responsibility as eldest, but we all helped. And mom was the best matriarch our Clan has ever seen. She grieved for our dad for the rest of her life, but she didn't let her sorrow take her away from her family or her Clan, and everyone loved her for her dedication and care."

"She sounds like an amazing woman," Serena offered. "I'm sorry I'll never get to meet her. She sounds a lot like I remember my mother being, though I was really too little to remember much. I just remember her warmth and acceptance. And so much love it could fill the world. It *did* fill my world. Until I was about six years old." Her thoughts turned dark, remembering when everything had changed.

"What happened?" Bob's question was direct but oddly, it

didn't feel like he was prying.

It felt more as if he was commiserating. He'd shared his sorrow and it felt right to tell him of her own experience. It had never felt so right to share such personal thoughts with anyone before. Bob was just easy to talk to and he really listened. Just listened and didn't judge.

"We were on a road trip from the Oregon coast, where we lived, to somewhere east, where I believe my father was from. The roads are very steep in those mountains, and a poorly loaded tractor trailer lost control and hit us. I don't remember much except the scream of metal and the horrible smell of burning tires and then I was in the air, thrown clear. I landed in the grass and was fine except for some bumps and bruises from when I was thrown from the car. My parents weren't as lucky. They were stuck inside and couldn't break free. The car rolled over and over…"

Bob squeezed her hand gently, taking her out of the memory and back to the pond and the quiet forest night. She was grateful for the distraction and smiled her thanks at him. Only then did she realize her face was wet with tears.

So many tears. So many years. The childhood trauma still had the power to make her cry, even after all this time. And what had come after was even worse.

She used her free hand to brush at her cheeks, a little self conscious, but Bob didn't say anything. He just held her hand and offered his silent support. He was solid in the night. Secure.

At least he made her feel that way. Which was something entirely new in her experience. She hadn't felt safe in a male's presence in…well…probably since the accident that had made her an orphan.

"The car exploded and I knew my parents were gone. Rescue crews came and someone picked me up and wrapped a scratchy blanket around me. I think it was a police officer. And then they took me to a hospital, but I wasn't really hurt. A lady from social services came and they put me with a foster family while they tried to find relatives. All they had was our address on the coast and we didn't have kin there. I was too little to know details, so when their inquiries failed to find relatives, I ended up in the foster care system. I was raised among humans for several years. After a while, I wasn't really sure what I remembered about my mother and father being able to turn into bobcats was real. The other kids' parents didn't turn into animals and the adults all seemed to think my little make-believe stories were cute, and maybe a little scary. Eventually, I stopped telling them and just accepted that nobody I knew now could change the way I remembered."

"I'm sorry you had such a tough time of it, kitten." Bob's voice was full of compassion and understanding. He was a good listener and she found herself telling him things she never expected to share with anyone else.

"I spent my formative years among humans and learned their ways, but eventually I was discovered and adopted by a couple from the Cascade Clan."

"That must've been quite a change to go from the human world back into our world after so long."

"Yeah. It was a shock at first. Suddenly, these strange, yet familiar-smelling people—bobcats—were there, adopting me and taking me away to live with them. I thought it was going to be so great, but little by little, it turned kind of ugly. Jack was nothing like I remember my father being. And his mate wasn't the motherly sort at all. I think she hated me from the beginning. The human family I'd lived with had been so much nicer, willing to let me grieve. They'd been supportive even when they thought I was a little weird compared to the human kids."

She knew Bob had to be surprised by what she'd been through. Most shifters were, when they heard her story. She'd heard it wasn't really normal for a shifter cub to be raised by humans, even for a little while. Most shifter groups kept track of their children, absorbing them into other shifter families if something happened to their parents.

"Jack always said he thought my time among humans

weakened me. And the fact that I was a late bloomer shifting-wise didn't help."

"What happened at your first shift?" he asked quietly.

She'd learned since coming here that the first shift was tough for most species of shifters. It also came at different times depending on the level of magic they had. Some—like bear cubs—shifted almost from the very beginning. Most other species didn't shift for the first time until puberty, or thereabouts.

"I didn't shift until I was seventeen. My cat had been dying to get out and run for years, but my human side was really confused and scared of what it would mean among the Cascade Clan. Eventually though, the cat would no longer be denied and I shifted all of a sudden. One of the other kids was teasing me and I wanted to run. My bobcat wanted to run too and it let loose, forcing the shift that had been so delayed and..." she trailed off, remembering.

"Let me guess. You ran." Bob's dry tone made her chuckle, as he'd no doubt intended, and the mood lightened.

He was good at that. Good at gauging her mood and doing things—little things—to alleviate the more somber times. Even on such short acquaintance, he already knew how to read her.

"My cat tasted freedom and didn't want to go back. I didn't either, really. But I had to, eventually. I faced the music and to my surprise, it was the one time that Jack didn't disapprove of what I'd done. He was actually kind of nice about it and let me off without punishment. I was so green, but after that, my bobcat knew what to do and it helped me through the first few months. When I turned eighteen, Jack wanted me to go to work for the Clan, but that's a whole other story."

She fell silent. She didn't really want to get into all that tonight. She'd opened up to Bob more than she'd ever opened up to anyone on such short acquaintance. Feeling vulnerable, she decided she'd done enough sharing for one night.

"It's getting late." She deliberately took her hand back from Bob's grasp and immediately missed his warmth.

"If you ever want to talk, while I'm here or even after I go home, all you have to do is call me," Bob offered in that soft, steady voice that nearly melted her heart. "I understand loss and I won't judge. From what you've told me already, you've been through more than most shifters, and at a very young age. You have my respect, Serena. And my thanks."

"Thanks?" That surprised her into looking at him. His face was solemn and oh, so handsome in the dark night. "What for?"

"For trusting me." He scooted closer and reached out one big hand to cup her cheek.

She allowed the touch because on some level, she realized, she did trust him. The thought should have alarmed her. Instead, it warmed her.

He moved closer and she didn't dare even breathe as his mouth hovered near hers. And then their lips met and warmth spread from that light contact, downward through her body to her core. When he pressed closer, she didn't resist. If anything, she met him halfway. Maybe more than halfway. It was as if she was starved for the gentle, yet erotic contact of his mouth on hers as he deepened the kiss into realms of pure pleasure.

His tongue stroked inside her mouth, the pressure easy, coaxing. His passion didn't frighten her, oddly enough. Instead, it seemed to spark something to life inside her she'd thought extinguished forever. She moved into his arms, wanting more, and he gave it to her.

He gave her all she asked for and just a little bit more, pressing his advantage, pushing her gently to the next level bit by little bit. She sighed as his teeth bit her lower lip when he pulled away. Damn, the man was sexy.

She'd practically climbed into his lap, but he paused to look deep into her eyes.

Not what she had expected.

He'd stopped to let her think. Or perhaps to verify that

she was thinking at all.

"You drive me wild, kitten," he breathed, his hands petting her back and roaming down to her waist. Only the thin layer of her cotton dress separated them and for an untamed moment, she wanted it gone. Then sanity returned.

Her breathing hitched. "You do the same to me," she admitted. "It's not something I'm used to." Shyness returned in a flash and she cringed at her own words. This Redstone Alpha was a worldly man. He lived in a place the rest of the world called Sin City. She must seem the most awful bumpkin to a guy like him.

She tried to pull out of his embrace, but he wouldn't let her go. He wasn't forceful about it, but he held her fast until she stilled.

"Look at me, kitten," he said in a very quiet, very serious voice. He was so gentle with her. It was enough to make her eyes tear. Why was this one man—this one, unattainable man—so good to her?

Looking up to meet his gaze, she felt horribly vulnerable. The look in his eyes though… It wasn't impatient or condemning, or even questioning. Any of those things would only have agitated her more. No, Bob Redstone's gaze held understanding. And patience. And most of all, compassion.

Sweet Mother of All, he was a special man.

"I think we might have something here, though I know you're scared." His deep voice warmed the cold places in her soul. "Heck, I think I'm a little scared too, if you want to know the truth. Now, big bad Alphas aren't supposed to admit stuff like that, so if you repeat it, I'll deny it." He moved one hand up to push a tendril of hair away from her face. The touch was so light, so caring. He touched her like she was made of spun glass, and it made her breath catch. "Just don't run from me, okay? If I push you too far, I promise I won't bite you if you push back. Well, not unless you want me to." He winked at her and just like that, his humorous little innuendo almost made her laugh.

"I'm just not sure… This is all so confusing."

He stroked her hair back again, pausing to lift her chin with his index finger so she would meet his gaze.

"I know. It's new to me too. New and beautiful, and something I want to explore. Don't you?" His gaze was full of hopeful understanding and a bit of very male satisfaction, if she was any judge. "We'll take this at whatever pace you set, kitten. But we will explore this thing between us. That's a promise you can bank on." His gaze turned serious and she felt the import of his amazing words in every nerve. "I've never felt this kind of instant attraction to anyone. It feels important to me. Don't tell me you don't feel it too." He moved closer and placed a gentle kiss on her brow and she shivered in response, the pleasure of his small touch working its way like lightning down her spine. "If you try to deny it, I won't believe you anyway. Your response to my kisses tells me all I need to know," he whispered before letting her go.

She didn't move far, though only moments ago she had wanted to flee. He had a way about him that forestalled her usual adrenaline-induced attempts at escape. She took a deep breath, wanting for once to deal with a situation rather than run from it.

"I can't make you any promises. My past…well…I'm the first to admit I'm more than a little damaged. There are still things you don't know about me." She looked away, watching the water flow sluggishly into the pond from the little stream before it flowed out again on the other side. "I'm not sure I'll ever be able to tell you about it all."

"You don't have to tell me everything," he answered from the darkness on her right. "But you should tell somebody. A healer or a priestess. Somebody who can help you deal with your past and recover from it. So you can move on."

She nodded, touched by his understanding. "I've talked to Bettina a couple of times, and it has helped. I'm just not sure I'll ever be able…" She trailed off, not knowing how to put her fears into words.

Bob put one arm around her waist, inviting her to lean against him. After only a moment of confused resistance, she did. There was nothing sexual about the touch and everything comforting. He was letting her—quite literally—lean on him. Being surrounded by his strength felt really good. Really safe.

"I'm glad you have someone you can talk to," he whispered, resting his chin on top of her head, nuzzling her hair a bit. "If you ever feel as if you can open up to me, I'm here for you. I just want to make sure you know that. At the same time, I don't want you to feel any pressure. I'm here if you need me. That's all. No questions asked. No pressure applied. Okay?"

She nodded against his chest. She liked the sincerity in his words and the fact that he wasn't pushing her on this particular topic. Her past was a minefield. A tricky place that she didn't like to contemplate or tell others about. She knew she still had to talk through some of the things that had happened with somebody. Her cat prodded her to do it, and Bob's words were a good reminder. Maybe she'd go look for the High Priestess, Bettina, and see if she had some time to spare.

But not right now. This time with Bob was special. Beautiful. She didn't want to taint it with painful memories of a past best forgotten. Not tonight, at least. Not when it was so new to sit in a man's arms in the moonlight with no demands being made, no pain, no anxiety, no worries.

"Thank you," she whispered, knowing he would hear. She wanted to give him something—a little piece of her past that just might have an impact on their future—if, indeed, they had a future together. She took a chance and revealed something very intimate. "I've never had sex in my human form, though my cat played with other bobcats during the frenzy, of course."

She referred to the time after a young shifter's first shift when the beast demanded sex. It drove young shifters into something they called the frenzy, when the beast wanted sex all the time, anytime, until finally it was sated. The frenzy lasted anywhere from a few weeks to a few years depending on the species of shifter and their personality. Hers had been really bad only for a couple of months and never had she been driven enough to do anything…extreme.

Orgies were not unheard of. Multi-partner couplings that lasted for hours or days were common. Again, it varied from shifter to shifter and among the various species.

She knew Bob was probably surprised by her admission. Sex wasn't taboo among shifters. Far from it.

When you had to get naked to become your beast, nakedness and attraction to the opposite—or occasionally the same—sex was nothing new. Until a shifter found their true mate, nothing was really frowned upon, as long as nobody got hurt. In fact, it was considered unhealthy among some species to abstain from having sex as often as your beast half wanted it. To deny the beast was to deny half of your soul.

A shifter had to make peace with both halves of their being. Satisfying the beast was not only a duty, but a necessity. Harmony between both halves was the goal.

"Did you have bad experiences?" Bob prompted when she didn't elaborate.

"Nothing awful. Just fumbling encounters with young guys around my own age. We were teenagers, answering the call of nature in our fur, but it wasn't anything like what I've heard sex is supposed to be, and I never cared enough about any of the guys I knew to want to do it with them when my human side was in control. A lot of them made fun of me because I'd been raised partly among humans. If the human family I lived with thought I was weird, the bobcats were even worse."

Bob was silent for a while, just holding her.

"I like humans," he said into the dark night. "I have a few friends and a lot of business colleagues who are human. My cougar side doesn't always understand them, but my human half sometimes wishes my life was as comparatively uncomplicated as theirs. Some of them have really big hearts and miles of compassion. That's nothing to make fun of. I think maybe your human foster parents were probably good ones, and if they influenced your attitudes, well, that's okay.

Half of you *is* human, after all. We just need to find a way to get your cat and your human working together, in partnership, instead of at odds with each other."

"That's more or less what the priestess said." She turned to look up at him. "How did you get so wise?" She smiled and he returned the gesture. She felt so safe with him. It was a feeling she cherished for its rarity.

"I'm an Alpha," he quipped. "Worse than that, I'm a Redstone. You don't grow up in my family without learning a whole lot about shifter nature." He stroked one hand over her hair in the darkness as his expression became more serious. "We Redstones have had our share of tragedy. All the losses have made me question my beliefs a few times in my life, and I've developed an interest in philosophy because of it."

She looked back at the pond, wondering about his philosophical bent. Probably like most people, she had expected one of the Alpha Redstones of Redstone Construction to be more brawn than brains. He was proving her wrong and she didn't mind it one bit. She liked the more cerebral side of him, even though it was easy to see he had plenty of brawn to go around.

The philosopher in him though, put her at ease. She had never been so comfortable with a man and she took the time to enjoy this beautiful moment. The trickling water, the loamy scent of the earth and the almost glowing beams of moonlight made this an idyllic moment out of time. A moment worth remembering.

She felt him kiss the top of her head again and they sat by the pond for a long time, watching the night and the dark flow of water.

CHAPTER FOUR

Serena woke the next morning feeling better than she had in years. Something about the night before with Bob had changed her on a fundamental level. She felt like a baby bird just pecking through its shell. Emotionally, she had started across a bridge and she could see the other end in sight.

She wanted to get to the other side of that bridge and find her future waiting there for her—whatever that might be. If Bob was in it, so much the better, but if not, she would always remember him with fondness for the way he'd helped her begin the journey across. He didn't have to do that. He didn't have to be so kind and gentle, so caring and patient. There was no doubt in her mind, he was a very special man. A true Alpha that protected the weak and nurtured those who needed his help.

But she didn't want to be a wounded shifter in need of his help. No, she wanted to be on more equal footing with him. Not that she'd ever be an Alpha. No, she just wanted to be more comfortable in her own skin and able to claim her own birthright as a shifter. That would put her on more solid footing for the future. Shifter to shifter, whatever other differences they may have, they were both shifters, and she needed to be comfortable with that part of her being before she could go any further on this journey of discovery.

That thought firmly in mind, she bounced out of bed, dressed quickly and set off in search of the High Priestess, Bettina. Serena practically hopped down the stairs in the Pack house to find the woman she was looking for waiting at the bottom, a broad smile on her elfin face. Serena laughed.

"How did you know?" she asked the first question that popped into her head.

"When the heart is ready, the teacher will come," Bettina replied with a teasing grin that belied her mystical words. "I hear they're making chocolate chip pancakes. Would you like to join me for a far too sugary breakfast and then we can take a little walk outside. What do you say?"

Bob resumed work with Rocky, giving his take on the different reports his Clan had sent to the Lords. Somehow it wasn't that tough to be grilled by the big grizzly bear shifter after spending those precious hours with Serena last night. She had a calming effect on his spirit. She brought peace to his world.

He was concerned about her past, but willing to let her come to him on that. She was healing. That was the important thing. She had crossed some of her self-imposed boundaries last night just by coming to him. Of that he was certain.

He would help her cross more, if she was agreeable. He would be there for her when she wanted to spread her wings. He would catch her if she stumbled and never let her fall.

He and Rocky finished discussing the second to last report about mid-morning and took a short break during which Rocky went out of his office briefly, to get more coffee. Bob stood and stretched, looking out the window. The room they were using was at the front of the house and the window looked out on the small cleared area which led to a gravel road that snaked around the mountain. It was a private road, open only to the locals and authorized visitors. The same road led past the cabin he was using, only his front door was on the other side, lower down the mountain.

Bob was looking at a tall, full evergreen that had been planted in the center of the clearing. It hadn't grown there naturally, he was certain. None of the surrounding trees were of the same variety and there was nothing nearby to indicate it had grown in place and simply been left when the rest of the area was cleared. Unless he was missing something, this one had been put there deliberately.

Allowing his thoughts to wander, Bob was almost taken by surprise when two sets of little paws landed on his booted feet. He looked down, careful not to move, lest he somehow trod on the little creatures.

Sure enough, two sets of baby grizzly paws were pinning his toes to the ground—or trying to. They were really too little to do much damage, and cute as buttons.

Bob let the baby grizzlies chew on his boot laces. The laces were reasonably clean, since the boots were new. He didn't mind the little scratches from the bears' claws. They were so tiny, it was kind of adorable.

"Well, hello there, little ones. Where did you come from?"

Two little faces looked up when he spoke and Bob had to blink a few times to make sure he was really seeing what he thought he was seeing.

"Twins?" he wondered aloud, sniffing to be certain of the scent of them. They were definitely shifters, and definitely closely related. Twins. Judging by the look of them, identical twins. "Sweet Mother of All," Bob whispered, shocked at their appearance.

"Damn." Rocky's voice came from the open doorway. "They're escape artists, I swear." He walked in and deposited a fresh carafe of coffee on his desk, then walked over to Bob, watching the baby bears the whole time. "You two." Rocky's voice brooked no argument. "Out. Your mama's probably looking all over for you."

The baby bears looked rueful and made little sorrowful grunting noises as they let go of Bob's boot laces and trotted toward Rocky on unsteady, baby paws. He bent and scooped them into his arms.

"Rock, have you seen—" A slightly frantic, feminine voice came from the doorway, the woman stopping short when she saw the bear cubs in Rocky's arms. She looked at Bob, her expression fearful.

"It's okay. I know what they are, and I will never divulge knowledge of their existence, even to my own family. Their safety is paramount." Bob lowered himself to one knee, which he could see surprised the woman. A human woman, by her scent. Rocky looked impressed as he held the two babies—one in each arm. The twins were looking straight at Bob as he put his hand over his heart. "I swear fealty now and for always to the Lady, Her Light and the Lords She has blessed to walk among us and guide us."

Bob bowed his head after speaking the vow. It was nothing new to him, but apparently Rocky hadn't expected it. They hadn't gotten that far in going over the reports yet, but he'd learn soon enough about the oaths all of the Las Vegas shifters and vamps had taken in recent months.

The moment the words were out of his mouth, Bob felt a little zing of magic that made him look up. The baby bears were both looking at him as just a little of their magic reached out to touch him. The bears turned into wriggling human toddlers in Rocky's arms, and they both laughed and smiled at Bob in a way that made him join in. They were such joyful children.

"I do believe they like you, Redstone," Rocky observed, breaking the spell. He handed one of the naked, laughing cherubs to the woman. "I'll just help get them settled and be back in a minute. Pour the coffee, will you?"

Bob got up, then poured the coffee as instructed, marveling at his discovery. He needed a sip of the bracing brew after what had just happened. It wasn't common knowledge that another set of Lords had been born. They had managed to keep it a secret and Bob understood why. The future Lords would be very vulnerable while they were growing up. Many twin pairs had been lost over the centuries to enemies. Others had been influenced and corrupted in subtle ways.

Bob was glad these two seemed to have loving and protective guardians who were well able to take care of them. The fact that they were bears was something unexpected. Bears were some of the most magical of shifters. Grizzlies even more so. If the Lady had chosen bear shifters to lead the next generation, Bob worried what it might mean for the world at large. Would their immense magical strength be a sign of bad times to come? He hoped not, for the sake of everyone—shifters, vamps, mages and humans. Everyone who served the Light, no matter what they called it, would be impacted if bad times were coming.

Still, the cubs were awfully cute. Bob couldn't help but be affected by the playful toddlers. In general, shifters loved babies. Shifters weren't quite as fertile as humans, so every birth was an occasion to be celebrated. Twins were almost unheard of. Identical twins happened only once in a generation, in each region of the world, and marked the next set of leaders for their people. At least, that's how it had always been for the *were*.

Other kinds of shapeshifters had other power structures, but the wild *were* had always counted on the Mother Goddess to appoint their leaders. Cougars, although they were big cats, had little in common with the more exotic cats who had founded their societies on other continents. Tigers, lions, panthers and others, had kings and queens that had fancy titles, but cougars had always followed the *were* Lords.

Rocky came back in and then sat down behind his desk. He took a sip of his coffee before speaking.

"You understand the need for secrecy." It wasn't quite a question, but Bob definitely understood.

"I swear I will do nothing that might put them in danger. As far as I'm concerned, I never even saw them."

"I appreciate that," Rocky said, but his expression was still troubled. Bob wanted to erase that frown from the grizzly's face.

"You need to hear the final report, and then you might feel a bit better about this. We were up to the part where my brother Mag got involved with the vampiress, Miranda van Allyn."

"I thought you were trying to make me feel better," Rocky quipped. "For the record, *were* mixing with vamps does *not* make me feel better."

"Just wait 'til you hear the whole thing," Bob answered with a grin. "I promise you'll like the ending."

Bob proceeded to go through the report of what had happened with Mag and Miranda, adding all the texture and nuance the dry, written report lacked. He talked about the vampire uprising in Las Vegas and the surprising results. Rocky seemed to be alternately impressed, surprised and ultimately pleased, just as Bob had hoped.

"So you see, at this point, the Master Vampire in Las Vegas has openly declared himself for the side of Light. He gave all his people the option to either do the same, or leave his domain. My family also instituted something similar for the Clan," Bob explained. "Any of the Others who come under the Redstone banner had to swear fealty—the same oath I just repeated to the little ones—or they were invited to leave. Our priestess and her mate, your friend Slade, oversaw it all. They have ways of knowing if anybody tries to cheat or lie their way through the oath. So far though, everyone has been honest. I take that as a sign my little brother Matt is doing his job. He's in charge of Personnel for the company, and he also does the dossiers on any shifter group seeking to join our Clan. He's very thorough. We don't let just anybody into the Clan, or allow just any shifter to work for the construction company."

Rocky let out a harsh breath. "You don't know how glad I am to hear it."

"I understand. We're all protective of cubs—especially those two. Are they yours?" Bob couldn't help asking. Their scent was similar to Rocky's but not quite the same as it would normally be in a familial relationship.

"Their father was my best friend and one of the most powerful grizzly shaman of all time. He was killed by a demon allied with the *Venifucus*." Bob could see the pain in the other man's eyes and his heart went out to the big man who had lost his friend in such a terrible manner. "Their mother—you saw her briefly—is now my mate. I claimed the boys in front of the Goddess. I'm their Alpha now." There was a world of joy and sorrow in the big man's voice. Bob felt compassion for the small family who had been touched by tragedy.

"I know how it feels to lose someone in horrific circumstances." He thought of the way his mother had been murdered. "Hell, I know how it feels to lose someone you love to the evil of the *Venifucus*. You have my sympathy, Rocky. And I'll make a further pledge to you, in addition to the oath I made to your boys. If you ever need my help, all you need to do is call."

Bob felt confident in making the promise. He'd been able to take Rocky's measure over the past couple of days and the fact that the Goddess had blessed him with the care of the next generation of Lords spoke volumes for his character. Bob knew Rocky would never abuse Bob's vow.

"I appreciate that," Rocky answered in that steady way of his. "With any luck, I'll never have to take you up on it."

Bob smiled. "Agreed. But I'm there if you need me."

They went on with their work until lunch, and this time, Rocky invited Bob to eat with him and his family in the kitchen. The boys made a mess in their highchairs until they decided they'd had enough of mashed peas and carrots, and shifted into grizzlies. At that point, there was really no containing them. They climbed down from their high chairs and scampered away, their mother following as best she could.

He'd been introduced to Maggie, the boys' mother. She was human, but handling the dual nature of her babies very well, if Bob was any judge. The cubs were just the cutest things, but Bob could already see how much of a handful

51

they were.

Rocky helped corral the toddlers before he and Bob headed back to his office at the front of the house. There were just a few last things to go over. Bob wasn't sure what they were going to do once they finished going through all the reports, but he was at the Lords' disposal. He had been tasked by his brother, Grif, to represent the Clan however the Lords wanted.

"So what haven't we covered? We did the last of the formal reports this morning, but there's this little matter of the notes from your brother Magnus's new vampire mate," Rocky said, pulling a final file from the pile on his desk. "You already told me about Miranda and Magnus. I know she was held prisoner by a *Venifucus* mage for an unknown length of time…" Rocky trailed off as he shuffled through the pages.

"It was several months, at least. Possibly as long as a year, but we don't know for certain. Her memories are foggy at best because of the way the mage treated her. He kept her starved and then bled her, using her magical blood to power some of his evil spells." Bob knew his disgust was coming through in his tone, but he couldn't help it.

He hated thinking of the way they'd found Miranda, half-crazed from starvation and blood loss. She had been very near death. She'd had enough energy left to launch one final attack, but that was about it. It had taken her months to recover fully from her captivity. During that time, she had been with Mag and they had renewed their relationship with the end result being that they were now mates.

It wasn't exactly normal for vampires and *weres* to intermarry. In fact, there was a pretty big taboo against it. But Mag and Miranda were true mates. She had tried to stay away from Mag, but when they were brought together again after her ordeal, there was no way to stop the mating from solidifying into something that would never come undone.

Bob had had his doubts, but he was glad now that she and Mag had found each other. Mag had been a sullen bastard and Bob hadn't known what had turned his formerly playful brother into a brooding mute. When everyone realized Mag had been searching for his lost mate for two whole years, Bob was impressed Mag had been able to hold it together and not rip someone's head off long before. It wasn't easy for a shifter to find his mate, then lose her all in the space of a single night. It had to have been hell for his brother.

Which was why Bob thought Mag and Miranda deserved a little happiness. Both of them. Miranda had been held prisoner and was just as wounded after finding, and having to deny, her One. That couldn't have been easy for her either. She was a hell of a woman. Even if she was a vampire.

Rocky finally found the right paper and began to skim. "These are things she remembered the mage saying while she was in captivity, right?"

"Yeah. She took some time after things had settled to write down everything she could remember her captor saying. As you know, he was proven to be affiliated with the *Venifucus*. Miranda collated her notes and then presented them to Grif. He shared them with the Master Vampire of our area and sent a copy to the Lords." Bob nodded to the papers in Rocky's hands.

"She's a neat little thing, isn't she?" Rocky mused as he went through the carefully organized notes. "I just saw this for the first time last night. Rafe and Tim read it when it came in and earmarked a few things they thought could wait until your arrival. This, for instance..." Rocky trailed off, lifting a sticky flag from one part of the document. A frown creased his forehead. "Miranda mentions a man called Devereaux. We have reason to believe she is referring to Jeremy Devereaux— also known as Jezza."

Bob waited for Rocky to go on as the bear shifter clicked open a document on his laptop. Bob couldn't see the screen, but from Rocky's movements, Bob could tell the other man was scrolling through a file, looking for something in particular.

"The twins' father, Tony, was a gifted shaman," Rocky said, losing Bob for a moment with the quick change of subject, until he clarified. "Tony foresaw his own death and prepared an external drive full of documents and information on people he was working with and things he wanted us to know after he was gone. He wasn't quite as organized as your little vampiress." Rocky chuckled as he paused to scroll some more. "But I knew Tony as well as I know myself. I've been sorting through his files for a while now and I've been able to make some correlations. Turns out, Tony was in close communication with Jezza and was in fact, the one who helped him move to the Cascade Range. Jezza has shaman blood, but has spent a lot of time kicking around in military circles. Most recently, he was part of the Wyoming wolf Pack's little conclave of elite soldiers."

"Jesse Moore's guys?" Bob asked, suspecting exactly who Rocky meant. The group of former Spec Ops soldiers who had gathered around the werewolf were legendary in shifter circles.

They hired themselves out for protection, and certain special operations that had little to do with the government. All those highly-trained, retired soldiers had formed their own mixed-species Pack of shifter soldiers with Jesse Moore as their Alpha. They were free to choose who they worked for now, and what missions they wanted to take.

They had, in fact, been of great help when the Redstones had needed backup after their mother was murdered. Grif and Steve, Bob's two eldest brothers, had both been Army Green Berets and knew a lot of the guys who now owed their allegiance to Jesse Moore. When the Redstone Clan had needed them, Moore's guys had come running and done their best—which was pretty damned impressive—to help keep everyone safe.

Rocky nodded in answer to Bob's question. "Jezza, from all accounts, has always been a bit on the mystical side, though he's a vicious fighter when needs be. He was working with Tony to figure out his path in life after retiring from the military. He didn't want to be a spook, though the Agency tried to recruit him. He ran a few missions for them, but decided against it when he began to feel he was needed elsewhere. Tony and he did a vision quest and the results were mixed, according to Tony's journal. All they knew was that Jezza needed to be in the Cascade Range for the next part of his journey to unfold. Where he went after that was uncertain."

"Do you think this Jezza Devereaux is being targeted by the *Venifucus*?" Bob remembered what he'd read in Miranda's notes about the way the mage had screamed curses down on Devereaux's head. The evil mage who'd held Miranda prisoner had definitely not been a fan.

"It's a pretty sure bet that if the mage in Las Vegas knew about Jezza, then so did his superiors in the *Venifucus*. Which brings us to the next part of our story." Rocky sat back in his desk chair and steepled his fingers, taking a thoughtful pose. "We know for a fact that Jezza has friends within the *Altor Custodis*."

"*Altor Custodis*?" Bob repeated, surprised. "We haven't had much to do with them in Las Vegas, though I've heard they've been active in California recently—at least among my little brother's vampire friends. To be honest, aside from what he's told us, I don't know much about them."

"Lucky for you, I've been brushing up on my history. Near as I can tell, the *Altor Custodis*—I call them the AC for short—was formed even before the *Venifucus* organized around Elspeth, the Destroyer of Worlds. While the *Venifucus* was always a group dedicated to helping in Elspeth's quest for world domination, the AC's motives were originally to simply observe and record the doings of the supernatural races. For eons, they allowed only non-magical humans into their ranks. Mages need not apply. Likewise, anyone with even a hint of shifter blood was barred from membership. They worked in the shadows and their records go back more than a thousand years. We believe they have dossiers on just about all of the really ancient bloodletters, as well as detailed histories of most of the larger Packs, Clans and Tribes of *were*. Which makes them a big problem now that we've verified their ranks have been infiltrated by *Venifucus* agents."

Bob frowned. "That's really bad news. Our enemies could use that information against us. Are you absolutely certain?"

"Unfortunately, yes. There's no doubt at all. Our information comes straight from Duncan le Fey."

Bob remembered the fey warrior who had come to their aid when he and his brothers had been fighting a group of evil vampires a few weeks back. Duncan was an honest-to-goodness Knight of the Light. An ancient *Chevalier de la Lumiere*. It was a position earned by service to the Lady Goddess, and such beings were beyond question, in Her grace. Anything Duncan reported about their enemies could not be questioned.

"So if the AC's information is being used by spies within their organization, we're all at risk," Bob thought out loud.

"Some more than others," Rocky agreed. "A while back, Jezza sent out a call for help to an old military friend. The guy was human, but had become acquainted with the supernatural world during his time in the service. Jezza trusted him to extract someone from a bad situation and bring them here. Only problem is, the man Jezza called was a former Navy SEAL named Ben Steel. I think your brother Matt might've told you about him. Steel is also a former *Altor Custodis* agent."

"Do you have suspicions about Steel? Do you think he's still working for the AC—or worse—the *Venifucus*?"

"I don't think so. Judging by recent events, he seems to be on the up-and-up. He's helped in a few cases since the one in Napa involving your brother." Rocky didn't pause to allow for Bob's surprise, but went right on. "I'd like to videoconference with your brother later, if we can, but for right now…" he looked out the window, watching something outside as he stood from behind his desk. "I've asked our local expert to come give us their impression of Mr. Steel."

Rocky went to the door and opened it. Of all the people who could have been on the other side, Bob hadn't expected to see the woman that seemed to have taken over a little corner of his mind and heart…Serena. She looked uncomfortable as she noticed him, walking into the office on hesitant feet.

"Thanks for coming, Serena. We'll try not to keep you too long," Rocky said with an affable smile, then turned to Bob. "Serena Wicklow, this is Bob Redstone," he introduced them. "Though I hear you two have already met." Rocky raised one eyebrow at them before moving away.

Bob took her hand and held it for a bit longer than was strictly necessary. His gaze locked with hers as Rocky settled back behind his desk. There were two chairs in front of the big wooden desk and Bob waited for Serena to be seated before retaking his own seat.

"Now," Rocky began. "I'm sorry to have to bring this up, but we're trying to connect some dots and your knowledge may help. This concerns Ben Steel. Can you tell us what you know about him and your first-hand impressions of his character?"

Serena gulped. Bob saw it and realized she was both nervous and scared. His heart went out to her but there was little he could do to alleviate her tension. It drove his cougar nuts that he couldn't protect her.

"It's okay," Rocky crooned to her, apparently seeing the same thing Bob saw. "Take your time. You know I wouldn't ask if it wasn't really important."

She nodded. "Yes," she agreed somewhat stiffly. "I'm okay." She paused a moment before finally answering the question. "Ben Steel was the one who brought me here. He said he had some familiarity with the region because he'd been sent to the Cascades a few years ago by the *Altor Custodis*, to watch the Cascade Clan that I was on the periphery of for years. He said he'd filed a report with the *Altor Custodis* about the Clan years ago, then moved on to his next assignment. As near as I can figure, right after that was when things turned bad for the Clan. Some key members of the most influential families got involved in bad things. One or two were approached directly and some were manipulated into positions where they had no other choice but to do things for these people. Not Steel, but agents within his organization that had gone bad."

She paused, swallowing reflexively, as if talking about the past was hard for her. "My adoptive father was one of them. Steel helped me get away from him and dropped me off here. Well...he dropped me at the base of the mountain. He never came into the Lord's actual territory. It was sort of a scoop and drop."

"Am I right in thinking that Steel found you through Jezza?" Rocky asked.

"The jaguar?" Serena nodded. "Yes, he mentioned Jezza, but I wasn't sure what their connection was. Jezza is kind of a ghost to my people, though he was nice to me the few times we crossed paths. He never came around when my adoptive parents were at the homestead. I got the feeling that was on purpose."

"Serena honey, I wouldn't betray your confidences for the world, but there are some things Bob here needs to know about the Cascade Clan—particularly the group up near Mount Baker."

"The drugs, you mean?" Serena went from timid to disgusted in the blink of an eye. "The Cascade Mountains run from Canada down to California and include several active volcanoes and other geological features," she told Bob. "Lots of rugged country with different groups of shifters that run certain territories. My adoptive parents—Lizzy and Jack— moved into the region near Mount Baker a year or two after adopting me. For all his faults, Jack is a strong son of a bitch. After a pretty spectacular dominance fight with one of the locals, the Alpha made him a lieutenant. That's about the same time they started running drugs across the border for a big cartel. The Clan makes money doing it, but the real profit goes to the humans who forced them into it. Though I don't know how hard they really had to be forced. Some of those bastards are the type to do anything for a quick buck."

Her bitterness came through in her tone, and Bob didn't

blame her one bit. Drugs were bad news. And the thugs who ran them were known to be brutal.

"My adoptive parents joined right in when they saw there was money to be made. They even wanted me to do runs across the border with sacks of heroin and cocaine when I was old enough. I refused. They beat the crap out of me. I healed and it started all over in a vicious cycle. It got worse when some of the couriers started to disappear. Others were caught by the DEA after having been maneuvered into position by a cunning predator. Nobody was really sure what was going on, but the whole Clan got spooked. Not enough to stop breaking the law, but enough to start sending out armed parties hunting whoever it was that was making their drug running business so difficult."

"You have your suspicions about who was doing it, right?" Rocky asked with a gentle, knowing lift of his lips.

"It had to be Jezza," she admitted quietly. "Nobody else really knew he was around—especially not anyone involved in the drug trade—but he showed himself to a few people, including me. He helped us where he could. And in my case, he arranged for Ben Steel to get me out of the region. We all knew I wouldn't be safe anywhere within the Cascades. The Clan is relatively small, but spread out over three states and two countries. There's a lot of money flowing through the Clan now too, with all the drugs. So they have a very long reach. My adoptive parents are stubborn people and Jack has risen in the ranks to one of the top positions of power. He's probably the heir apparent by now," she frowned at the thought. "My continued disobedience became an obsession with him. He tried to break me more than once. He's just sadistic enough to drag me back and keep trying. Which is why I sought sanctuary with the Lords. Now that I have their protection, Jack can't touch me without bringing down their wrath on his dishonest head."

Bob detected more than a hint of satisfaction in her voice. He was proud of the way she had bounced back from what had to have been a horrible ordeal. No wonder Rocky had been so protective of her. And no wonder she'd been so shy at first. She'd been through a hell of a lot in her time.

CHAPTER FIVE

"Thank you, Serena," Rocky said in a respectful tone. "You know I wouldn't have asked you to talk about this if it wasn't important."

"Are you going to try to stop them?" She looked stronger than Bob had expected. Serena was finding her backbone and he felt inexplicably proud of her.

Rocky looked from her to Bob and back again, his expression tight. Bob knew he couldn't tell her too much about what they'd been discussing before she had come in. As a general rule of thumb, the fewer who knew about a plan, the better. But it was a tough call in her case. Her life had been turned upside down by the people in her past and she was still healing. Perhaps knowing that the Lords and their lieutenants were not ignoring the situation would help her heal faster. Bob was hoping Rocky would give her at least that reassurance.

"We haven't decided what we're going to do yet," Rocky said finally. "We think Jezza might be in trouble and we'll do our best to warn him—though as you say, he's a hard man to track down."

"Have you tried the caves up on the eastern ridge near Mt. Baker? Or the old mine on the southern slope of Eagle Peak?

Or the old ghost town in the valley?" Serena seemed eager to help them track the elusive soldier-shaman.

"Tell you what," Rocky said, shuffling through the papers on his desk until he found a folded map. He handed it to her and she accepted it with a curious expression on her face as she turned it around and looked at it. "Mark up the areas you think we should search, and give them rankings. Number one is your most likely place for him to be, then work your way up from there. Take some time. Think about it overnight. Mark up the map and give it back to me tomorrow. Meanwhile, we're prepping a team to go in and look for him. Any locations you can give us to search would be a great help."

Serena looked determined and Bob was glad Rocky had given her a task. Having something to do that could actually help would make her feel useful and possibly help keep her mind off the bad times in her past.

"I think he has a sat phone," Serena volunteered.

"I've heard that before, but nobody seems to know his number," Rocky said with a bit of his frustration showing. "I've called all around the country to people who might've had reason to have his digits, but no dice. And the numbers in my file on him are disconnected with no forwarding. He's off the grid."

"Then you really do have to find him the old fashioned way," Bob surmised.

Rocky nodded, shuffling his papers together into a neat stack on his desk. "I think that's all for today. I've got a meeting, so you're on your own for dinner, Bob. They'll welcome you at the Pack house as long as you're here, or you can make your own meals down at the cabin. Your choice."

Bob didn't reply as he rose from his chair. Serena was getting up too and Bob planned to leave with her. Rocky didn't need to know Bob's plan to coax Serena into sharing the evening meal, though the grizzly shifter probably already guessed.

They said goodbye to Rocky and Bob ushered Serena out

into the late afternoon sun. It was a little early for dinner, but the time would roll around soon enough. He might as well ask her...

"I don't suppose you'd like to have dinner with me?" Bob asked as they walked slowly along the path that led from Rocky's home down to the road. "Maybe at the Pack house?" A nice, neutral, public location ought to make her feel secure.

Serena seemed to think about it for a moment before replying. "We can start there, but if you'll trust me a bit, I know a place that I think you might enjoy."

"Like a picnic?" Bob liked the way her eyes sparkled, even though she seemed uncertain, and he was surprised that she'd venture out of the comfort zone of the Pack house. Maybe she was a little less fragile than he'd thought. He'd wait and see—and treat her as gently as possible. The very last thing he wanted to do was frighten her off.

"Yeah. I guess you could call it a picnic. Sort of." She looked down at her feet, but she hadn't rescinded the invitation and he wasn't fool enough to say no.

"Then I put myself in your hands," Bob said gallantly, playing along. "How about I meet you at the Pack house in a half hour? Is that a good time?"

Bob would have liked to go with her immediately, but he had to secure his laptop back at the cabin and freshen up a bit. A male didn't go courting a lady without taking care with his appearance. Bob might share his soul with an animal, but his animal was a cougar, and even big cats occasionally prided themselves on how well-groomed they were. A little spiffing up was in order after spending all day working in the bear's den.

Serena practically skipped all the way back to the Pack house. She had a dinner date with the cougar. She wasn't sure if she was ready for such a big step, but the more she was around him, the more comfortable she felt with him. That had to be a good sign.

And the talk she'd had with the High Priestess had gone a

long way toward helping her realize that she was no longer the injured, abused bobcat she'd been when she had arrived here. No, she had come a long, long way since then. She was able to stay in her human form a lot longer than anyone realized. In fact, she really didn't have a problem staying human anymore, though nobody but Bettina seemed to notice. Serena just enjoyed prowling in her fur. The freedom to be herself in a safe environment was pretty intoxicating.

"Someone looks happy." Bettina's musical voice broke through Serena's jumbled thoughts as she climbed the stairs to the wide front porch of the Pack house.

Serena looked to her right and saw the ethereal High Priestess sitting in one of the rocking chairs in one corner, lighting the whole area with her presence. There was something incredibly magical about the older woman and Serena really liked being around her.

"Do I?" Serena smiled as she walked over to the High Priestess and perched on the porch rail facing her.

"You have the decided look of a cat who is about to be let loose in a cage full of canaries. Both excited and a little apprehensive. What's going on?" Bettina's kind voice invited confidences.

"I'm having dinner with Bob." Serena couldn't help the silly grin she just knew was spread all over her face.

Bettina smiled brightly and leaned forward, patting Serena's hand. "Good for you." Bettina's approval meant a lot to Serena. "What are you going to wear?"

Serena felt her heart speed up. She hadn't thought about it. She hadn't gotten past the happy feeling that had filled her when Bob had asked her to have dinner with him.

Bettina stood up and took Serena's hand as she turned them both toward the front door. "Come on. I'll help you pick something out. I know how you cats like to look your best. Let's find something that will knock his socks off without looking too eager. You have to make him work a little bit for your favor."

Serena felt better having the High Priestess's help. They

went up to her room and proceeded to raid her closet. Once they'd settled on a nice outfit, Bettina left Serena alone to dress with a motherly hug and a whispered "Good luck. You're a lot stronger than you think you are. It's about time for you to roar."

Bob arrived at the Pack house just as dinner began to be put on the big buffet tables in the dining room. Serena met him on the wide front porch with a shy smile. She had changed into a skirt and looked pretty and feminine. He felt like purring, knowing that her inner cat had dressed up for him, as he had for her. Bob took it as a good sign.

"You look nice," he said softly, wanting to say more but afraid to scare her off. In fact, she looked gorgeous. Sexy, yet innocent at the same time. And absolutely delicious.

"Thanks," she replied with another of those shy little smiles that so enchanted him. "So do you." A slight blush touched her high cheekbones as she looked down at her hands.

They walked into the house and down the hall toward the big dining room together. It was a buffet-style setup tonight, so they were able to pick a few things and pack them to go. Bob let Serena do all the choosing while he stood beside her and took the packages out of her hands as she filled them.

The Pack house seemed to have all sorts of supplies for those who wanted to take their meal to go. Bob snagged a paper shopping bag to place the smaller containers in and Serena carried the drinks as they left the dining room together, heading outdoors. She seemed in a playful mood as they walked along, moving into the twilight of the forest behind the building.

They'd gone uphill for a few minutes when she turned down a game path to the left, into an area of the mountain that Bob hadn't yet seen. They had kept him pretty close to the immediate area around the bear shifter's home since he'd arrived. Bob assumed he would be allowed to see more of the Lords' territory once Rocky delivered his decision on Bob's character. It made sense to be cautious. The Lords were the most important shifters in all of North America.

They were shifter royalty, though the *were*, as a group, didn't go in for crowns and such. No, the *were* left that sort of stuff to the fancier animals. The more exotic big cats had all sorts of monarchs, from what Bob had heard, modeling their society after the politics of Renaissance Europe. *Were* were simpler folk. They let the Mother of All show them who was meant to lead and it didn't matter what family or bloodline they came from. If the Goddess chose them, they were the leaders. End of story.

Serena led the way toward what Bob could now hear, sounded like rushing water. They rounded a thicket of bushes and there in front of them was a gorgeous little waterfall and pool surrounded by big, flat stones. One was large enough for them both to sit on and still have room for the food containers.

"This is nice," Bob said, loving the fine mist of humidity in the air, even though the night was coming on and the mountain air was cooling. It was so different here from the desert. So lush and loamy.

"There are a few spots like this around the mountain, some bigger, some even smaller, but this one is my favorite. It's also the most convenient to the Pack house. I come up here a lot." She led the way to a big, flat rock at the water's edge.

They sat in the last few rays of the setting sun and ate their picnic dinner enjoying the peace of the waterfall and stream. Bob felt comfortable with Serena. A little bit of the edginess that had never quite left him since the murder of his mother seemed to fall away with the rushing of the water—and Serena's calm presence at his side. There was something about her that placated his pacing cougar. Something that made the cat want to purr.

The thought was startling. There were stories about cat shifters purring in their human form. It was said that the one who could make the cougar purr while it was trapped inside the human body was the shifter's true mate. A rare and wondrous thing.

Three of Bob's brothers had found such magic recently. They had mated with women who made his older brothers happier than Bob had ever seen them. It was nice to see his brothers paired off with women who made them truly happy. The Goddess knew, their family had had more than their share of heartache in the past few years.

"I come here when I need to think," Serena offered, breaking into the peaceful sounds of the falling water. "Lately, I've been coming here a lot."

"Heavy thoughts weighing you down?" Bob quipped, hoping to lighten the pensive mood.

She sighed. "Yeah. You could say that." She nibbled at her food for a moment before continuing. "I've spent a lot of time in my fur in the past. It was easier letting the cat's instincts rule over my confused human brain for a while." She cast a few crumbs into the pond and some fish obligingly rose to the surface to eat them. Serena concentrated on the fish just below the surface of the water while she spoke. "Just recently though, I've been walking on two legs more than four. The cat has retreated a bit to give the human side of me time to come to grips with the change in my circumstances."

"The cat protected you while you found your feet again. It's not uncommon for our kind. My little sister spent a lot of time in her fur after our mother died. The cougar helped her cope. I'd guess your bobcat did the same for you," he observed in a quiet tone. He wanted so much to pull her into his arms and offer comfort, but he didn't want to stop her from talking. It seemed like she needed to talk.

"After everything that happened, I guess I was just a bit overwhelmed. I've never known such kindness among shifters as I've found here. Not since my parents died. It was a little hard to deal with at first. I know that sounds strange..." She tore off a small piece of bread and threw it to a particularly large fish. The dusk settled around them but they could both see well in the dark. Still, an air of intimacy surrounded their little hideaway and the words that passed between them.

"I can understand it. And I can curse the people who abused your trust." He let just a bit of his anger at her adoptive parents out in his words and her gaze shot up to meet his.

Silent communication passed between the predators that lived in their souls, the cats understanding each other on a more basic level than human comprehension. The smaller bobcat seemed to recognize the larger cougar and its protective instincts where she was concerned. It also recognized the Alpha who had enough strength to back up his words.

"That's in the past," she finally managed to say after a long, silent moment where many things were said without a single word being spoken. She looked away, focusing on the water once more. "I need to learn to leave it there."

Bob finished the last of his meal and reclined on one elbow, adopting a casual pose. Inside, he felt anything but casual, but he was trying to calm any residual fear she might have.

"That's probably a good attitude. Moving on is hard, but necessary. We all had to learn that after our mother's killers were brought to justice." Bob didn't normally open up about such private matters, but Serena had shared her past with him. He felt it only fair to allow her to hear some of his tale of woe. Somehow, it might help her to know that everyone faced tragedy in life. It was how you dealt with it, and came out on the other side, that was important.

"What happened to her?" The question was quiet, testing, as if she was afraid to ask. It was also respectful, which Bob appreciated. He hadn't talked much about his mother since her death. He hadn't been able to bring himself to put his pain into words.

"She was murdered in her own garden by two mages with *Venifucus* ties. They partially skinned her." He let that statement stand and he could feel the horror of Serena's reaction. That sort of defilement was one of the worst things that could happen to a shifter. Taking a part of a shifter's pelt, it was believed, prevented the spirit from passing easily from this world to the next.

"But you caught them, right? You brought them to justice?"

"There was a male and a female. The male was captured first and his magic drained. He's not much more than a shell now and remains under guard. My cougar still wants to taste his blood, but he's been useful for the information he can provide about the enemy. He's told us a lot about the *Venifucus*, though not easily. Some of our best interrogators have been working on him for a while now. He's just smart enough to hold some information in reserve because when he's told us everything he knows, there's little reason to keep him alive—and a lot of reasons to tear him to shreds."

He watched Serena's face carefully and knew she understood the savage need of the cat to claw and rend its enemy. She seemed to accept his bloodthirsty statement without passing judgment.

"Were you able to make her spirit whole?" she asked quietly.

"Yeah. We finally cornered the female magic user who had possession of my mother's fur and retrieved it. The sorceress was killed in the chase. She either jumped, or perhaps fell, down an open elevator shaft. We're still not sure which. Maybe she didn't know it was there. Or maybe she didn't want to be taken alive. I guess we'll never know." Bob thought about that for a moment. Either way, he was glad the evil woman was dead. "Our priestess found my mother's pelt in a bag the woman was carrying and reunited it with my mother's body. We were able to hold a ceremony for her and see her off to the next realm. I think that was probably the saddest day of my life."

Serena surprised him by moving closer until she was right next to him. She put her arms around his waist and snuggled into him, resting her head on his shoulder and hugging him.

She felt so good there, nestled against him. He put his arms around her and hugged her back, liking the way she offered comfort.

"I'm sorry," she said quietly, her words muffled against his shirt. "I know what it's like to lose a parent. The pain never quite goes away, does it?"

Bob rubbed her back with one hand, offering what comfort he could in return. "No, it doesn't. I had my brothers, of course, and little Belinda was so traumatized. We all tried to help her but eventually Grif just packed her up and went to a cabin he owns in Wyoming. He thought the change of scene would be good for her, and it was. Though we never thought he'd meet his mate up there. Lindsey has been better for him—and for Belinda—than I ever would have guessed. Finding his mate has brought him a measure of peace. I see it in him and I'm both happy, and a bit envious. Lindsey is his true mate and she is Goddess-touched."

"Sounds like quite a woman."

"She is. She's becoming a true matriarch to the Clan. Not exactly the way my mother was, but Lindsey is forging her own path. I'm glad Grif found her. For his sake and for Belinda's. My little sister is slowly coming out of her grief and blossoming into the girl she once was."

"I like the way you speak about your family," Serena observed, still clinging to him. "I can tell you care deeply for them."

"That's the way it should be for our people. What happened to you, Serena, is not normal. Most Clans care for orphans. They foster them with loving families. Your adoptive parents should be shot."

She reached up and placed one finger over his lips, meeting his gaze. Time froze for a moment.

"It's over now," she said finally, her simple words belying the fire that started in the depths of her eyes as she looked at her finger, resting over his lips.

Her little tongue peeked out and licked her lips and a moment later, they were both moving toward each other, their mouths meeting in the middle. It was a kiss of little finesse but a whole lot of fire. It was unexpected and powerful, and Bob had to catch his breath as his heart went from zero to sixty in no time flat.

Whether he kissed her or she kissed him, he didn't really know. He just knew they were joined at the mouth, their bodies pressing closer and need blossoming between them in an eruption of fire he never could have predicted. Serena was a wildcat in his arms, taking as much as she gave, driving him into a near-frenzy of need.

Passion drove him, making his skin hot, his blood coursing through his veins at rapid speed. He tried to read her responses, unsure if she was on the same page as him. He wanted to take this all the way, but he didn't want to rush her.

"Kitten," he gasped, moving his mouth away from hers, although she tried to follow. "Are you sure about this? Do you want this?"

"I want you." Her gaze met his and the molten fire in her eyes told him what he needed to know, even as her words confirmed it. "I need to feel whole. I need you, Bob." She reached up to nibble on his jaw. "I want to know what it's like in human form and I choose you to show me. Is that clear enough?"

She backed up to lift her shirt up over her shoulders and off, tossing it on the rock behind her. She was bare beneath, the little vixen. It looked like she'd been planning seduction all along when she invited him on this little picnic. Bob grinned.

"Well, what are you waiting for?" Her voice shook even as it challenged him. He prowled closer to her, a growl of pure joy sounding in his throat as she bent backward, reclining on the flat stone under him. Yielding. Waiting for him to claim her.

Oh, yeah.

"Picnic, my ass," he teased in a low, rumbling tone that he couldn't quite control. She brought out the playful side of his beast. "You brought me up here to seduce me, didn't you, kitten?"

"Is it working?" She smiled up at him and he could only shake his head in wonder at this new side of her. Far from a shrinking violet, he began to learn that when Serena knew what she wanted, she went after it with both hands.

He lowered his body over her, allowing her to feel the hard length of him against her softness. There was fabric separating them, but he knew she could feel the evidence of his desire when she gasped and her eyes widened.

"Feels like it's working to me," he answered back in the same spirit of playfulness. "How does that feel to you?"

Her head tilted coquettishly. "It feels...intriguing," she answered. "But I think I need to know a bit more before I can make a final decision."

Bob growled as he bent down to lick her neck, nipping, then laving the small hurt with his tongue. The cat inside him liked to bite, but she didn't seem to mind, and the biting wasn't about pain, but about shared pleasure. He didn't want to hurt her. He never wanted to hurt her. Far from it.

"That can be arranged," he whispered against her skin, as he moved one hand to the button on his trousers, releasing it. Her little hands were pushing at his shirt, moving it up so her fingers could glide over the muscles of his abdomen. He wasn't ticklish, but his response to her touch made him growl again as the cat inside him enjoyed her petting.

He lifted up so she could push the bunched up shirt over his shoulders and off completely. Then he set to work on the floaty, gypsy-type skirt she was wearing. He soon discovered it had an elastic waist. He pushed it down over her hips and was pleasantly shocked to learn that she wasn't wearing any panties.

Sweet Mother of All.

She'd definitely come prepared to seduce. She'd gone commando and he hadn't even realized it. He had thought it would take a lot longer and a lot more effort to get her to this point, but he hadn't counted on her taking the lead. *Damn.* The more he got to know her, the more he liked her.

She'd surprised him. And challenged him. He found he really enjoyed that. Bob couldn't really remember a time when another woman had so completely captured his full attention so effortlessly. That she had planned to seduce him tickled his sense of adventure.

All along, Rocky had been warning Bob how fragile she was, but here Serena was, proving him and everyone else wrong. She might still have sore spots—and who wouldn't with her background and recent history? But she was more than her past. She was more than the experiences that had led her here.

She was overcoming the problems of her past and grabbing hold of her future—shaping it in the image she wanted. It seemed that being with Bob was part of that and who was he to argue? It's what he wanted too.

That she was confident enough to reach out for him meant a lot. It meant that she had thought this all through and deliberately set out to be with him tonight. He would have to wait and see if it led to more private time with the woman who was fast becoming an obsession, but he would do everything in his power to have her in his arms as often as she allowed it.

Now it was his job to convince her. Knowing she had no experience with sex in her human form didn't help. He felt both honored and anxious that she had given him the task of introducing her to fucking as a human.

One thing he didn't have to worry about was hurting her with his entry. She had told him she'd had sex in her fur during her frenzy. So that part was taken care of. You could only lose your virginity once, thank the Goddess.

But there was still quite a burden on his shoulders—a delightful burden, but a burden nonetheless. He had to make this so good for her that she would want to do it again. And again. And again. With him, and only with him.

He was feeling really possessive of her already and he hadn't done much more than kiss her. He liked kissing her, so he did it again. He climbed up over her body, having removed all trace of fabric between them and just held himself over her, their bodies separated by no more than an inch while he took her mouth in a gentle seduction of the sense. He wanted everything to be perfect for their first time together.

His warmth surrounded her. His strength impressed her. And his technique totally collapsed her every defense. She didn't have the will to deny him anything when he treated her so gently, with so much intense care. But why would she? She had planned this.

Okay, maybe the plan had been hastily formed, but it was her choice. She had set out to seduce him and test her newly rediscovered strength. Bettina's gentle words had helped Serena find her courage and the strength to reach out for what she wanted.

And what she wanted most right now was Bob. She wanted to know what it would feel like to be with him. She had been curious about human sex for a long time and Bob felt like the right man—the only man—to try it with. She trusted him, odd as it may seem. Even on such short acquaintance, she knew in her heart that he was special.

Even now, he treated her like a treasure. He kept his full weight from her, letting her feel only his warmth and the strength in the rock-solid arms that kept his muscled chest and torso just a few inches from her. He dipped, allowing his chest to meet hers, rub and then retreat as his mouth continued to tantalize her with drugging kisses. He repeated the maneuver a few times until her nipples were pebbled points of sensation, a jolt of sexy lightning zipping through her body from those little points of contact every time he dipped to touch her there.

Sweet Mother of All, Bob was something else when it came to pleasing a woman. She didn't want to examine too closely how he'd gained his skills. Her inner bobcat was a jealous bitch and didn't want to think about *her* Bob being with anyone else. Ever.

Whoa.

The unexpectedly serious nature of this encounter was just dawning on her when Bob retreated from her mouth, only to take his lips lower, kissing a slow, sexy path down her neck and over the upper slopes of her breasts. She actually moaned, wanting him to move lower, to the little points that needed relief so desperately.

And then he was there. His mouth covered one nipple while he engulfed her other breast with one large, warm, calloused hand. He had shifted his weight a bit lower and to one side, freeing one hand and allowing him access to the rest of her body. She couldn't wait to see what he had in store for her next.

Her hands went to his head, tangling in his hair, loving the feel of the soft golden silk under her fingers. Her head lolled back as he sucked on her nipple, that lightning of pleasure streaking through her again and again. She had never felt this way before. Fucking in her fur hadn't been anything like this. Not at all.

Bob spent a lot of time on her breasts—first one, then the other—making her writhe beneath him. When was he going to get to the fucking part? Did it always take this long when doing it in your skin? She had no basis for comparison, but she thought maybe Bob was making this something special. Just for her. The thought made her feel all warm and gooey inside—in addition to hot and bothered—in the best possible way.

On some level, he had to care for her. He obviously cared enough to make his own pleasure secondary to hers. The boys she had been with in her youth hadn't been thinking much about her comfort. No, they had been focused on their beast's need to mate. As had she, if she was being honest.

But Bob was different. She had instinctually known he was a very special man, and she had trusted him enough to want him to be the one to introduce her to human-shaped sex. She wasn't sure exactly where this was all going to lead, but she was glad she had chosen him.

And then all thought fled as Bob moved downward once more, pressing kisses into her navel, then over the slight curve of her belly and then lower. He settled himself between her legs, his hands urging her thighs to part even wider for him. Making room for him.

She looked down and his gaze flashed up to meet hers. She felt heat flood her cheeks. For a moment, she had been in a place where nothing was awkward and nothing mattered but the pleasure he gave her. Then she had met his gaze and suddenly, she was embarrassed. But he didn't give her time to dwell on it. Instead, he lowered his lips to her body once more, using his hands to spread her wide. With unerring accuracy, he found the little nubbin at the apex of her thighs and went for it, distracting her back into that place where nothing mattered but the pleasure he gave her.

Serena panted and moaned as a flush stole over her entire body. The lightning buzzed through her again and it was leading her toward…something. Something she had never felt before.

And then it was there. She was there. Yowling a bit as she crossed over some previously unknown precipice and fell into pleasure. Bob growled against her skin, the sound of his dominance sending her even higher.

Damn, that felt good.

While the lightning still gripped her body, Bob moved again, sliding upward and positioning his hard cock at her entrance. He waited until she opened her eyes and met his gaze to slide in. Slowly. Inch by inch, he joined them, holding her gaze, making the moment special. Important.

She couldn't look away. She thought she saw something in his determined gaze. Something soft and fragile. Something vulnerable. Just the idea of it entranced her. Bob was so strong. He was such an Alpha in every way, but she was quickly discovering he was also a man. A man who had been through traumatic times in his family and had weathered the storm. She liked knowing that they had some common ground—a shared understanding that life wasn't always perfect and nice. She felt like he was a bit of a kindred spirit…and so much more.

Her cat wanted him forever. The bobcat didn't care that his cougar could eat her for lunch. It didn't care that he was more than twice her size when in their fur. It didn't care that he was a different species of cat. It only knew that he was an honorable being, a protector who wouldn't hurt her, but instead, would care for her in both her forms.

The cat's instincts were to curl into his arms and never leave. And the woman wasn't far behind.

He began to move, still holding her gaze. She saw the change in his eyes as the lightning began a new round of tremors through her body. Small at first, they built steadily as his pace increased.

"Do you feel it?" he asked, his breath fanning her skin, making her shiver.

If he was talking about the incredible connection forming between them, then she definitely felt something. If he meant the pleasure, there was no way *not* to feel the riot of sensation he was causing in her body. She nodded and a little whimper escaped her lips.

"Tell me, kitten. Do you feel this thing between us?" he insisted.

She nodded again, though her movements weren't neat. Her body was too sensitized by his possession. Everything was almost too intense, but she wouldn't change a thing. She finally realized what she had been missing all this time and she didn't want to go back. No, she definitely wanted to feel this again—with Bob. And only with Bob.

"Say it," he whispered, his head dropping close to hers as he pushed deeply into her body.

Her breath hitched as he increased the penetration. She felt totally possessed, totally his in that moment. It wasn't scary. In fact, her cat craved the feeling like its next meal. Her body guided her as the electric jolts of the lightning that only he seemed able to produce in her tried to send her into orbit again—only this time a lot higher than she had gone before.

She was learning something here. She was learning there were different levels of pleasure and Bob seemed to be the master at showing her just how far he could take her. She wanted to go all the way.

"Say it," he breathed, the intensity almost overwhelming as he retreated, then pushed deep once more.

"I feel it!" she gasped.

He had slowed to speak, but her response seemed to break the dam that had been holding him back. His possession was deep and total. She almost wept when he pulled back, but whimpered in pleasure when he shoved back home. His key, her lock—somehow they were made for each other.

His pace increased again and the buzz of electric pleasure was non-stop in every cell of her body. Where it was leading, she didn't really know, but she knew she wanted to get there. *Oh, man, how she wanted to get there!*

Bob lowered himself over her completely, enveloping her in his warmth, his strength. His hands clasped her shoulders, helping her accept the deep, hard thrusts of his body as the intensity threatened to overwhelm her. She had never imagined anything could feel like this. Like dying and finding nirvana at the same time. The ultimate pleasure. The ultimate thrill.

She was crying out on every thrust now, little whimpers of straining pleasure, little sounds of need. She needed him to take her to the next level. She didn't think it was possible to get there alone. Only with him. Only with Bob.

She clutched at his shoulders, her claws coming out unintentionally. The sharp coppery scent of blood hit the air at the same moment the lightning of completion struck and made her entire body spasm around his. With his.

Bob stiffened around her and she could feel the warmth of his seed bathing her from within. Her cat craved the possession, wanting to mark him with her teeth, but Serena knew biting was something reserved for mates. She didn't want to cross a line or get carried away with her first lover. She didn't know where he stood on the whole relationship issue. He was just passing through and she was still recovering, learning more about herself every day.

She looked at this encounter as part of her healing. Bob had come along and made her want to try something she never would have considered with any other cat. He had made her want to be just a little more daring, a little more whole emotionally than she had been before they'd met. And her risk had paid off in ways she never would have expected.

The pleasure coursed through her, making her muscles spasm even as her mind turned to mush. The last coherent thought she had was that she was glad she'd waited. Bob was in a class by himself when it came to making love. Even with her limited experience, she knew that much.

Bob had felt the sting in his shoulders as her little claws came out and it had sent him straight over the edge. To have driven her that wild on his first attempt meant something. It was a major boost to his ego and brought out all sorts of protective, possessive thoughts in his cougar half, and his human half as well. Both sides of him wanted Serena with an intensity that would not be denied.

The miracle that had happened just now humbled him. Timid as she was, she had let her inner huntress out and pursued him. The cougar didn't usually like being the object of a woman's hunt, but it made all kinds of exceptions for Serena. His inner cat liked everything about her and would humor her every whim. For Serena, his cougar became a pussycat.

The fact that she had passed out from pleasure stroked his ego a little further. He had stayed inside her as long as he could, but eventually, he'd had to move. He couldn't let her go far, so he had rolled them over, putting his back against the hard rock beneath them and draping her luscious body over him like a blanket. He fished for the picnic blanket with one hand and managed to pull it over her back so she wouldn't be cold.

He basked in the moment until his own eyelids started to

droop and sleep claimed him.

How long they laid there, under the dark sky and cover of the forest, he didn't know, but when she scrambled off his body sometime later, he woke instantly.

She seemed shy and he thought he understood. This had been her first time making love as a human and probably her first time playing the temptress. He liked that she had let her wild side come out to play with him, but he was concerned about the way she scrambled into her clothes and began packing up the picnic things. Her movements were almost frantic and he didn't like the way she wouldn't meet his gaze.

He stood and dressed, then stilled her movements by the simple expedient of taking her into his arms. She resisted a little, but he wasn't letting her put distance between them.

"It's okay, kitten. I just wanted to thank you and let you know how special you are to me." When she didn't relax in his embrace, he tried to find better words to soothe her. "You make me feel so good, Serena. And I know you enjoyed what we just did."

Dammit. Bob—the most loquacious Redstone brother—was having a hell of a time finding the right words. Then again, he'd never been in quite this situation before. He'd never had a woman mean so much to him before. And that thought stopped him dead. Something fundamental had changed inside him and it would need examination before he knew where he stood.

"You're so special to me, Serena," he tried, one last time, kissing the crown of her head as he rocked her a little in his arms, but she didn't respond.

And then she was gone. Out of his arms.

Bob was still trying to figure out what had just happened and Serena was standing five feet away, her lithe body trembling the tiniest bit.

"I'm sorry," she whispered before turning and fleeing into the night, her expression one of fear and longing mixed during the short glimpse he had of her face.

Bob wanted to go after her but he knew she would come

to no harm on the Lords' mountain. Plus he wasn't confident he could find her. She knew the area a lot better than he did and bobcats were as fast as cougars. She also probably wouldn't exactly welcome him chasing her down. Something about their interlude had scared the bejeezus out of her and part of him knew he shouldn't push her too hard—even if another part of him wanted to chase her down, catch her and tie her to his bed, never to be released.

Bob sank to his knees on the flat rock and stared up at the stars visible through a break in the trees. Serena had launched a sneak attack and he felt like he'd been completely overtaken. She had definitely won this round, but he wondered if she realized it.

One thing was for certain—now that he knew what it was like to be with her, he vowed there would be more lovemaking in their future. He just had to plan his strategy and find a way to help her conquer her fears.

To do that, he would have to figure out what had caused her to flee, but Bob could be a patient man. When he discovered something he wanted, he usually found a way to get it. He had time to plan and plot, but soon, he promised himself, the pretty little bobcat female would be his.

CHAPTER SIX

Banging on the cabin door at oh-dark-thirty woke Bob from dreams of a certain luscious bobcat woman. From the intensity of the pounding, it was probably Rocky. Bob threw off the single blanket he had slept under and armed himself before heading toward the door.

"What?" he called out, cautious and picking up on sounds of all kinds of movement outdoors. Shifters scurrying through the woods around his cabin at a fast clip, vehicles on the gravel road, and a few people running around near the road as well. Something was definitely up.

"It's Rocky. We have a situation."

Bob pulled open the door. The bear-man was clearly agitated. His hair was flat on one side as if he'd just rolled out of bed himself.

"What's wrong?"

"We just got reliable intel that an attack is imminent. It could come at any time in the next few hours. We're evacuating everyone who can't fight and prepping the rest for action." Rocky spoke fast, his expression tight.

"Where do you want me?" Bob was ready to help defend the Lords' domain.

"Serena needs to go but she's hard to place. Can your Clan

take her in? I think she'll be more comfortable with cats, and she seems to like you. Plus, your Clan is big enough to protect her."

Bob didn't hesitate. "I'll take her. And I can get reinforcements up here within a day, if you need."

"Look to your own Clan. We've already got Jesse Moore's guys mobilizing. They'll be here in a couple of hours, but the non-combatants need to go now. This could go down any time."

"I'll get my stuff and go get Serena. We'll be out of here in fifteen minutes or less." Bob was already thinking about what he needed to do to prepare. "We'll drive."

Rocky nodded, already looking back toward his house across the road and up the mountain. "Safer if nobody knows where you are. I don't trust planes we haven't vetted and the few we have are already busy taking our people out and bringing in Moore's guys."

"What about Jezza?" Bob thought to ask, even though he knew Rocky was antsy to get back to his family. "Anybody going to find him?"

"Can't spare the people right now." Rocky shook his head, genuine regret in his eyes.

"Don't worry about it. I'll get the map from Serena before I drop her off with my brothers, then I'll double back and take care of Jezza. One less thing for you to worry about."

Rocky clapped him on the shoulder. "Good man. I'll owe you one when we meet again. Communications blackout until you're over the state line, okay? Be safe, my friend, and good hunting."

"Understood and good hunting to you too," Bob replied. It seemed he'd made a friend in the grizzly bear, though he hadn't really realized it.

Rocky took off back across the narrow gravel road toward his house and Bob didn't waste any time in packing his few belongings. He gave the cabin a quick once-over and hit the road toward the Pack house, which was just up the road a ways. He double-timed it, covering ground quickly with his rucksack of possessions over his shoulder. He passed a few vehicles heading down the mountain and could see they were mostly full of women with small kids and the few really elderly shifters that lived here.

Bob sent up a silent prayer for the safety of each of those vehicles and the shifters inside them. The threat had to be damned serious for the Lords to take this drastic step. Bob didn't know where the SUVs full of the weaker members of the community were headed, but he'd bet good money the Lords had a secret place to stash them that had been arranged long before this emergency. The evacuation was too orderly not to have been planned well in advance. The Lords definitely knew how to look out for their people.

Bob arrived at the Pack house to find Serena in the thick of things, helping pack supplies into a vehicle that was mostly full. When she saw him, she gave up her place in the relay line and picked up a big duffel bag that had been leaning against the porch. She ran forward to meet him as he neared.

"Rocky called ahead to say I was to go with you." It wasn't quite a question, but it was clear she was puzzled by the directive and doing her best not to tremble with fear.

Bob cursed inwardly and pulled her into his arms for a quick hug. "I'm taking you to my family. We're strong enough to protect you from just about anything and Rocky wants you well away from any fighting. So do I."

She pulled slightly away to look into his eyes. The world around them stopped for a minute while she seemed to teeter on the brink of a decision… And then she nodded, slowly.

"Okay. Let's go."

Bob squeezed her once in silent approval, then let her go. He bent to sling her duffel over his shoulder and then took hold of her hand as he led her back down the road he'd just run up. He had left his vehicle in a communal lot roughly halfway between the cabin and the Pack house, slightly lower on the mountain. The fastest way to get there was through the trees and, in fact, Bob saw quite a few shifters using various shortcuts to the hidden lot where more than a few vehicles were kept.

He kept hold of her hand as they made their way through the dark trees. Dawn hadn't even begun before they reached Bob's vehicle. He had driven an SUV here that he'd done quite a bit of work on. The outside looked like an older model vehicle that had seen better days, but inside was a different story.

He opened the passenger door for Serena. She climbed in while he stowed her duffel bag and his rucksack in the back. He had installed special compartments for storage back there, as well as a few other things that made this vehicle perfect for road trips. It would come in handy today while they made a quick escape.

Bob ran around to the front and got in on the driver's side, starting the engine and checking the various instruments. Everything was in good working order and it looked like nothing had been added or taken from his sophisticated electronics systems by the Lords' technical people who had gone over the vehicle with a fine toothed comb when he had arrived in their territory. The Lords were careful folks. They believed in the old *trust but verify* style of leadership and Bob couldn't really blame them.

He pulled out of the lot without turning on the headlights. Shifters could see in the dark and it was best not to bring any more attention to the stealthy movements on the mountain than they had to. All around him, other vehicles moved without lights, shifters at the wheel. A few waved as he passed and he returned the gesture. Only sharp shifter vision could see through the specially tinted glass he had installed on his vehicle.

The front glass was tinted within legal limits, but a special coating gave the safety glass an almost impenetrable gloss that humans couldn't easily see around. The back glass was as dark as he could make it within legal limits, which was to say *dark*. It also had a more reflective coating that kept prying eyes from seeing all the changes he had made back there. Tinkering with cars was one of his favorite hobbies, and he had put a lot of modifications into this particular vehicle.

Bob itched to call his brothers, but he had promised Rocky not to use his phone or any other communications devices until he was beyond the state border. It was a wise precaution. If enemies were planning an attack, they would be stupid not to monitor all transmissions. Bob's equipment was encrypted, but he didn't want to take any chances. He would sooner die than betray the Lords in any way.

As long as they were on the road and in this vehicle, they should be fine. This little honey had a few tricks up her sleeve, including Kevlar in the door panels and a few offensive surprises of her own.

"Did you bring the map Rocky wanted you to mark up?" Bob asked as he negotiated the dirt road that led down the mountain. It took a lot of his concentration. The Lords deliberately kept the road rough to discourage unwanted visitors. It was just one of many little tricks they had in store for anyone fool enough to attack them in the heart of their own territory.

"It's in my bag," she replied in a small voice as she stared out at the dark road, worry etched in the set of her brow. "Do you think they'll be all right?"

"Honey, they've got an army up there and another *en route*. They'll be okay. Our job is to stay out of the way and prevent ourselves from becoming a liability."

"*My* job, you mean," she gave a derisive snort. "If you didn't have to babysit me all the way to Las Vegas, you'd be up there helping them defend the mountain. Don't lie to me and tell me you would be running like a scared rabbit."

"I won't ever lie to you, sweetheart," he said very seriously. "You're right. If I didn't have you, I'd be alongside the other soldiers. But the thing is, I'd rather be with you. Now that I've met you, if I wasn't seeing to your safety, I'd be worried. And a worried soldier is a distracted soldier. I'd be that liability we're trying to avoid becoming." He chuckled as he made a steep hairpin turn down the mountain. "All in all, everyone's better off with this arrangement."

"You're really taking me to Las Vegas? To the heart of your Clan?" She seemed skeptical.

"Don't worry. My brothers and their mates are going to love you. I think you'll like them too." His new sister-in-laws all seemed to have a soft spot for those who needed protection.

"But what about Jezza?" she asked in a small, pensive voice.

Bob's stomach knotted. He didn't want to tell her the plan they'd come up with on the fly. He knew she was genuinely concerned about the other man's safety. A little flare of jealousy hit him at that thought, but Bob tried his best to squash it. He had to try to remain objective for both their sakes.

"Rocky can't spare anybody, but I'm going to—"

"No. If your plan is to take me to Las Vegas and then double back, it'll take too long. Jezza could be dead by then."

She was quick, he'd give her that. "Once we cross the state line I can call my brothers and have them send a plane. I could hand you off to one of them and then go find Jezza."

"Why wait? Oh—scanners, right?" She answered her own question. "Okay. What's the nearest airport?"

"Probably Idaho Falls."

"If you go south. But what if you go north and west? Toward the Cascades?" Her voice held an excited edge. If he didn't know better, he'd think she was eager to get back to her home range.

Bob had made it down the mountain and onto the back roads that would eventually lead him to the main highway. By that point, he'd have to make a choice.

"I guess we could aim for Spokane. If one of my brothers can get a plane up there that we can trust, I could drop you off on my way. But it's going to take hours and hours to get there. Hell, it'll take a few hours just to get across the Montana border so I can make some calls. If we commit to this plan, it's going to be a hell of a juggling act."

"But it'll get you to Jezza faster. I don't want my safety to

87

come at his expense. He risked a lot to help me. I can do no less for him." She was adamant in her stance and Bob had to respect her feelings.

There was a streak of nobility in her that he hadn't quite expected, but found enchanting. Everything about her enchanted him. *Damn.* He had it bad.

Bob followed the winding back roads, having turned on his headlights as soon as he'd joined the country road off the mountain. Now his job was to blend in. The battered appearance of the outside of his SUV did that very well—as long as he didn't do anything to draw attention, like drive through the night with no headlights. Or speed. Or drive aggressively. He had to keep it slow and steady. Under the speed limit. Nonchalant.

It was going to be a long trip to the border before he could start making calls.

Dawn was a bit of a non-event, Serena decided later. Their slow progress toward the border with the skinny part of Idaho was made even more tedious by a drizzle that brought with it dark gray clouds and not even a hint of sun. The only difference between night and day was that the sky had lightened to dark gray rather than pitch black.

"I don't like the look of those clouds," Bob had said once the sky had gotten about as light as it was going to get. "If the weather gets too bad, nothing will be flying."

Serena chose not to comment. As long as Bob was going north and west, she wasn't going to rock the boat. Jezza needed help and she was going to do whatever she had to do to get him the help he needed. Even if it meant going back to her old territory.

She would be in danger if certain members of her old Clan saw her, but she would be careful. She had learned a thing or two about stealth from the classes she had been taking on the Lords' mountain. They had let her train and learn how to defend herself. She wasn't an expert by any means, but she knew a lot more now than she had before. Learning new skills had helped her feel empowered, and if the weather kept misbehaving, they might also come in handy. Because there was no way she was going to wait around for a ride to Nevada when every minute of delay could cost Jezza his life.

The man had been too good to her to let him die like that. She owed him. And Serena always made a point to repay her debts.

"If you lift the lid on the console between us, you'll find cold drinks. Snacks are in the glove box. We probably won't have a lot of time to stop for breakfast. I'd rather press on, at least until we're over the border and I can call my kin," Bob said into the silence.

Serena lifted the hatch on the center console and was surprised to find it went a lot deeper than she had thought. A little LED light came on inside and she could see that the container was actually a refrigerator. Cool air drifted over her hand as she reached in to select a bottle of water for herself.

"Would you like anything?" she asked politely.

"Any cola left? I think there was at least one in there."

"I see it. There are two actually." She retrieved the red can and popped the top before handing it to him. She stowed her water bottle in the cup holder on her side of the SUV and closed the hatch on the console. Then she went after the snacks he had mentioned.

The glove box had a spot up top for papers that was neat and tidy. Below was a larger compartment that held various small bags of cookies, crackers, cheese puffs and chips. She took a bag of raspberry centered cookies for herself, then looked over at Bob.

"Can you snag a bag of chips for me?" He sent her a smile and she had to catch her breath. His smiles were potent.

Even under the circumstances—with all the worry that ate at her gut, the tension in her muscles, and the anxiety about getting where they needed to be—she had to admire that smile. It melted her bones and made her heart stutter a little in appreciation. Bob Redstone was just too good looking for his own good.

She fumbled a little with the bag of chips, but recovered as best she could. She opened the bag and handed it to him so he could snack as he drove. Flustered, she turned to her water bottle and spent more time than absolutely necessary focusing on unscrewing the cap. She chewed a cookie, not really noticing the burst of raspberry flavor and swallowed some water, staring out the window at the sparse traffic and worsening weather.

"If the weather is too bad and you can't get me out of here by air," she whispered, staring out at the rain, "I'll go with you."

She could feel the intensity of Bob's gaze on her profile, but she couldn't meet his eyes.

"I won't take you into danger, sweetheart. Please don't ask it of me. I have a burning need to protect you."

Something in his tone touched her and she finally turned to look at him. He was watching the road, but he kept shooting her glances when he could. There wasn't much traffic on the road with them, thankfully.

Not wanting to argue, she let it go for now. There would be time to argue if and when it became necessary. Her brain wanted to focus on why he was so protective of her. Was it just because he was an Alpha and had a strong need to care for those who were weaker—as she had learned a good Alpha should be? Or was it something deeper? Something more personal?

She was almost afraid to let her mind go there. What would it be like to have a relationship with a cougar Alpha? Her inner bobcat was a little intimidated by his larger size and incredible brawn, but cats were proud—and a little vain. Her cat knew it was prettier than his. It might be smaller, but the bobcat was tough. Resilient. And fluffy.

Her animal side knew it could hold its head up high, even next to a cougar. But would the cougar ever look at her as anything but a smaller, weaker, distant cousin of sorts? That was something their wild sides would have to work out. As for their human sides...Serena felt comfortable with Bob when they were talking. And when he turned that certain look on her, she felt an excited quivering inside. She had never felt that way with another man. Only Bob seemed to be able to evoke that kind of response.

It scared her a little, but not in a bad way. It was more the fear of a woman who had never really found anyone she was truly attracted to before. An untried woman who finally found a man who pushed all her buttons. She was confused by the reaction and a little afraid of the consequences, but she definitely didn't want to run away. In fact, she was eager to see where the attraction might lead.

But only if he was serious. She didn't want to be just another conquest to a handsome man. She wanted whatever was happening between her and Bob to mean something. Even if it was just a brief affair, she wanted to know that for this short time, she was his focus and that he felt something for her that went beyond animal attraction. Not pity or protectiveness, but actual caring and admiration if it couldn't go any deeper.

She thought they had already crossed that bridge. They had gotten to know each other and formed a bond of intimacy. The High Priestess had really helped her break that final bond of fear that had held her back for so long. Bettina's words, combined with Bob's sudden entrance into her life had combined to bring out the courage her inner cat had used to sustain her in her fur for so long. Only now, she felt that courage in her human form as well. It was a huge breakthrough and something she would always thank Bob for helping her achieve—even if he didn't realize it.

She respected the man he was. She thought he probably had found some things to admire about her as well. They had made a good start, but where would the incredible attraction between them go now? Would he forget her if he managed to get her on a plane to Las Vegas? Would he not make it back?

The place he was going—the wild part of the Cascade mountain range—was dangerous. She knew it well and knew just how deadly the people she had left behind could become.

Bob could get into serious trouble pretty quickly and he didn't know the terrain. There were caves and hidden places all over those mountains.

Fear ran through her as she thought of him out there alone. Even the best instincts might not save him from her former Clan mates. They were ruthless when it came to protecting the smuggling routes and hidey-holes that were their livelihood. A stranger in their territory would not only stand out, but be ripe for hunting.

Even an Alpha cougar could be brought down by enough vicious bobcats working together.

CHAPTER SEVEN

When they finally crossed the border, Bob started making calls. His SUV was wired for sound so he didn't have to stop the vehicle in order to talk. With her sharp, shifter hearing, Serena would probably hear the conversation anyway, so he just went ahead and made the calls within the confines of the car, knowing she would hear all.

The first person he contacted was his brother Grif. As Alpha of the Redstone Clan, he was at the highest level of the hierarchy, the strongest link in the chain. He had to get Grif's approval for Serena to be admitted into the Clan neighborhood and put under their protection. It was mostly a formality. As a general rule, if Bob, or one of their other brothers had given his word, Grif would go along with it, trusting to his brother to have thought things through and not to have made any offers lightly. Unless there was something going on that Bob didn't know about, all would be well on the topic of his promise to keep Serena safe in Las Vegas.

He hit the speed-dial button, the audio playing through his SUV's sound system. The phone rang twice and then a female voice answered.

"How are things in Montana?" the youngest Redstone

asked. Teenaged Belinda lived with Grif and Lindsey.

They had all lived in the same house with their mother when they first moved to Las Vegas a few years ago. Little by little, the younger brothers had built their own places in the area, but the house where the Alpha lived was still considered the family homestead. It had become a place of warmth and light again when Grif had brought Lindsey home to stay.

"Things are a little rough at the moment," Bob answered his baby sister. "I'm on the road. Is Grif around? I really need to speak to him." Although he tried to temper his words, he also needed to convey the urgency that drove him.

"I'll get him." Belinda seemed to understand his tone. Bob could hear her bellowing Grif's name in the background as she scampered through the house. He could easily hear her soft footsteps and the jostling of the phone as she sought their eldest brother. A minute later, Grif's voice came over the SUV's speakers.

"What's up? You weren't due to call in for another day or two."

"Code Red on the mountain," Bob reported. "There's some kind of assault underway. They're evacuating the non-combatants. I'm on the road with one and she's listening in on our call. I've promised her we'd look after her. Rocky asked and I agreed. Is it okay with you, Alpha?" Bob asked formally. He couldn't go into too many details over the phone. It was always possible someone might be monitoring the airwaves, even though he had scrambled his signal.

"I'll want to know more when you get here, but if you promised, it's okay with me." Grif's response was all Bob could have hoped for. The fact that his brother trusted him so completely was something he never took for granted.

"Thing is, there's someone else in danger. Someone I agreed to find and warn. He's off the grid in the Cascades. Is there any way we can get a secure flight to meet my friend at Spokane? The Lords are unable to help and every air asset they have is already in use. Added complication is some nasty weather moving in."

"Let me check with Steve and see what we can scramble," Grif sounded doubtful. "I've seen the weather reports and the storm that's heading your way might pose a problem for air travel in the whole region. You can probably still get through on the ground though."

"I had hoped to drop off my friend and continue on to the Cascades. Originally, I was going to drive her home, then come back, but she convinced me the person I need to warn may not have that kind of time."

"Your friend is one of us?" Grif asked.

"Related species. You're gonna laugh, but she's a bobcat."

Sure enough, Grif did laugh at the irony of Bob—a cougar shifter—making friends with a bobcat shifter when he'd been called "Bobcat" almost all his life as a sort of nickname. At first his brothers had used it as a teasing insult because bobcats were so much smaller than cougars. It was also a play on his name, of course, and the fact that he could turn into a big cat.

"Yeah, I know," Bob cut into his brother's laughter. "Should I call Steve or will you?"

Grif was still chuckling when he replied. "I'll do it. You concentrate on driving. Stay safe little bro. One of us will call back when we know more about the flight situation."

Grif was still chuckling when they signed off. Bob switched the radio on to seek the weather report and left it on low volume in the background while he waited for the announcer to get back around to the heart of the forecast.

"Your brother sounds nice," Serena offered from the passenger seat.

"He's a damn good Clan Alpha," Bob agreed, adjusting the windshield wipers as the rain intensified.

"And the girl, was that your sister?" Serena seemed to want to talk.

"Belinda. Yeah, she's the youngest of us all. Still a teen. Going rapidly from cute as a button to femme fatale. Lady help us all when she starts dating." He rolled his eyes comically, but it was only half in jest.

He, like all his brothers, was intensely protective of Belinda—the only female left of their direct line. They had already lost their older sister a few years before their mother had been murdered, so Belinda was watched extra closely. Nobody wanted anything to happen to her. The brothers couldn't take another loss like that. Bob especially, wanted Belinda to live a long and healthy life and have a few children of her own that he could spoil as their Uncle Bob. He looked forward to it, though he didn't look forward to vetting the young men who were bound to come around, wanting to date his little sister.

It was going to take a very special guy to run the gamut of the five Redstone brothers and be allowed to mate with their little sister. They had time yet. Belinda was still young. But in a couple of years, the boys would start testing their luck, asking her out. It was going to be a hellish few years until she grew up enough to find her true mate.

"It must be nice for her," Serena said in a wistful voice that made Bob glance at her. "Having a family that cares, I mean," she clarified when she caught him looking. Her voice was quiet, carefully contained, but Bob could hear the sadness and pain in her tone. He reached out to cover her hand with his.

"Belinda has been through tragedy and come out stronger on the other side. You have too. She had her family to lean on, of course, but now sweetheart, you have me. I've promised my protection and that's not something that will change anytime soon."

She stilled, watching him, her eyes filled with wonder...and suspicion.

"Why? You just met me. We're not even the same species."

Bob knew the way he answered could either reassure her or frighten her off. He didn't want to reveal too much in case the depth of his feelings scared her away. He had to play this cool, for now. Let her work her way up to the same intensity of feeling he was discovering inside himself where she was concerned.

He shrugged, though his feelings were definitely *not* as casual as he tried to appear. "Close enough. We're both cats. And I've been called Bobcat by my friends and family for most of my life." He chuckled a bit, trying to be nonchalant. "As to why..." He allowed his words to trail off as if he was considering how to respond. And in truth, he was. He had to find the right words, but was afraid he would fail miserably. "Let's just say, I like you. A lot. More than any woman I've met in a long time. And though it may sound strange, in some ways, you remind me of my older sister. I sort of wish she'd had someone like me around, willing to help her when she was in trouble. Or you could say I have a fondness for small, defenseless things."

She growled at him in the first real show of spirit her cat had given him. "I'm not totally defenseless." She looked away, training her gaze out the window. "And I'm not your sister."

On that he could agree. "Thank the Goddess for that."

He might've said more but the phone rang through the car speakers at that moment. He checked the number and realized it was Steve. He hit the button to activate the call.

"If you're heading for the Spokane airport, don't," Steve said in lieu of hello. "In fact, don't go near any airport in the region, even the small ones. The Lords sent an urgent message to all Clan leadership. Their people have had serious trouble getting out by air. A few are dead. Many injured. Running battles in and around the local airstrips and the Lords themselves are pinned down on their mountain. So far, they're holding their own, but the enemy is well prepared and has a lot more resources than anyone expected. Worse news—this seems to be a simultaneous strike on all shifter monarchs in North America. It might possibly extend farther, into Europe and South America, but I don't have confirmation yet. So far, we've heard of strikes against a few of the big cat kings and queens and a possible attack on the tiger stronghold in Iceland. We're waiting for confirmation on that and on a rumored strike in the Balkans. Information from South America is coming in now and it looks like something's going on there too. This is bigger than anything we've seen before, Bob." Steve's voice sounded grim.

"Sweet Mother of All," Bob swore under his breath as the news sank in. He thought fast, trying to figure out what his next step should be. He could turn around and try to help the Lords, but it probably wouldn't do any good, and it would put Serena right back into danger. And if shifters were being targeted in such a big way… "What about the Clan? Do you need me to come home?"

"We're fine for now. On high alert and keeping everyone close. Grif said you have a need to go into the Cascade Range." The statement was more of a question.

"How secure is this connection?" If anyone would know, it would be Steve, the Clan's security expert. "Can I speak openly?"

"Just put new scrambling tech on my end last week and I know your vehicle has the latest. I upgraded your software before you left. Speak freely. We're as safe as I know how to make us."

Bob breathed a sigh of relief. Communication was key and he had felt hampered in the last call he'd made home, unsure of how much he could say.

"We analyzed some of Miranda's notes in light of information the Lords had. There's a former Spec Ops guy named Jeremy Devereaux—goes by the name Jezza—who helped my friend Serena get out of a bad situation in the Cascades. He's off the grid. Apparently he has a sat phone but nobody has the number. He's been working against shifter drug runners near the Canadian border and piecing our information together, we believe he's being targeted by the *Venifucus*. The Lords were going to send out a team to find him and warn him, but then the shit hit the fan this morning and we made a run for the border. They asked me to get Serena to safety. I'd rather not take her back to the Cascades. It was hard enough for her to get out the first time.

Jezza called in that guy Ben Steel—the former SEAL and ex-*Altor Custodis* agent. Matt knows him. He helped Serena escape the first time, but if I bring her back into the area, it's possible we'll run across some of her old Clan, and that wouldn't go over too well."

"I can handle myself if I have to," Serena said to Bob, though she had to know that Steve would hear it too over the phone. Her voice was small, but strong. Almost resigned.

"You might have to," Steve said over the SUV's speakers, his voice deadly serious. "I know Jezza. I served with him. And before you ask, no, I don't have his sat phone number. It's been a while since we've spoken, but if he's gone native, it's going to be hard to find him. Dude's like a ninja and extra sharp in the woods. The fact that you know the area, Serena, will be invaluable to Bob in tracking him."

"Hey—" Bob began, but Steve cut him off. Bob was surprised his older brother would talk over his head, as it were, to address Serena directly. It stirred Bob's protective instincts, even though he was probably overreacting.

"I know you're a damn good tracker bro. I'm not dissing your skills. But if it's the lady's home range, she'll know where to look. You won't. If she goes in with you, you'll have an advantage. Besides, there's not much other choice unless you want to come south first, drop her off—even if one of us meets you halfway—and then go back north. It'll take too long. The *Venifucus* are on the move as we speak, and a lot better organized and manned than any of us thought. If Jezza's been targeted, he might already be dead. Somebody's got to either confirm that or warn him so he can take precautions. He's an important man to have on our side, Bob. You don't know him like I do. He's got serious skills. Skills that rival Slade's. Magical stuff. Things we'll need if this battle continues to escalate—which I believe it will."

"Damn." Bob thought about the situation. All airports off limits. No way to get Serena to safety and a very big need to get to Jezza. They really did have no other choice. "Serena, honey, I know I promised to take you to safety—"

"Don't sweat it." She surprised Bob with her strong tone. It sounded like his fluffy little kitten had found her backbone. "I owe Jezza for getting me out of there in the first place. I'm not quite the same girl who escaped the Cascade Clan. I've grown and I've learned. I'm stronger now, and this is important. It wouldn't be right for me to leave Jezza in danger when I can help you find him. With any luck, my adoptive family and the rest of the Clan will never even see me. We can get in, and get out again, without anyone the wiser. If we're careful."

"I like her already," Steve put in after a short moment of silence. His humor-laced tone broke the mood a bit. "I'm Steve, by the way. Is it true you're a bobcat?"

She cocked her head to the side and gave Bob a quizzical look at Steve's question. "It's true. The Cascade Clan is all bobcat. There's a wolf Pack farther south in the range, but the bobs keep to their own territory most of the time and chase others out. There's not a lot of inter-species interaction."

"Things are a lot different down here. Our Clan is multi-species. I think you'll like it when you finally get here," Steve offered. Bob's inner cat liked the way his older brother spoke with such confidence, as if Serena's place in the Redstone Clan was a foregone conclusion. "You know, it occurs to me, that I may be able to send you some help. Not shifter." Steve was quick to add. "But there are some friends I can call that might be able to help. For one, I'll see if we can locate Ben Steel. If he's still in the area, he might be a good resource, since the lady already knows him. I never worked with him personally, but I've done some research since Matt told us about him and I've heard good things."

Bob wasn't sure about trusting anyone who had worked for the *Altor Custodis*, but he could definitely use some help, and beggars couldn't be choosers. There was also still one other avenue they could try that hadn't really been mentioned.

"Do you know anybody else who might have Jezza's sat

phone number?" Bob asked. "Maybe some of your old Army colleagues—or some of Slade's Agency connections?"

"I'll work on it, but don't hold your breath. If Jezza doesn't want to be found, he's not going to be found easily. The only real way is the old fashioned way. Put yourself in his path and if he recognizes you as friendly, he might show himself." Steve's reply wasn't what Bob wanted to hear.

"So I guess we're heading into the Cascades whether we like it or not." Bob finally put the distasteful thought into words. He reached across the center console to place his hand over Serena's. "I'm sorry to have to take you back there, sweetheart."

"It's okay," she answered in a small voice. That she was trying so hard to be brave was like a kick to his gut. He had promised to keep her out of danger and here he was, driving her right back into the teeth of it. "It'll probably be good for me to face some more of my fears."

"That's the spirit," Steve said in an encouraging tone. Bob wanted to tell his older brother to shut the hell up, but Serena seemed to gain strength from Steve's confident words. "You know, Bob, this attack on the leadership is serious," Steve went on. "The *Venifucus* are way better organized than anyone thought and they have a lot more manpower. This is probably just the first volley. Do what you need to do, then hightail it back here. It just might be time to start circling the wagons."

"I hear you, bro," Bob answered, his thoughts grim.

They had been dealing with the *Venifucus* threat since the murder of their matriarch, but nobody had thought the group had such reach or power. Until now, there had only been sporadic skirmishes with small groups or single perpetrators who had *Venifucus* ties. But this... It was large-scale and might span a good portion of the globe. The true length of their reach didn't bear thinking about.

"We'll do this as quickly as possible and then we head for home," Bob reassured his brother. "I'll be in touch and you can reach me anytime we're in the vehicle. I have some equipment in the back, as you well know, and you have my numbers. It would be best if we did pre-arranged check-ins. I'll call you on twelves and sixes, okay? Morning and night. Even if I have nothing new to report."

"Good man," Steve approved the plan. "I'll be watching for your calls and if you miss one, I'll send out whatever cavalry I can manage. Just be careful. The good guys are spread pretty thin at the moment." He paused for a beat then his tone changed. "I'll look forward to meeting you in person, Serena. Keep my little brother safe, okay?"

She laughed at that, as Steve had probably intended. For all his serious-soldier demeanor, he certainly did know how to charm females. Thankfully, he was newly mated and posed no competition for Serena's attention. Even so, the cougar inside Bob bristled a bit.

"I think it'll be more the other way around," she quipped, "but I'll do my best."

They signed off without much more ado and that left Bob and Serena enclosed in the quiet cab of the SUV. The rain outside was worsening and made them feel even more isolated.

"You don't have to do this, you know," Bob insisted, breaking the silence after a while.

He was tense. He really didn't like taking her into danger, regardless of what she said. Her brave act wasn't fooling him. He knew she didn't want to go back, but her sense of honor wouldn't let her do anything less to help the man who had risked so much to help her.

"I know," she answered in a careful tone after a moment's thought. "Have you ever considered that sometimes circumstances force you to face things you otherwise wouldn't want to even think about? Like maybe we're guided to do things that we don't want to do? Like it's fate or something?"

"You think fate is making you go back to the Cascades?" Bob didn't like that thought one bit. "I've seen the Goddess in action a lot lately and I have to tell you, you don't want any part of that business. It's too dangerous."

He thought about the bloody battles his brothers and their mates had fought and the way the Lady Goddess seemed to guide their paths. Those paths had not been easy ones and he didn't want that kind of struggle for Serena. She had already been through enough as far as he was concerned.

"I wouldn't presume to say that the Goddess even knows I exist," she was quick to clarify, "but it does seem strange to me that there's no other reasonable choice. Not if we want to warn Jezza. I mean, there *is* a choice. I could choose to be selfish and put my own safety first. Or I could choose the noble path—the right thing to do—and put myself out a bit to try to get word to him."

"Put yourself out a bit?" His voice rose as he repeated her words. "Honey, going back to a place you needed help to escape in the first place is doing more than just *putting yourself out a bit.*"

She laughed, much to his consternation. This was *not* a laughing matter.

"Can't you see? I don't have a choice." She seemed to sober as she turned to him in the confines of the SUV's cab. He glanced at her occasionally while he continued to drive. "Not if I want to be the person I am working to become. Not if I want to have integrity and pride. Not if I want to be strong."

"Serena, there are other ways to be strong." He had to admit though, she had a point. If she was male—and not a woman he was interested in romantically—he probably would have admired her spirit. Hell, he already *did* admire her spirit, even if it also scared the shit out of him. "Okay. I see your point...but I really don't have to like it."

She laughed again and he just shook his head. This wasn't an argument he was going to win apparently.

They avoided anything even resembling an airstrip on their way through the mountains of eastern Oregon. They had stopped for fuel—both gas for the SUV and food for themselves—just inside the Idaho state line, then hopped right back on the road.

They still had a ways to go. The Cascade Range was a bit farther west, almost right up against the coast and included some famous—or rather, infamous—volcanoes such as Mount Saint Helens and Lassen Peak.

The position of the mountains right near the coast meant lots of weather. In the winter, that meant lots and lots of snow, but thankfully the year was warming up nicely. Although a few of the peaks stayed covered in snow year-round, the area they were aiming for on the lower slopes of Mount Baker would probably be clear. Especially with all the rain that was falling, melting any last little tidbits that remained.

Once their course had been decided and Bob accepted the fact that Serena would be coming with him, he had asked her many pointed questions about her former territory. She had been willing to talk—it was a good way to pass the time as the miles flew by and she seemed to understand how important it was that he have a grasp of the area they would be covering.

It also helped him focus. His mind kept going back to their encounter the night before and how good it had felt to hold her in his arms and be with her. She tasted like ambrosia and her honey scent drove him wild. That scent permeated the cabin of the SUV and made his inner cat want to purr, but there were important things at stake—among them, both of their lives. In the grander scheme, the safety of Jezza, the Lords, the Redstone Clan, *all* shifters for that matter, and even regular humans should the *Venifucus* succeed in their foul plans.

"There are three possibilities we should check first," Serena had told him. "The ghost town, the caves, or the old mine. In that order." She went on to describe the geography of each location and how they could get there with the least possibility of being seen.

Bob was glad to learn she had thought it all through very carefully. She was being cautious, which boded well for their chances of success. Just when he had thought she couldn't surprise him, she did. He found not only did he admire her beauty and courage, but her intellect wasn't anything to discount either. She was very smart, he discovered as they talked out their strategy, with good instincts.

"We'll have to stop somewhere for the night. I'm not sure I want to chance a motel," Bob said as they drove down the road. Twilight was upon them already and soon it would be full dark. "But it just so happens, the back of this SUV can double as a sleeping area in a pinch. We'll probably be safer in here than anywhere else. We just need to find a good place to hole up for the night. What do you say? Are you up for a little camping?"

Serena looked back into the rear of the big SUV with a doubtful expression. "I'm all for safety," she said. "But it looks like a bit of a tight fit. Are you sure it'll work?"

Bob smiled. "Trust me."

An hour later, they had found an out of the way wilderness area with dense forest on state land. With a little luck, nobody would see the dark SUV parked among the trees, well off the road. Bob had taken care to go out and erase any sign of their passage through the tall grass and parked the vehicle in such a way so that any hint of a gleam off its surfaces was dampened. He even smeared mud on some of the shiny bits, to help the vehicle blend in a bit more with its surroundings.

He scouted around the area and found only wildlife and a few curious fish in a small stream to the northeast. Dinner, if he could catch a few fat ones. But they had stocked up at the last rest stop and had a cooler full of food and drinks that should last them a few days, and a full tank of gas. He had installed an extra large capacity tank as part of his upgrades, so they could go a lot farther than most other SUVs of this type. With any luck, they wouldn't need more fuel until after they had accomplished their mission.

"Everything looks okay out here if you want to stretch

your legs," he reported when he crept back to the SUV.

He had asked Serena to wait inside while he checked out their surroundings and she had agreed, but they had both been cooped up for most of the day inside the vehicle. It was time to stretch, answer the call of nature and prepare for the dark forest night.

"Is it safe to shift here?" she asked in a low voice. They were both speaking quietly.

"I think so, but don't go far. There's a little stream about twenty yards to the northeast. I'll meet you there after I set up the back of the truck." The delay would give her a chance to stretch a bit while he put the back seats down and got out the supplies they would need.

He turned to the back of the SUV and started working while she undressed by the passenger side door and left her clothes neatly on the seat. He allowed her a bit of privacy, but wasn't surprised when she, in bobcat form, looked up at him from under the back bumper of the SUV. All the interior lights had been shut off and he was working using only his superior night vision. She blinked up at him before slinking out from under the vehicle and trotting away toward the stream he had told her about.

She was bigger than the normal bobcat, probably because she was a shifter, but still petite compared to him in his shifted form. He thought she was adorable, even with her stubby tail. Bobcats were named such because of their bobbed tail that was about half the length—allowing for body size—as his. It had looked a little funny to him at first, but the rest of her was just so damn gorgeous, he found it more amusing than odd.

He finished pulling supplies out of cleverly hidden storage areas and completed the setup for the night. He then locked up the SUV, shed his own clothing and shifted shape, moving toward his lady in the woods.

CHAPTER EIGHT

After being cooped up all day in the car, Serena really enjoyed stretching her body and getting a chance to let her wild side out. She admitted to herself that she was frightened about going back to her old territory, but she was equally frightened by the concerted *Venifucus* attacks. There was no other way to put it except to say the world had changed drastically in the past eighteen hours.

She wasn't the only one in danger. The Lords and the other shifter monarchs all over the world were in deep trouble. In fact, the whole world was in deep trouble if the *Venifucus* had managed to get that organized and that big without anyone knowing about it. The shit had just well and truly hit the fan. Nobody was safe.

The humans didn't even realize what was going on, but if the shifters fell into disarray, humanity could very well be the next target. While shifters weren't the only thing standing between the darkness the *Venifucus* served and humans, they were a big part of it. Humans for the most part, had no idea what was really out there in the world, looking to rule over them. She didn't think humans truly understood the concept of evil, or the ongoing battle to prevent it from overwhelming the Light. Not the way shifters did.

She almost envied their ignorance. Shaking, she tried her best to put such troubling thoughts aside and focus on the moment. The night. The forest.

She took care of her personal needs, then stretched and ran around a bit. She didn't stray too far from the SUV. It represented safety to her, as did the incredible man who owned it.

If her instincts were right, Bob was something she never expected to find and still didn't quite believe. Her inner cat was telling her strange things about the much larger cougar. Her bobcat recognized the feline and the Alpha in him, but it went further than that. It recognized a man it liked on every level. A cat that didn't threaten. A man that promised only protection and respect. Her inner bobcat liked that very much.

So much, the feline heart of her wanted to keep him. Forever. The cat had found its mate.

But the woman wasn't so sure. They weren't the same species, even if they were both feline. She wasn't sure how that would work. Would he feel the same mating call for a woman of a different species? Could he? Did he want to? Or would he not feel the same deep need to be with her as she was feeling toward him?

She was so confused. How could she ask him such things? How could she not?

They had shared so much in just a few short days. She felt things with him that she felt with no other. She trusted him with her body in ways that she had never trusted another man. Dare she trust him with her heart? She was afraid it was almost too late to prevent it.

But did she want to? Her new-found confidence was telling her to take the chance. To grab for happiness with the cougar. The High Priestess's words repeated in her mind, encouraging her to step out of her comfort zone and rejoin the land of the living. She'd already come so far, but Bob had made her want to come all the way back into the light—to be with him.

She had loved every minute of their time together and wanted to make love with him again and again. While she had fled in confusion the night before, Bob hadn't held it against her. She had almost feared her reception—when she had a moment to think about it—today, but he hadn't brought it up. He merely kept going, accepting her. Keeping her as safe as he could under the circumstances. Allowing her to make her own decisions.

That respect was precious to her. If he could love her, she would probably never find a better man. Her cat wanted him for its mate and her human half wasn't far behind, but she had to find out where he stood on the matter...and that would take some doing.

Her cat form yowled low in frustration as she approached the bank of the small stream. It caught movement in the flowing water and pounced, acting completely on instinct.

A fat fish flopped onto the shore. Serena felt a pulse of satisfaction and turned back to the stream. It was time to be a cat and not worry about the human side of things. Good thing cats liked sushi.

By the time Bob arrived at the stream a few minutes later, three fat fish lay at Serena's feet. He padded over to her on his much bigger paws and tapped her nose in play. She swatted at his paw and then pushed two of the fish toward him.

The cougar sank onto his belly and sat opposite the bobcat as they feasted on fresh fish. For the moment, they let their animal sides rule while they filled their bellies. The cats loved the fresh seafood and after finishing the meal, they prowled around a bit together, working off the stiffness from the long car ride and allowing time for dinner to settle.

When they were both feeling relaxed and a bit weary, Bob herded her back toward the SUV. She didn't need much coaxing. She stayed in her cat form to see what he had in mind. She had noticed a chain around his neck, mostly hidden in his fur, but she could see that the key fob for the

SUV was attached to it. He had left his clothes under the vehicle, she saw as they returned, but he had kept the key with him. Smart. But it needed human fingers to work the buttons, didn't it?

That question was answered as he pressed a sensor under the bumper with his paw. The proximity of the electronic fob and the pressure in the right place seemed to combine to pop the hatch open.

Bob took a moment to lift the neat pile of his clothes in his teeth and stow them in the back of the vehicle before he jumped up into the roomy cargo area. She hopped up, following him. Her clothes were already within easy reach on the passenger seat, where she had left them. She wasn't sure if they were sleeping in their fur or their skin yet, but she would follow his lead, whatever he decided.

He didn't seem inclined to shift, so she sat on one side and watched him as he hit another sensor with his paw and the tailgate closed automatically. The tinted windows enclosed them in darkness, but they both had excellent night vision. She saw him do a few more things. He touched a small panel on the side of the SUV's body and it slid out and down, showing a peephole of sorts that had been built into the lower part of the body of the vehicle.

Another press of his paw slid a tiny part of the back roof up at an angle to allow for fresh air to circulate in the enclosed space. There were already dark-colored blankets spread on the floor under them and a few dark pillows along the side of the compartment. All the comforts of home.

After showing Serena where the control was for the viewing panel on her side, he settled down, his face near the small viewport. It was clear he was choosing to sleep in a place where all he had to do was open his eyes to see what was outside on his side of the vehicle. She realized he probably wanted her to do the same.

It made sense. They could watch a good sized area from the little ports without moving a muscle, and in their fur, their senses were extra-sharp. They would hear the slightest sound from outside and the fresh air circulating through the open hatch would allow them to smell intruders from a long distance away. They could sleep and guard at the same time.

Realizing they were as safe as they could be given the situation, Serena gave in and slept.

Sometime before dawn, Serena woke to find herself encased by strong, bare arms. Bob. His big, naked body was spooned against hers, his front to her back, and his arms were around her as if they belonged there. One hand cupped her breast and the other was over her belly, dangerously close to the apex of her thighs—the place that wanted his touch desperately.

They must have shifted form sometime during the night. Both of them. And then snuggled together.

Had he taken her into his arms consciously or was it some kind of instinct that had made him curl around her? All sorts of questions flooded her mind as she came slowly awake. Dawn was starting to trickle through the dense trees. They had slept through the night—or at least she had—with no disturbances. Had he awoken to find her in her human form, then shifted to take her into his arms? Or had he been as weary as she and just did it in his sleep?

Did it really matter? They were both naked. Human. Wrapped together in a cocoon of body heat with the dark blanket thrown over them. Had he done that? Had she?

She wished she knew what it all meant.

A kiss on her shoulder made her mind still and her racing thoughts scatter.

"Good morning." Bob's voice rumbled near her ear, deep with sleep. *Sexy.*

A little thrill went down her spine. When she didn't move away, the hand on her breast began to stroke and pluck. *Oh yeah.*

Even if she could have made her boneless body move, it would have flatly refused. It was enjoying what he was doing too much.

"You know I think you're beautiful, right?" Bob's whisper sent warm heat across the shell of her ear. The weight of his words landed a blow to her defenses—what little was left of them. "You're cute and sexy and smart. All the things I've always dreamed of in a mate."

That last word made her breath catch in her throat.

"Mate?" she croaked, at a loss for air. Her body froze, waiting for his answer, but he continued stroking her.

"Yeah, I think so. Don't you? There's something really special going on here. My cat is truly happy when in your presence and your scent drives him mad with desire and protectiveness. He wants you, even though he doesn't really understand why your tail is so short." He chuckled and placed little kisses along her shoulder and part-way down her arm.

"What about your human side?" She held her breath, anxious to hear what he would say. Both halves of a shifter's soul had to be in alignment, or any relationship they tried would never work.

"My human side was attracted to you the moment I first scented you in the woods. That attraction has only grown since getting to know you. My heart breaks for what you've been through and I'm proud of the woman you've become. I'm enchanted by your little cat form and my human arms long to hold you all night, every night. For as long as you'll let me."

He stilled this time, seeming in anticipation of her reaction. Her heart had melted into a puddle of happy goo. Her brain had finally stopped harassing her with so many anxious questions. All seemed right with her world for this short moment out of time. They were both thinking in terms of mating. Their thoughts—and hearts, she hoped—were aligned.

She turned to face him, rolling over within the loosened circle of his arms. She raised one hand to his face, cupping his stubbly cheek and looking deep into his eyes.

"What if I want you forever?" she whispered, not really believing she was being so daring, but Bob had a knack for bringing out her inner wild child.

"That can be arranged." He moved closer, sealing their serious words with a wondrous kiss. It was gentle and strong at the same time. A lot like Bob himself.

When he pulled back after long, breathless minutes, a smile spread across his lips, crinkling the corners of his eyes. This was a man who smiled a lot. He would bring joy to her world and more than that, she sensed he would bring love. So much love. Her heart yearned for it and wanted to give so much in return. Finally, she had found a man she knew she could have that sort of relationship with. He was a cougar, but her inner bobcat seemed fine with that.

After the hell she had faced at the hands of bobcat males, her cat saw most of them as the enemy. It was always doubtful she would have been able to change the cat's opinion, or her human reactions to males of her own species. If she was ever going to find anyone to share her life with, she had thought maybe she would be forced to spend the rest of her life living among humans, hiding her true nature.

But Bob had changed everything. His cat didn't frighten hers, even though he was so much bigger. His human side had won her admiration as well. And there was something indefinable going on in her heart and soul. Something almost magical. Something divine. Goddess-touched, though she had never really experienced anything like it before. Somewhere down deep inside, she instinctively recognized her mate.

She loved the feel of his hard muscles against the soft spots on her body. His hard pecs flexed against her breasts as he moved her closer. His thigh insinuated itself between hers, the sinuous movement encouraging her to ride his hard-muscled leg. His tongue danced with hers, lulling her senses and sending her into a place of bliss—where only they two existed.

He trailed his hand down over her thigh, reaching under to coax her leg over his hip and then he was just...there. His cock ready at the entrance of her straining body. There were no real preliminaries this time, but none were needed. She was ready and eager to accept him into her body. In fact, she reached between them to help line him up. She wanted him more than her next breath and if his hushed growls were any indication, he wasn't far behind.

Bob pushed inside, the angle making it a bit of a challenge, but he was up to the task. She wrapped her leg around him tighter, moving to accommodate his entrance. Their coming together this time was primal, hungry, intense. Rain poured down around the vehicle, but they were encased in a little bubble of warmth that hid them from the rest of the world. Nothing else existed.

Bob used his muscular thighs and braced one foot against the wall of the SUV for purchase, holding her body to him with strong hands. One kiss ended and another began, one blending into the other as he possessed her totally, sending her body into an orbit of need and want.

But he didn't leave her wanting for long. His thrusts brought her pleasure so intense that she began to make soft little noises each time he filled her, her body clenching around him, wanting to keep him deep within.

She was desperate now, breathing hard as she reached for the pinnacle, just out of her grasp. But Bob was there. He brought her with him, urging her higher and higher. And then they exploded in a shower of sparks she swore she could see, though her eyes were shut tight. It was magical and ecstatic. Sublime and almost divine.

Being with the man who might just be her mate was like nothing she ever could have predicted. And her inner cat was purring, wanting to keep him with her forever. The human woman was tempted to agree.

She must have dozed for a few minutes because the next time she woke, the rain had stopped and dawn was definitely lighting the sky in the east.

"Good morning again, kitten." Bob's voice was full of the low rumble of his purr. Sexy as all get out.

She reached up, kissing him as she took stock of the happy

lethargy in her limbs. She had slept well and been well loved the first time she had awakened. Maybe they had time for a repeat before they had to get on the road?

Bob seemed to be thinking along the same lines, his hands roaming over her body. She was starting to heat up again—

And then the screech of an owl sounded almost right above their vehicle and both of them stilled. She was breathing hard, as was he. His gaze held hers even as he moved slowly to separate their bodies. He looked upward, out the small vent at the top of the roof of the SUV and then out the small viewports on either side of the vehicle.

The owl screeched again and then the sound of wings could be heard moving away. A moment later, something small squealed. The owl had made a kill despite all the noise he had been making.

"That doesn't seem quite right," she whispered so low that the sound wouldn't carry beyond the cabin of the SUV.

"Yeah, I know," Bob agreed, pulling on his pants with deft, quiet movements. She reached for her clothes and did the same. "It's too close to full daylight to risk going out four-footed. I'm going to take a quick look around out there. Stay here, close up the ports, and be ready to leave. If I don't return in five minutes, drive away and head to Las Vegas, okay? My family will take you in and I'll join you there, if I can. Promise me."

"But—" she tried to object.

He reached out to her, cupping her cheek. "Promise me, sweetheart. I only just found you. I want you safe." His gaze held hers and there was so much being said between his impassioned words. "Please?"

She sighed and nodded. "Okay. But you be careful." It was the *please* that got her to agree in the end. She knew big, strong Alphas like Bob didn't often plead with anyone. They were more into giving orders and expecting obedience. That he bent so far for her meant something. Something important.

Bob took off through the woods on two legs, using every skill he had for stealth. He might not have actually served as an Army Green Beret, but his two eldest brothers had, and they had made it a point to teach the other three brothers everything they knew. The five of them were a well-oiled machine when it came to field work. They had put in long hours practicing until they each had developed skills that exceeded most regular shifters.

He scouted on foot and finding nothing, he took to the trees. Cats were naturally good climbers and he was no exception, for all his size. He saw the owl that had been so loud above them and followed its flight path. The higher vantage point and pearly gray light right before full dawn showed him things he hadn't seen the night before.

Not too far away was the reason for the owl's odd behavior. Intruders. Several dark-clothed men stalked through the forest as if looking for something, but not really expecting to find it. They were far enough away that he judged they wouldn't hear the engine of the SUV—if they left now.

Bob hopped down from the tree and raced back to the vehicle. Serena was in the front passenger seat and she looked relieved when she saw him until she realized he was running. Smart girl.

He hopped into the driver's seat and started the engine as quietly as he could. Making sure to check the mirrors and look over their campsite carefully, he moved rapidly toward the road.

"I think we got away clean," he said as the SUV rolled onto the pavement. "They'll see depressions from the tires and might even get a few impressions of the tread, but I made sure to buy a very popular brand of tire that fits multiple vehicles. They won't get very far trying to trace us that way."

"Who won't?" she asked. She seemed more baffled than upset, for which he was glad.

"Whoever sent out a search party in that forest. There was

a team of about five guys in dark gear beating the bushes, looking for something. They weren't dressed like forest rangers or campers. They looked like foot soldiers."

"Do you think they were looking for us? How could they have traced us? We were so careful." She seemed more alarmed now and he hated having to add to her worry.

"It's possible. We had to get gas. People saw us when we stopped. And other motorists saw us on the road, though with the tint on this glass, they probably didn't get a good look. But it's equally possible those guys were looking for someone else. That owl might've been one of our kind, which would explain why it screeched a warning in case the SUV it saw parked in a strange place had shifters in it. Or maybe those foot soldiers were just searching any area where *were* might've hidden after the shake up yesterday. We're not the only ones on the run from the Lords' mountain. By now they've gotten word out through the Alpha network to warn every affiliated Tribe, Pack and Clan. Everybody on our side of this conflict is laying low and regrouping, preparing for the worst. Or at least, they should be."

"I wish we knew for sure what was going on."

"It's almost six a.m. I've got to call Steve to check-in. We'll get a sit rep from him."

Bob touched a few controls that would connect him with his brother in Las Vegas through the phone. The magic of Bluetooth connectivity allowed the audio transmission to play over the speakers in the SUV so they could both hear the call ring on the other end.

"Bobcat, how's it going?" Steve answered on the second ring.

"Somebody was beating the bushes near our overnight parking spot this morning, but I don't think anybody saw us. We're back on the road. Most they'll get is a tire impression. What's going on in the wider world?"

"The Lords are still pinned down by a large force. It's an old fashioned siege up there with magic flying every which way, but I've got my money on the good guys. If this were my op, I'd say the siege of the mountain is a distraction maneuver. Something else is going on here. The less protected shifter leaders were fair targets, but the *Venifucus* had to know they'd never be able to take the mountain with the force they sent. The best they could hope for is exactly what's happening now—keeping the Lords in place and less effective than they otherwise might be."

"They haven't managed to stop communications though, right?" Bob asked.

"No. The Lords have multiple redundant systems in place to communicate down the chain of command through the Alphas that report to them. There have been a few reports through the network of hunting parties out looking for stray *were*. That could be what you encountered this morning. So far, I haven't heard even a hint that anyone is looking specifically for you, but I'll keep channels open and alert you if that changes."

"Good. We have a couple of locations to search for Jezza. I'll check in again at noon. Say hi to Trisha and the rest of the family for me."

"Will do. Stay safe, you two. Don't take too many chances."

Steve signed off with little fanfare and Bob ended the call.

"Sounds like they weren't after us specifically, which is something to be thankful for, I guess," Serena observed after a moment of thoughtful silence.

Bob nodded, thinking through what Steve had told him. "I wonder what the bigger objective is though. If this is really some sort of distraction tactic, it's a hell of a big operation to use that way. Whatever they're doing behind the scenes must be even bigger." Bob frowned. The only thing he knew of that would be bigger was something he didn't even want to contemplate.

"Their stated goal is to bring Elspeth back to this realm," Serena said in a small voice.

That was exactly the thing Bob didn't want to think about, but he had to face facts. "All the attempts up 'til now that we're aware of have failed." He had to keep believing in the good guys and their ability to foil the *Venifucus's* plans.

"What if this time is different?" Serena's statement hung in the air between them as Bob drove through the light rain, toward their target.

By the time they reached the dusty valley where the old ghost town lay almost hidden among tumbleweeds and rocks, the rain had stopped and sun began to break through the clouds. They approached cautiously, uncertain of what they might find.

Bob parked the SUV a short distance from the nearest building and got out. He had arranged the vehicle so that the driver's side door faced the road, which was some distance away. He wanted to take a look around before he exposed Serena to possible danger.

"Seems deserted," she observed, looking out the windows of the SUV.

"Maybe it is. Then again, maybe it's not." Bob stretched his limbs and knew Serena had to feel as stiff as he did. "You can get out of the car, just stay behind it for now, out of sight of the road. Keep your feet hidden behind the back tires. I don't think we were followed, but we can't be too careful."

They were in a long, flat valley between two rolling foothills. There was little vegetation except the scrubby high desert grasses that characterized parts of this side of the mountain range. Because of the higher elevations west of their location, most of the rain in the area fell on the other side of the big mountains. So they had pretty good visibility on Serena's side of the vehicle. With their shifter eyesight, they could easily spot any movement up on the hills.

Bob had done a thorough scan of the area as they drove in and continued to sweep his gaze over the perimeter. He didn't see any threats on Serena's side of the tall SUV, but when he looked at the road again, he saw a telltale plume of dust. Somebody was coming.

CHAPTER NINE

"Get back in the car and stay out of sight," Bob said, able to see the approaching vehicle more clearly by the second. Luckily, Serena was still hidden on the other side of the SUV.

She didn't argue, just hopped into the vehicle and into the comparative safety of the dark-windowed back of the vehicle. Bob shrugged out of his flannel shirt, leaving himself clad only in a sleeveless T-shirt in case he needed to shift. His lower half could shift out of the jeans and boots with relative ease, but the fewer layers he had on top, the better if he needed to become his cougar in a hurry.

He stowed the shirt on the driver's seat of the SUV while he opened a compartment in the dash and took out some equipment. Photography was a hobby of his and he always kept one of his top-of-the-line cameras with him, in case he came across something worth shooting. In this particular situation, it might come in handy to have an excuse for being near the old ghost town.

He could see the approaching vehicle clearly now and there was definitely some sort of official emblem on the doors. Police or park ranger or something else official. Maybe this wouldn't turn out to be a shifter problem, but he wasn't taking any chances.

"Cover up back there and if anyone searches the vehicle, pretend to have been taking a nap, okay? It looks like we're getting a visit from somebody in an official vehicle. Could be just a human cop of some kind wondering what we're doing here. Or not. Won't know for sure until I can size them up in person, which won't be long now."

Bob knew Serena could hear him through the wall of the vehicle, but she didn't make any sounds, to her credit. She knew how to hide, apparently, which was a good thing in this situation. Bob sent a prayer up to the Mother Goddess, hoping the vehicle contained just a nosy human official of some kind.

The vehicle drew up a few yards away and parked. The emblem on the door read US Border Patrol. So the lone man inside worked for the federal government. *Interesting.*

The man got out of the light-colored truck and took a long-barreled rifle with him, holding it casually over one arm. He wore mirrored sunglasses and black cargo pants, boots and a dark camouflage shirt. For a human, Bob supposed he looked dangerous. He was obviously comfortable with the rifle and Bob would bet he knew how to use it well.

"Got a report of a strange vehicle in the area," the man began, walking a little closer, but halting far enough away to have time to bring up his rifle if he sensed a threat. The man was cautious and Bob was on his guard.

Bob had been bent over his camera bag, but rose to face the man, the chain that he usually wore tucked inside his shirt falling out as he moved.

"I hope I'm not doing anything wrong," Bob said, putting on his best innocent act. "I heard about this ghost town and wanted to get some photos. Is that all right? Do I need a permit or something?"

The Border Patrol agent took off his sunglasses and squinted at Bob's chest. It took Bob a moment to realize the man was looking at the chain that had slipped out from inside his shirt. The chain was silver-toned metal and held a stylized cross. Bob wore it as a memento of a friend who had touched his life in profound ways. He had worn it off and on for years now and thought of it as a sort of good luck charm.

"Photos?" The agent looked at the well-used and expensive camera equipment in the bag, then back at Bob. "You a Christian?" His chin jerked toward the cross on Bob's chest.

Bob's hand went to the chain. "I got it in Italy when I visited the Vatican," he answered indirectly.

The agent nodded knowingly. "Catholic then. Made of silver?"

Bob thought the question somewhat telling since most magical races had serious problems with the poisonous metal. The cross *was* silver, but it was also blessed by a rare and sacred magic that allowed Bob to wear it and other shifters could touch it without fear. As far as Bob knew, it was one of a kind.

"Yeah. It's got a Latin inscription on the back, see?" Bob grasped the cross and turned it over in his hand.

Something strange happened then. Bob stilled as his vision seemed to change. He could see a dark, almost malevolent glow about the other man's left hand. Bob studied it covertly as the agent's attention was focused on the cross, and a cold chill ran down Bob's spine. He saw the mark of the *Venifucus* tattooed on the back of the guy's hand.

Slade and his priestess mate had claimed to be able to see invisible tattoos on some of the *Venifucus* fighters the Clan had killed or apprehended in battles they had fought recently. A hand-drawn image of the various tattoos had been circulated among the Clan and Bob wouldn't quickly forget what the evil patterns had looked like. An inverted V in a circle with magical glyphs all around shone on the back of the agent's hand. It glowed a dull, pulsating red on the man's skin, its poisonous taint flowing sluggishly through his entire body.

"What's it say? Do you know?" the agent asked, referring to the cross still held in Bob's hand.

"In remembrance of He who made the blind to see," Bob quoted

the Latin inscription's translation, truly understanding it for the first time.

He'd never really comprehended the full meaning before, but now he thought maybe he finally was in a position to appreciate it. The cross—the symbol of the Christian God, who had performed miracles such as curing blindness—was also a powerful magical talisman. Maybe this talisman's real magic was in allowing someone like Bob, who had no magical sight of his own, to be able to see magic—or at least the hidden tattoos the servants of the *Venifucus* often wore.

"Nice," the agent answered noncommittally.

Bob let go of the cross and the vision of the evil tattoo dissipated. Yeah, this cross was more than just a gift from a treasured friend. No doubt about it now. Bob was on his guard, and grateful yet again to the human priest who had befriended him and given him such a useful gift.

"We've had reports of wild animals around here. Wolves. Could be rabid. Stay away if you see any. Don't stop for photos." The agent's eyes scanned the ghost town, then returned to Bob.

"Wolves?" Bob tried to sound timid, but it was a stretch for an Alpha cougar. Still, he tried to act the part of a scared, city-bred human. "Is it safe to stay here for a bit so I can get some photos?"

"You should be okay for a little while, but you need to get off the mountain before dark, just to be safe." The man lowered his rifle so that the barrel pointed to the ground. With any luck, he had bought Bob's act.

"Thanks for coming out to check on me. I appreciate the work of federal agents such as yourself. Am I close to the actual border here?" Bob looked around, gesturing to the wild mountain slope to the north, playing his part to the hilt.

"Close enough," the man almost grunted. It appeared he didn't like being questioned, so Bob backed off a bit.

Clearly, the agent was overstepping the scope of his authority by hassling Bob, but he wasn't going to push it. They weren't anywhere near the border, which was on the other side of the big mountain in the distance. And since when was the Border Patrol in the habit of warning people about rabid wolves?

Yeah, this guy had an altogether different agenda. He was looking for shifters, if Bob guessed right. Only the human man's seeming inability to detect magic and Bob's silver cross had thrown him off the scent.

Still, he could be playing a deeper game, but Bob thought not. If this guy suspected Bob was a shifter, he would probably have used that rifle by now. Any human warrior who knew about shifters, knew enough to never lower their guard around one. This guy had lowered his gun, his guard and everything else when he decided Bob was *safe*.

The fool.

And not only was he a fool, but he was in league with evil. Bob scratched his chest, touching the cool silver of the cross and his vision changed again, confirming what he had seen before. The Border Patrol agent wore the mark of the *Venifucus*. Bob would let him live for now, but there would be a reckoning. Eventually.

"Thanks again, Agent…" Bob trailed off, hoping the miscreant would supply a name.

It wasn't strictly necessary to have his name, but it might help track him down later. It would also be helpful to report back to Steve. Bob knew his brother could work his computer magic and come up with all sorts of information on the erstwhile federal agent. Some of it might prove useful in the future.

"Parker," the man replied automatically.

He pulled a business card from his shirt pocket and stepped closer to Bob to hand it over. Sure enough, it had the official seal of his office on it, as well as an office address and phone number.

"You see them wolves, or anything else strange out here, you give me a call." He stepped back while Bob pocketed the card, then turned back. "What was your name again?"

"Sorry." Bob smiled and reached into his photography bag

to take out a card of his own. "Robert Painter," he replied, handing over a stylish business card that sported one of his photographs of the Grand Canyon. "I mostly do landscape photography. I've had a few gallery shows in Portland and Seattle. After seeing this place, I'm hoping to do a series on ghost towns. I think it'll be unique."

Bob had used the photographer ploy a few times before and kept the bag stocked with documents that would prove he was somebody else. In fact, Bob truly had done exhibitions of his photos under the assumed name and kept anything to do with his hobby under that name on purpose.

Too many people would court him because he was one of the rich and famous Redstone brothers. He had wanted his art to speak for itself, so the false identity had started as a way to do that. Eventually it had turned into a convenient alias to use in tricky situations. Nobody seemed to realize that in some parts of the country, cougars were known as *painters*. It was a little play on words that amused him.

The agent pocketed the card after reading it and started back toward his truck. "Just don't stay too long. And don't go into the structures. I can't vouch for how safe any of the construction might still be after all these years."

Bob almost laughed at that. If anybody could judge the soundness of a structure, it would be a Redstone. Construction was their business, after all.

"I'll be finished in about a half hour. Maybe less. I just want to get a few shots of the exteriors of these buildings against the sky while the light is right. As soon as the sun shifts, the image I want will be lost." Bob was tempted to add some more flowery, artistic description, but the agent was already getting in his truck.

Agent Parker waved as he pulled away and Bob touched the cross one more time to get a third confirming look at the tattoo on the man's left hand. Yep. There it was. No doubt about it. Agent Parker was in league with the devil.

Bob fussed with his photographic equipment for a little

while longer until he was sure the Border Patrol agent was well out of range. He let his senses out to their full extent, sniffing the wind and listening carefully. He scented wolves had been here, but not within the past few hours.

He walked back toward the SUV and opened the door, reaching for a skinny, folded tripod he kept alongside the seats on the floor. He used the motion to look into the back, meeting Serena's gaze.

"He's gone, but I don't think you should get out of the SUV. Sorry. He could easily have a scope aimed at us right now. I'd prefer it if he didn't get a chance to spot you."

"What was all that about?" Serena asked, her brows knit in concern.

"Agent Parker warned me about wolves, and asked if my necklace was silver. He knew about shifters. He figured I wasn't one since I could touch silver and am wearing a cross. He took me for human."

"I noticed the chain before, but I figured it was some other kind of metal," she said quietly, looking at the piece of silver that lay outside his T-shirt. "Is it really silver?"

"The chain is steel, but the cross is pure silver. It was a gift from a priest who helped me a lot when I was younger. I wear it out of respect for him and as a sort of good luck charm, though I really only wear it when I'm traveling. When he gave it to me, Father Vincenzo said to wear it when I was away from home and that it would always help bring me back safely. I've never had reason to doubt his advice, so when I packed to go up to the Lords' mountain, on it went." Bob touched the cross and rubbed the inscription as he often did.

"How can you wear it? I mean, if it's silver..." she trailed off, clearly puzzled.

"I'm not really sure, but I always assumed this thing had to have a hell of a lot of magic coursing through it to allow me to wear it. I guess I thought maybe it had to do with the man who gave it to me or maybe the fact that he said it was an ancient relic."

"Why would he give something like that to you?"

"Why indeed?" That was the crux of the matter that had Bob thinking overtime. "I think I just found out why and you're not going to believe it until you get a chance to see it in action for yourself." He paused, trying to find words to explain what he had just experienced. "I'm not a very magical guy. I have the basic shifter magic that allows me to shapeshift and that's it. Since meeting Slade and Kate, our priestess, and my brother's mates, I realize I'm kind of low on the magic scale, even for a shifter. But when I touched this cross and looked at Agent Parker, I saw..." He didn't know exactly how to put it into words.

"What? What did you see?" Serena prompted.

Bob looked straight at her. "I saw a *Venifucus* mark on his hand. Clear as day. When I took my hand off the cross, it was gone. I did it three times, just to be sure. Touching this cross somehow allows me to see the evil magic marks like the priestess and Slade can."

"Marks?" Serena looked confused and he realized she probably hadn't been briefed on such things.

Bob explained briefly about the drawings that had been circulated around his Clan. "It's a rare talent to be able to see hidden magic, but a few of our people have it. The marks aren't visible to normal eyesight. I've never seen one before except in those drawings, but I definitely saw one today."

"So what do we do now?" Serena looked upset, but there wasn't much he could do about it right now. Not with the possibility that they were being watched from a distance.

"I'm going to putter around and take some photos. I'll also be doing recon while I'm at it. I want you to stay in here and lay low. He could be watching. Open the little panels in the back and keep an eye out. I won't be far. If you see anything, tap twice on the side of the SUV. I'll come running. I should only be about fifteen or twenty minutes, then we can move on."

He wished he had better words of reassurance for her. She looked scared, but determined at the same time. *Ata girl.* She was made of strong stuff, this mate of his. She would hold tight for a few more minutes before he could get them someplace where he could take her in his arms and calm her fears the way he wanted to—with soft words and loving caresses.

"Don't worry, sweetheart. Parker thinks I'm human. Catholic too, if you can believe it." He chuckled and she seemed to find the humor in the situation.

Most shifters worshiped the Mother of All. While Bob respected his priest friend's beliefs, he knew most Catholics would view shifters as pagans of the first order. But shifters were more accepting of other beliefs, most acknowledging that there was no one true way. They followed the Goddess, preferring to see the hand of the divine in the sacred feminine, but Bob had respected Farther Vincenzo's devotion to the male God he had dedicated his life to.

Who was Bob to put limitations on the divine? Such things were way above his pay grade and he had learned there were many paths that led to the same place. As long as a person believed in the Light—in doing good and shunning evil—then he was okay in Bob's book. And some, like Father Vincenzo, were even more okay than others.

The older man had had a shining spirit and a kind face. He'd been willing to guide a confused young shifter—even though they had never really discussed Bob's true nature—and help him figure out things about life that had helped shape him into the man he had become. Only now, years later, did Bob fully understand the value of the good Father's guidance—and the extraordinary nature of the gift he'd given Bob when he had left Rome.

"When you get back, I want to hear all about the man who gave you that cross."

Bob thought about it for a moment, and then nodded. If he was going to share the story with anyone, it would be Serena. The cougar inside him was possessive of her and the man wanted to earn her love. Both parts of him wanted her…forever.

He knew that meant sharing things he wouldn't readily tell

others. If he wanted her to trust him, he would have to do the same for her.

"All right. When I get back." He wanted so badly to kiss her, to hold her and reassure her, but it just wasn't possible at the moment, while the might be under observation. He sought and held her gaze, laying a little part of his heart on the line. "You're so incredibly special to me, Serena. I hope you know that."

She nodded slowly, a dazzled smile breaking just slightly over her gorgeous mouth. As if she was unsure. As if she was hopeful. He could pretty well guess what she was feeling because he had to admit, he felt just about the same way, if he was being honest.

"I'll be back shortly. Sit tight and keep watch."

He knew he had to leave now or he would blow their cover and climb into the back of the SUV with her. If that Parker guy, or any of his ilk were watching, that would cause problems, but Bob was just about at the point that he didn't give a damn.

Forcing himself to leave her, he stepped back and closed the door. Each step he took away from her was like a chore. Resolutely, he set up his lightweight tripod and attached the camera. Moving quickly now, he took a few shots of the ghost town, moving steadily through, using his viewfinder and his nose to tell him the story of the place.

Wolves had been there recently, but not within the past day or so. He could smell their presence all over the site, but these weren't just any wolves. No, these were werewolves.

Something had brought the Pack Serena had mentioned up from the southern part of the Cascades. Bob didn't know what could've caused such a migration, and he didn't dare hazard a guess. It could be any one of a number of things— all of them bad.

Either the werewolves were servants of the Lady and Her Light, or they were in league with the *Venifucus*. If the former, they were probably on the run. If the latter, they were doing the chasing.

Bob didn't want to chance running into them until he knew for sure one way or the other. He took photos and did a full circuit of the town in as little time as possible. He also took several shots of the surrounding area. He could study them on his screen later and look for visual clues. He could also forward anything interesting he might find to his brothers. If there's one thing his older brothers had taught him, it was that good recon was never wasted.

As a result, Redstone Construction kept files on many and varied locations all over the globe. Bob's interest in photography had started because he had been told to record observations of his travels when he had gone off on his own several years back. Being young and foolish, he had bought a camera and figured the lens could do his work for him. What he hadn't counted on was finding a love of the gadgetry and skill it took to make a good photograph.

What had started out as a small rebellion against his older brothers nagging turned into an enjoyable and somewhat successful hobby that he had never outgrown. His photos nowadays went both into the family archives and the Clan's files. Dual purpose and doubly useful both artistically and informationally.

He finished up and packed his gear, heading for the SUV. Serena hadn't made any sounds and Bob didn't see anything out of order, so he packed up casually, then climbed into the vehicle, aware he could still be under observation.

"Stay in back until we're under some cover. We're more exposed out here than I'd like and a good scope might possibly see through the light tint on the windshield. You're better hidden back there for now."

"Okay," came Serena's quick answer.

Bob didn't speak again until he was back on the road. There wasn't a lot of traffic on the road, but there was some, which was both comforting and a little worrying. The other cars could contain just innocent humans going about their business, or they could contain those in league with the bad guys. Drug runners. Hostile shifters. *Venifucus* agents.

"I smelled werewolves in the ghost town. They were probably there within the past day or two. What can you tell me about the wolf Pack that lives farther down the range?" Bob asked once they were on the road, heading in the general direction of their next target.

"Not much. Our Clan hated them. There were occasional border skirmishes and we always managed to push them back into their own territory. There was one incident though…" her voice trailed off as she seemed to think back. Bob could see her in the rearview mirror and she met his gaze in reflection when she spoke. "It was a bad business. One of their young women was caught in our territory she was hurt bad before she escaped."

"Was she attacked? Raped?" Bob asked in a firm, quiet voice.

Serena nodded, her eyes sad. "I think so."

"Do you know who did it?"

CHAPTER TEN

"I'm very much afraid my adoptive father, Jack, had something to do with it," Serena admitted, feeling both shame and anger. "And I think it was Jezza who freed her and helped her get back to her Pack. I know she made it home because Jack was up in arms when the wolf Alpha sent a message stating that the Pack would seek justice for their injured daughter. He laughed, but I could see he was nervous about having pushed the wolves a little too far."

She paused only a moment before continuing. "Lizzy was worried the argument between the Pack and our Clan would interrupt the drug trade. The humans they were dealing with who supplied the drugs to carry across the border weren't the forgiving type and they knew what we are. Lizzy said they carried silver ammunition in their guns. She was terrified they were going to shoot Jack, while I was secretly hoping for it."

Bob reached back and grasped her hand, squeezing lightly. He was such a good man. So ready to offer her comfort. She didn't feel weak with him. No, his strength helped her find her own and she finally understood how things should be between people who cared about each other.

She had been learning about friendship from the Lords and their people—especially the High Priestess, Bettina. But

Bob took it deeper. His kind gestures were a thousand times more meaningful and his encouragement brightened her world. A simple smile from him lightened her heart and made her feel as if she could handle just about anything—as long as he was by her side.

"So the wolves aren't on good terms with the bobcats?" Bob's quiet question dragged her back from her reverie as he removed his hand and put it back on the wheel. He was driving, after all, and the position had been awkward with her still in the back of the vehicle.

"Not by a long shot. The last I knew, the wolves had sworn blood feud on my former Clan. The girl was just the most recent—and most heinous—of the conflicts between the two groups." She met his gaze in the mirror and saw a speculative gleam enter his eyes. "Is that helpful?"

"Not sure. It could be. I'd rather not get in the middle of a blood feud, but it's possible it could work to our advantage in some way. For now, it's just good to know."

He quieted and she knew he was thinking about what she had told him. They entered a section of road where the trees were thick and he pulled over, stopping the SUV.

"You can climb up front if you want. I'm going to check something." He got out of the vehicle and jogged around the back.

She maneuvered herself back into the passenger seat and waited. He wasn't long in returning and he had a deep frown on his face as he climbed back into his seat.

"What's wrong?"

He held up a little black plastic thing with a wire coming out of it. She didn't recognize it, but the look on his face said it was nothing good.

"I thought I felt a little impact as we rejoined the road. Somebody shot this at us and it adhered to the back rear panel. If I'm not much mistaken, it's some kind of tracking device. And I think our friendly Border Patrol agent is probably the one who tagged us."

"Oh, no." Her stomach twisted with knots of worry.

"What do we do now?"

He shrugged, but his gesture didn't allay her fears. "He can track us this far. Probably knows I stopped for a bit. When we get going again, I'll drop the tracker out the window once I spot a good sized bump in the road or big pothole. If he checks, he'll probably think it came loose on its own. We haven't met up with the main road yet, so he doesn't really know which way I'm heading yet."

"Do you think that's the only tracker or might there be more?"

"Now that I know they're playing dirty, it won't matter. There's a gizmo in the glove compartment that should block the signal. Only drawback is we can't listen to the radio or make calls. It blocks everything." He looked at the clock on the dashboard. "It's almost noon. I'm going to check in with Steve, then switch on the jammer until we get to the caves. With any luck, we'll find our quarry there. If not, we'll figure out what we do from there. Cell phones will work if we get about twenty yards from the vehicle while the jammer is on, so if we stop someplace relatively safe, I can still check in with Steve."

He leaned over, reaching for the glove compartment. His muscular arm brushed past her and made her remember more intimate moments they had shared. There was no denying the attraction that sizzled between them, but she knew now was not the time to be thinking about getting busy with the sexy cougar. With any luck, there would be plenty of time for them later—when it was safer.

Bob took a small device from inside the glove compartment that looked like a tiny transistor radio. He held it in one hand while he placed the noon call to his brother.

"Hey Steve," Bob greeted his brother when the other man picked up the phone. They exchanged a few words before Bob got to the meat of his report. He told his brother about the Border Patrol agent and the tracker. Steve agreed with his plans to use the jamming device.

"It looks like the attack on shifter leaders was even more

extensive than we thought," Steve told them. "Reports have been trickling in. A few leaders were killed or injured globally, but the seconds and heirs are stepping up in most cases. The Lords are coordinating North American efforts, even though they're still pinned down in their territory. So far, they're holding strong, but it's definitely a siege up there right now."

Bob told Steve their plans for the afternoon and they ended the call shortly thereafter. He then plugged the device he had taken from the glove box into an outlet hidden in the center console. He pulled back onto the road and before long they spotted a pretty big pothole. Bob lowered his window and threw the little black tracker out of it without slowing down.

He rolled the window back up and reached toward the console. The jamming device activated with the push of a button.

"There. That should do it. We won't have any comms until we shut that off. For now, we're running silent."

"You've got the spy lingo down pat, haven't you?" she joked, feeling a moment of humor despite the desperate situation.

The news about the Lords and their continuing troubles on the mountain had hit her pretty hard. If the enemy was that well armed and coordinated to launch simultaneous attacks all over the globe, then they were up against something a lot bigger than anybody had expected. The picture became clearer with each new report and it kept getting worse.

But somehow, being with Bob helped. He was the first man in her life who made her feel like a desirable woman. Not only that, but he made her feel valued and like she was part of something important. Like she was important to him on a personal level she had never wanted before with any other man.

Bob was different. He was good and strong and kind. He had patience with her insecurities and encouraged her in a gentle way to be stronger than she ever thought she could be.

In just the short time she'd known him, he had managed to bring out the best in her and she really liked the person she was when she was with him.

If the world ended tomorrow, she was glad she'd had what little time they'd had together. In their brief time together, he had changed her for the better and there was no going back to the timid, scared mouse she had been. Somehow, she had found her courage with his help. She had discovered the heart of the wild cat in her soul, the spirit that would not surrender to fear or intimidation anymore.

And she had discovered desire the likes of which she had never experienced or expected. Bob made her want him without even trying. Just by being him—by breathing—she desired him. She wanted to claim him as her own and never let him go. For whatever time they had left, she wanted to spend it with him.

"Penny for your thoughts?" Bob teased her as they drove along in silence.

"Not sure they're worth that much," she replied, hiding the true direction of her thoughts out of habit. She didn't feel quite secure enough yet to talk about their relationship—such as it was—out in the open, so she decided to change the direction of her thoughts and their conversation. "You promised to tell me about the cross," she prompted, as if that was what had been occupying her mind.

"Ah, yes." Bob paused, checking their surroundings and the road before glancing her way briefly. "I suppose that's only fair." He made a turn onto the road that would lead them closer to the caves and drove at a steady pace. "I suppose you know how cats like to roam. Cougars are no exception. After we got out of school, all of us took off for a year or two, one by one. Grif joined the Army. Steve followed in his footsteps. Mag traveled through South America for a while and a year or two later, I headed to Europe. I bounced around from country to country for a while until landing in Italy, of all places. In Rome, I met a Catholic priest named Father Vincenzo. He was a funny little fellow, kind of grizzled and old, and I was honest with him from the beginning, explaining that I wasn't a Catholic."

Bob glanced at her before continuing. "I was attracted to his church because of the architecture. It was really old and he told me the foundations of it went all the way back to Roman times. We began talking that first day and I asked his permission to take some photos. He wanted to know more about my skills before he agreed to let me shoot inside the church, so we made arrangements to share lunch the next day so I could show him some of my work."

The smaller road became more challenging and he negotiated some tight curves before continuing his story. "We had lunch and he liked the images I showed him. He asked that I return the next day to attend a mass. He didn't care that I wasn't Catholic, but he wanted me to see the true function of the church before he would agree to let me take pictures of it. He said he wanted me to understand the soul of the building and the people who cared for it. He claimed it would help me understand how to capture its essence in my photographs."

"Sounds like he was an artist at heart," Serena observed. "And a bit of a romantic, as well."

"He has the soul of a poet," Bob agreed fondly. "I attended the mass as requested and felt... Well, it's hard to describe. The mass was in Latin and I don't know much of the language, so it pretty much flew right over my head, but that hour was one of the most peaceful hours I've spent anywhere on earth. Whatever else was going on there, the spirit of the place was one of comfort, understanding and acceptance. It just felt...good. In a way I can't really describe adequately."

"Sounds like it really made an impression on you." She looked at his face, so strong and sure. His eyes were full of memories of a place he had come to love, if she wasn't much mistaken.

"I spent a few weeks shooting interiors, exteriors—shots from the belfry, shots from the roof. I climbed all over that old church and attended mass almost every day. It didn't matter that I didn't understand a word of what was going on. I just sat in the back and soaked up the peace of the place and the magic of the man who brought it forth. Every afternoon, Father Vincenzo would sit with me for a while and we would talk. Mostly about unimportant things, but there were a few conversations that will stick with me for the rest of my life."

"How so?" She was intrigued by his words and the almost awe-filled tone of his voice.

"Being a Redstone can be a little overwhelming at times. When I set out on my journey, we had just lost my older sister. She died violently and it rocked my world. She and I had been especially close as children, but when she moved to live with her mate's Clan, we lost touch. I blamed myself for that. And for what ultimately happened. Her death weighed on me along with my grief and sorrow. Father Vincenzo helped me work through it and put me on the road to being a better person. He helped me heal, when I thought I was beyond repair. He gave me back my hope, which had been lost along with my sister. And he never asked anything in return. Father Vincenzo did this for all of his flock. He is a truly great man."

"He's the one who gave you the cross then?"

"Yeah. Eventually I got a call from Grif, asking me to come home. I know Grif wouldn't have asked such a thing lightly. He had taken his time away from the Clan, and I know he respected the rest of our rights to do the same, but the construction company was at a critical stage in its growth and he needed all hands on deck. Right before I left for home, on that final day, Father Vincenzo gave me the cross. I tried to turn it down at first when I opened the plain wooden box and saw the silver inside. He stopped me, placing his old, gnarled hand over mine and met my gaze. He said, *I know what you are. I have always known. The Holy Mother looks after your kind as the Father tends His flock. Accept this gift in memory of me. It will bring you good fortune and it will protect you and always return you safely to your home. Wear it when you travel and do not fear the metal.*

Touch it and you'll see, he told me. I didn't know what to think, but I reached into the box with one finger. I touched the cross and it didn't have that icy burn I associate with silver. In fact, the metal felt warm in a comforting way, not painful at all."

"I can't even imagine that. Silver is something I've always avoided." She shivered, thinking about it. "But I see how you wear that cross next to your skin. I can't believe it's real silver."

"I know, but it really is. This thing is so old, there are no maker's marks, except for the Latin inscription. Father Vincenzo told me what it said and wouldn't let me refuse his gift. I haven't worn it all the time. When I'm home, it stays in its little box. But when I travel, I always seem to take the thing with me, just like Vincenzo cautioned me to do. I guess I'm more superstitious than I realized, but I sure am glad I had it with me today."

"Do you think the priest knew about its magical properties? Do you think maybe he had some kind of foresight or clairvoyance to know that you would need it in the future?" She wasn't overly familiar with such things, but it did seem truly odd that the old priest would press such an important and rare gift on a shifter who had been just passing through his territory.

"I guess anything is possible."

They arrived at the first cave about two hours later, after noshing on some of the food they had picked up the day before. The gas tanks were still more than half full and Bob didn't want to take a chance on stopping at a gas station or restaurant again unless they really had to. For now, they had plenty of munchies and a few sandwiches left. That should hold them for a day or two.

Serena had warned him about the cave complex. There were a series of caves that were mostly connected, the largest being at ground level. The entrance was huge. Big enough to drive right into if he wanted. As inviting as it sounded to hole up inside the cave, truck and all, Bob would have to be certain the place was safe first.

He parked the SUV and scanned the area first, before even attempting ground reconnaissance. The place was deceptive. There could be quite a group hidden within the side of the mountain and he would never know it until they were upon him.

In fact…

"There's somebody watching us," Serena said in a nervous little voice. "Up there." She pointed with a subtle movement.

Too late, Bob saw the lookout lying prone along a rock ledge. "Damn."

And then a man stepped out of the cave, boldly facing them. He had long, dark brown hair hanging almost to his shoulders and an angular, Native American cast to his features. His skin was golden and he was well over six feet tall.

"I don't recognize him. He's not a bobcat," Serena reported.

"But he is a shifter." The size and musculature of the guy gave that away easily.

Bob's hand went to the magical cross around his neck. He grasped it and looked carefully at the man and the guy up on the cliff. No dark red miasma surrounded them, but they definitely didn't look friendly.

Bob rolled down the window a bit, enough to allow the breeze to bring him the scent of the two men.

"Wolf." He knew the scent well. There were many wolf shifters in the Redstone Clan. "But which side are they on?" he thought aloud.

There was nothing for it. These wolves didn't carry the *Venifucus* taint if his talisman was to be believed, and Serena had told him how the wolves around here were practically at war with the bobcats. Bob would have to chance talking with them to see if he could establish their loyalties.

"Stay here. I'm going out to talk to him."

To Serena's credit, she didn't try to talk Bob out of it. She merely reached over to squeeze his hand as he opened the driver side door. He met her gaze and tried to reassure her, but they both knew the inherent danger in what he was about to do.

Bob closed the door after one last look at the woman who had changed his life so dramatically in such a short time. If he'd blundered into a situation that could hurt her, he'd kick himself from here to the next realm. But Bob was by nature, a bit of an optimist. There was every chance these wolves were okay. He just had to do his best to find out. Sending a silent prayer up to the Lady, he stepped closer to the wolf-man.

"Hi." Bob thought it never hurt to be friendly. The wolf didn't even nod.

"You're trespassing." The man's deep voice was definitely *not* friendly. His stance remained combative and challenging.

"I thought this was bobcat territory," he challenged. It wouldn't do to show any kind of weakness to an angry wolf.

The man looked from Bob to Serena—still seated in the SUV—and back. "She tell you that? She's one of them, isn't she? But what are you? You don't smell like a bobcat, though you're probably a damned feline too."

"Cougar," Bob supplied, figuring there was no harm in revealing something that would be obvious to most shifters who had run across one of his kind before.

For all his size and toughness, the wolf shifter that faced him seemed on the young side. Looking closer, Bob could see the big guy was probably only in his twenties, though his eyes held a sort of grim wisdom that belied his years.

"You're not from around here," the wolf raised his chin, looking suspicious.

"Nope," Bob agreed. He was the older, more experienced Alpha of the two of them. It was clear the younger wolf was an Alpha just from the way he carried himself. They could either fight for dominance or establish some kind of truce. It would all hinge on the next few minutes. "We've travelled from Montana where my companion was given refuge on the Lords' mountain. Do you follow the Lady and the Light?"

The young wolf's head cocked at the bald question. That wasn't something shifters went about asking each other in the normal course of business.

"Of course we do. What about you?" he challenged.

Bob took the offhanded question seriously, repeating the essence of the vow he'd made over and over. "I am Her servant, against the coming darkness. I serve the Mother of All and oppose any who would try to extinguish Her Light."

The wolf looked confused for a moment. "Why are you talking like that? Are you a holy man?"

Bob laughed, sensing the release of tension in the air. "No. I'm just a cougar. Nothing magical about me. But you do realize there's a war on, right? We're fleeing from the Lords' mountain, where they've been under siege for the past two days by agents of the *Venifucus.*"

Shock showed clearly on the young wolf's face. "You can't be serious."

"I'm afraid so."

The wolf seemed to regroup. "What brings you here of all places? Did she trick you into coming here? You'll find no friends or sympathy among the bobcats."

Bob's mouth tightened in a frown. "I know. We're looking for someone. I was tasked by the Lords' to find the jaguar and deliver a warning. Once that's done, we're out of here, headed for the safety of my Clan. Though, if what we suspect is true, nowhere will be truly safe after this."

The wolf seemed skeptical, but at least he was listening. "How do I know anything you say is true? You're a damned cat, travelling with one of *them.*" His emphasis on that last word as he gestured toward Serena made his feelings about the local bobcats clear.

Bob didn't know what to say. How could he prove his words? How could he prove Serena wasn't in league with her former Clan? He just wasn't sure what would bring the young wolf around.

And then a beautiful young woman stepped out of the cave behind the guy and moved to his side. They shared ancestry, if Bob wasn't much mistaken.

"It's okay, John. Don't you recognize her? That's Jack and Lizzy's girl. She disappeared last year, but I remember her. Poor thing was almost as much a prisoner as I was." Her words were soft, but laced with steel.

Bob knew then who this young woman was. She had been the girl the bobcats had captured and savaged. Bob looked at the woman, liking the way she stood tall and strong. She had been through hell, but she seemed to have come out of it at the other end, whole and probably a lot stronger than she had been before.

Unbidden, Serena left the SUV and came over when she saw the other woman. Bob wasn't happy about it, but he saw the way the women looked at each other, with sad understanding in their eyes.

"I'm glad you're okay, Giselle," Serena said first. "And I'm so sorry—" her voice broke as emotion nearly overcame her. "I'm sorry I wasn't able to help you."

Giselle moved closer, taking Serena into her arms. They hugged fiercely, tears flowing. "It's okay. I saw how they treated you. You had broken bones and could barely walk and they still kicked you around."

The man she had called John seemed to relax, though his expression was pained. He probably didn't like the reminder about what had happened to Giselle. Bob understood.

"I never understood how parents could beat their own cubs," Giselle went on, as teary as Serena was, but at her words, Serena drew back.

"They weren't my parents," she said in a firm voice. "They adopted me a few years after my real parents were killed in a car crash. I was born on the coast. None of the bobcats here are my kin."

"Well, thank the Goddess for that," John intoned. He looked at Bob and some of his wariness had left. "You'd better come in. Looks like we all need to talk."

The younger man clearly didn't like the idea of talking, but Bob had always been the loquacious brother of the Redstone five. He liked talking, where most shifter males seemed to be more the strong, silent type. John fit that mold precisely and Bob had to stifle a grin.

They were ushered into the cave and Bob was surprised to see about twenty werewolves inside, sitting around performing various tasks. A few women were preparing sandwiches on one side of the huge cave. Some of the men were cleaning their personal equipment—sharpening knives or cleaning guns. They were all armed, but they seemed peaceful enough for now.

One thing Bob found interesting was that this wasn't a permanent camp. It looked more like the group had stopped here for lunch while hiking. When they left, there would be little evidence of their presence left behind.

John invited them to sit on the ground near the entrance of the cave. Bob judged the situation and knew he would have to bend a little, to show the other Alpha he was willing to trust him to a certain extent. Putting himself on the ground, in a more vulnerable position, even momentarily, showed that he was extending a little bit of trust. It was a start.

Serena and Giselle sat first, there seeming to be no question of dominance or trust between them. It was the men who held out a bit longer, wanting to establish who was in control here. Bob deferred to the younger man—for the moment—because he clearly had more right to this little bit of territory than Bob did. Plus, Bob was good at negotiation. He knew he had to give a little in order to get something in return. It was a concept most young Alphas had little acquaintance with, sadly.

They all sat, the wolf male last of all, but there was a sort of wary respect in his gaze when he met Bob's eyes.

"I'm Bob Redstone," Bob offered, breaking the silence that had fallen between them first, offering the hand of friendship.

"John Lightfoot," the other man replied after only a moment's hesitation, reaching across to shake Bob's hand.

"My sister, Giselle," he motioned to the young woman who sat at his side.

"My mate, Serena," Bob proclaimed, loving the way that sounded. *His mate.*

Serena looked up at him sharply, but didn't argue with his statement. It was all so new to both of them, this being-part-of-a-couple thing.

"Tell me why you seek the jaguar," John demanded bluntly.

Here was the crux of it now, Bob thought. Do they trust the wolves or do they demur? It was Serena who answered, taking at least part of the decision out of Bob's hands.

"Jezza helped me escape from Jack and Lizzy. He got me out and had me delivered to the Lords' mountain. I owe him so much. When the Lords were attacked two days ago, Bob was asked to get me to safety, but he was also asked to warn Jezza that we believe he's being targeted by the *Venifucus*. The plan was to get me on a plane to Las Vegas, to be with Bob's Clan, but all the airports were being watched and the weather was bad anyway, so we decided it was more important to get to Jezza first. Then we'll go south, to safety."

"Las Vegas?" Of all the parts of the story to latch onto, Bob was a little surprised that was the first thought that came to John's mind. Bob waited for the inevitable question about his family. "Do you know a wolf Alpha named Buddy Garoux? He's our mother's brother."

The question took Bob by surprise, but pleasantly so. Bob smiled. "I know Buddy. He came in under the Clan banner with his wolves about five years ago when we were working a big construction job in Louisiana. He retired to Las Vegas with his mate last year and brought a small Pack with him. He's one of the elders among the wolf shifter leadership in the Clan."

"Good," John said, rising to his feet. "Then we can settle this matter of trust more easily than I'd hoped. Let's call Uncle Buddy." John headed toward the cave entrance, already pulling a small sat phone from his pocket. It wouldn't be able to get a signal inside the cave. "Come with me, Bob."

Bob looked at Serena, torn. He didn't want to leave her vulnerable in case these wolves were playing some elaborate game.

"It's okay. I'll stay with Giselle," Serena offered. He could tell by the look in her eyes that she knew there was still a possible threat from these wolves, but she was being brave.

"You have my word as Alpha that your mate will come to no harm," John said. Bob didn't like it, but he had to take the word of the Alpha. To do otherwise in wolf territory would be an insult, and tantamount to a challenge.

Bob nodded curtly and followed John out of the cave, praying that all would be well and that the wolves were on the level. He caught up with John a few feet outside the cave as he was heading in the direction of the SUV.

"Don't go near the vehicle. I've got a jamming device scrambling all signals within about twenty yards of it."

John looked at Bob suspiciously, so he explained.

"Some asshole Border Patrol guy tagged us this morning. I got rid of the tracker, but I didn't want to take any chances I missed something."

"The asshole have a name?" John asked, still seeming to weigh every word Bob spoke.

"Parker," Bob replied. "And if my instincts are correct, he's a *Venifucus* agent." Bob didn't want to go into how he could see the mark on the guy's hand, but John just nodded.

"He's no good, that's for sure. He's been hassling us for years, but just lately it's gotten really bad. Like he's off the rails or something. He's not even pretending to be Border Patrol anymore."

That didn't sound good, but Bob let it go as they walked a little farther away from the SUV. He didn't like being parted from Serena, but he had to trust that the Alpha was true to his word.

The call went through and Bob heard John greet his uncle. Then he turned the phone's speaker on and Bob talked with the older wolf for a while, assuring the other man that Bob really was who he claimed to be. Buddy even called Steve and conferenced him in on the call to verify everything Bob had said. With Buddy vouching for Steve and Bob, the call soon took a grim turn as John reported the reality of his Pack's situation.

"Jezza was captured last night. I've gotten word from my scouts that he's being held in the old mine. We've been working on a rescue plan, but we're spread really thin. Two days ago, our Pack house was raided and the settlement overrun by bobcats and humans with silver bullets in their guns. We lost about a quarter of our Pack and we've been on the run ever since. Jezza was helping us. He led the bobcats away while we ran for the caves. The only good bit of news is that the human hunting parties seem to have left the mountain altogether."

Steve reported on the full list of attacks they knew of that had gone down simultaneously two days ago. Mostly, it was shifter leadership that had been targeted. The Cascade Range wolf Pack didn't seem to fit the pattern. They weren't even the dominant shifter group in the range.

"So why attack a Pack of wolves way out here?" Bob asked the question they were probably all thinking.

"Because of the border, maybe," John answered with a bit of uncertainty. "The bobcats control it only because we haven't challenged them for it, but the truth is, my Pack was stronger and more organized than the cats before the attack two days ago. We could've taken them out a long time ago, but Giselle didn't want us to. She didn't want to be the cause of bloodshed and I respected her wishes because I didn't want to put her through any more trauma."

"And now with your Pack on the run and the Border Patrol in league with the *Venifucus*, the bobcats and whoever is pulling their strings have no opposition left here," Bob said. "There has to be something important here, in this region, for them to want it so much."

At that moment, they heard a rumble in the distance and the ground beneath them trembled.

Of course.

"The volcano is waking up," Bob reported to the men on the other end of the phone call.

"Koma Kulshan is not happy to be disturbed," John intoned, looking up toward the mountain in the distance.

"The tiger shifter king makes his home on the side of a volcano in Iceland," Steve reported, sounding like he was leafing through reports. "They just had a big dust-up and change in leadership. It's said the new king up there can actually draw on the power of the volcano. I wonder if the *Venifucus* are trying to do something similar."

"Shit," Bob cursed. He would bet that was exactly what was going on. The power of a volcano was the vast power of the earth itself. "There's probably more than enough energy there to pull Elspeth from the farthest realm back into our world. Crazy bastards are just nuts enough to try to control a volcano." Bob's disgust was clear in his tone. "If they fuck up, they could blow the volcano and kill a hell of a lot of people. And if they succeed, they still kill a hell of a lot of people, only less localized."

"We have to stop them," John said.

"How?" Bob was at a loss for a moment. How did you stop someone from tapping into the power of a volcano, for heaven's sake? That had to require a shitload of magic and Bob wasn't really a magical sort of guy.

"I'm going to try to get in touch with the new tiger monarch," Steve said quickly. "He survived the attack on his stronghold two days ago and could be of help, since he knows volcanoes. I'll let you know what I find out."

"What about the jaguar?" Buddy asked. It was the first time he had spoken since he'd vouched for Bob and Steve, but he had been listening the whole time. The elder's wisdom could not be discounted. "I've known a few jaguars in my time and they usually have a better grasp of magic than most *were*. If you free him, he might be able to help."

"You're right, Elder," Bob said respectfully. "Freeing Jezza should be our first task. After that, maybe we can form a plan to do something about the mountain."

"She is called Koma Kulshan in the Nooksack tongue. My father's people knew a lot about the mountain in the old days. I'll see if any of the tribal elders have information that might help," John volunteered.

"All right," Steve said. "We'll gather intel on both ends and reconvene after you've freed Jezza."

Bob liked how Steve just automatically assumed success. Bob wasn't so sure rescuing Jezza was going to be that simple.

CHAPTER ELEVEN

When the earth shook, Serena gasped. Giselle looked as startled as she did and both women jumped to their feet as small pebbles rained down from the ceiling of the cave.

"Inside a cave probably isn't a good place to be during an earthquake," Serena said as they joined the rest of the wolves heading for the exit.

To Serena's shock, there were children and mothers with babies running from the deeper recesses of the cave complex. They had been hiding back there, keeping quiet. Things were much worse for this Pack of wolves than Serena had thought if they had taken what looked like most of the Pack on the run.

She bent to pick up a toddler who had fallen over. The child's mother was nearby, holding an even smaller baby as they moved toward the exit. Giselle helped the woman while Serena kept close with the toddler, knowing the mother would want to keep her eye on her baby, especially when held by a stranger.

They got out of the cave and away from the entrance to clear ground. Rocks rolled down the side of the hill, piling up on the lower slope. By the time they reached the open area, the ground had stopped shaking.

A few brave souls went back into the caves to bring out their supplies and packs, but all the mothers and children stayed well clear. Serena let the toddler down onto the ground and the mother took hold of her child's hand while carrying her baby with the other. They nodded to each other in acknowledgment, but Serena knew the wolves would be hard-pressed to trust a bobcat. Her people had done savage things to the wolves in the past. Things that wouldn't easily be forgotten…or forgiven.

Serena was getting nervous when she caught sight of Bob and John walking toward them. Everybody else seemed to still, watching their leader and the newcomer as well.

"Cascade Pack," John raised his voice and everyone listened. "I welcome Bob Redstone of the Redstone Clan and his mate, Serena, among us." That settled that question, Serena thought. The Pack now knew they were the good guys as John went on. "I've just heard upsetting news about the enemy who would try to summon the power of Koma Kulshan, the great mountain, to use for evil deeds. It's the same enemy that drove us from our homes. The same enemy the bobcat leadership serves."

"How do you know we can trust this man and his words?" one of the older males asked.

John held up his sat phone. "Because I just had a conversation with my uncle, who lives among the Redstone Clan. He vouched for him. I've also spoken with Bob's brother Steve, who some of you probably remember from your Army days. He's working the intel on this and what he told me wasn't good."

Murmurs went through the crowd and Serena realized that quite a few of the wolves had the look of soldiers. They were older than the Alpha and more careworn, but they deferred to John. Either the older men had chosen not to lead, or John had a lot more power than she guessed. He was young to be leading the Pack, and the men he led didn't look like the type to suffer young fools gladly.

"Judging by the earthquake we just felt, I think we ought

to evacuate the caves. Gather your families and settle them in the open for now, in case there are more tremors. Then I want all the soldiers to join me by Bob's vehicle. You need to hear what we've learned."

A few minutes later, an impromptu strategy session was being held next to Bob's SUV. This day had already taken more twists and turns than he could have guessed. Now he found himself aligned with a ragtag group of wolf shifter refugees. He was surprised to find a full platoon of older men who were ex-military. A few came up to him and said they were friends and former colleagues of his brothers, Steve and Grif.

Bob laid out the situation as he knew it, explaining what had happened in Montana and throughout the world. He also talked about the theories they had arrived at concerning the volcano. The vets weren't happy with the report, but they were men of action. They began formulating plans.

Bob also mentioned the tracker that had been shot onto his SUV and a small man toward the back of the group of soldiers came forward. He introduced himself as Chico, a comms specialist and everybody stood back to watch as he did a thorough inspection of the SUV. Everybody waited while Chico did his thing, even climbing under the vehicle to check the chassis.

When he popped up, he shook his head. "Looks clean. I can tell you for sure though, if you want to take the chance and drop the jammer signal." He pulled a little box from one of his many pockets. "I can detect and stop any tracker with this, but there might be a split second where a signal could get through." He turned to John. "Your call Alpha, but we need to clear the vehicle so we can use comms."

John nodded, his expression grim. "All right. Let's do this the right way. Lewis, split up your men as you think best," John addressed the oldest of the vets. "I won't leave what's left of the Pack without a few protectors. See how many you can fit into the vehicles we have. We'll need to find a safe place."

"I might be able to help there," Bob put in. "We have building projects all over and I know for a fact there's a new housing development going up in eastern Oregon. If you have adequate transportation, you can send your people there for the time being. The places aren't completely finished, but it's got to be better than a cave, right? Plus, the crews are all shifters. Might even be some wolves there, though I don't know for sure."

"I'll take you up on that offer," John said decisively. "How far away is the site?"

Bob thought about it. "Probably a four or five hour drive. I can call ahead and have the crew ready to meet your people. Maybe escort them in from the highway?"

"Sounds good. Let's organize the Pack into their vehicles. I want them ready to roll when you drop the jamming signal just in case."

What followed was a few minutes of organized chaos as a small parade of cars, pickups and minivans rolled quietly out of well-hidden caves. The Pack hadn't traveled here on foot. They had cobbled together a small fleet of vehicles of every shape and size. Family cars and hatchbacks. SUVs and small trucks. Even a few luxury sedans. It looked like everybody had pitched in with whatever vehicle they had.

Bob thought that was a good thing. They would look less conspicuous on the road, as long as they drove sensibly and didn't bunch up or form long lines like a convoy. He trusted to the military guys to know what to do, though. None of them looked like greenhorns at their first rodeo.

While the Pack was getting organized, Bob took a little walk to make some calls, Serena by his side. Before long he had the directions and contact information for the foreman at the construction site and Grif's agreement to take in the refugee wolf Pack while they were in need. He walked back and gave the information to John, who disseminated it to Lewis and a few of the others, who in turn gave the driving directions to those who would be going on the long journey to safety.

It wasn't long before Lewis came back to report in. "Everybody's mounted and ready to roll," he told John.

"I know it's a lot to ask, but I'd like you to go with them," John said to the older man in a strong, quiet voice. "You're the most experienced man we have. If anything happens to me, you're the best choice to lead the Pack. I'm trusting you to keep them all safe on the road and well hidden once they get to their destination. Are you willing to take on that responsibility?"

"You know I'd rather fight than hide, but protecting civilians has always been my thing," Lewis smiled ruefully. He walked up to John and stuck out his hand. John took it, pulling the older man into a back-pounding hug. "You be careful out there, son."

"You too, old man," John said with clear affection for the powerful older wolf.

"I'm leaving you Joe and his lot. They're used to working as a team and their skills are sharper than the rest of us. Goddess go with you, and good hunting," he said, making room for the man he'd indicated.

Joe was younger than Lewis, and Bob recognized him as one of the guys who'd claimed to know Grif and Steve. Chico, the comms guy, stood at his side as he faced the Alpha wolf.

"My platoon is at your disposal, Alpha," Joe said respectfully, his hand resting on the butt of a large weapon that he wore with casual familiarity. He was also dressed in desert fatigues that looked well-worn. The small group of guys behind him was dressed in various bits of similar camo gear and all were armed, Bob was pleased to note.

"Thank you, Lieutenant," John said as he turned with the other man toward where Bob waited with Serena. She'd been quietly watching everything, probably trying to avoid drawing attention to herself among the Pack. "Joe and his friends were visiting Lewis when this all went down," John explained. "If not for them, a lot more of my Pack would be dust."

"Right place, right time," Joe tilted his head, nodding, as if taking no credit for the feats of bravery that had no doubt been involved in the Pack's escape.

"Lieutenant Joe Merchant has relatives among my Pack, but he lives in Wyoming and is one of Jesse Moore's officers." John dropped the little bombshell on them and Bob couldn't help the smile that spread over his face. The Goddess was indeed smiling on them today.

"Moore's guys were a big help to my family a while back," Bob said to Joe. "Were you part of that action?"

"Sadly, no. My platoon was on another job, but I heard about some of it. The new ladies in your family are very impressive, and of course, I served with Grif and Steve for a while. So did a few of my guys." Joe motioned toward the small group of men who stood a short distance away, watching everything that transpired.

"You travel as a platoon at all times?" Bob was only half-joking when he asked the question.

"I've got kin here in the Cascade Pack and we all just came off a job, so I invited them along. They're part of my family too." Joe shrugged.

Bob knew from his brothers that comrades-in-arms were sometimes closer than blood relations. Sometimes Bob regretted that he hadn't followed his brothers' footsteps into the service, but that particular ship had sailed a long time ago.

The first of the civilian vehicles were getting underway and Bob knew time was ticking down. They needed to finalize their plan of action and get moving as well.

First things first. "Do you want to try that electronics sweep?" Bob asked Chico, the comms guy. He stepped forward while Bob reached into the SUV. "I'm switching it off in three...two...one. It's off."

Chico was busy watching his equipment and after only a moment he gave a thumbs up. "You're clear. Looks like the tracker you found was the only one. We're good to go." Chico turned off his little black box and stowed it back in one of the many pockets on his cargo pants. Bob thanked the man as he stepped back to stand with his cohorts.

"Chico, bring our truck around," Joe ordered quietly. "Get everyone mounted up. We leave in ten."

The rest of the men trotted off to the remaining vehicle—one of the largest SUVs currently on the market. The rest of the guys would fit in that if John and Joe rode with Bob and Serena. Bob checked his watch and realized it was nearing time for the evening check-in with Steve.

Bob paused to watch the last of the civilian cars drive away, and for a moment he wished he could've sent Serena with them to safety. But he knew she belonged with him. He wasn't ready to trust her care to the hands of others he had only just met. It might be dangerous for her to be with him, but it felt like the entire world was dangerous for shifters right now. At least Bob and the small group with him were going to try to do something about it.

For now, it was better for his concentration and his heart to have her by his side. Plus, she knew this part of the mountains better than anyone else—even the wolves. This was her home range. The wolves were interlopers here who only knew the land as visitors, not as residents.

Bob's phone rang and he turned on the ignition so the call would be routed through the speakers and mic inside the cabin of his SUV. It was Steve. Bob figured the others would want to hear whatever he had to report.

"Hola, bro," Bob said as everybody piled into the vehicle. "I've got Serena, John Lightfoot and a wolf guy called Lieutenant Joe Merchant with me," Bob reported, so Steve would know who was listening.

"Son of a bitch, Joe," Steve sounded happy, though his words were harsh. "What the hell are you doing there?"

"Lucky accident. I was visiting kin and the rest of my guys came with," Joe answered easily. "How you doin' Red?"

"Better now that I know my little brother's got some skilled backup. Thank the Goddess you're there." Steve finished the small talk and got into the facts he had been able to uncover. "I've spoken with the tiger king. Hell of a nice guy. Former Royal Guard. Good with strategy and tactics. He told me a little bit about the volcano magic. He was non-magical until he was poisoned and ended up almost dying. Then the Mother of All started messing with his life in a big way. The long and short of it is, you're going to need someone magical because it's almost a certainty the *Venifucus* have a mage working on the mountain."

"Jezza," Serena breathed, speaking for the first time. "He's a holy man. If anyone's got magic, it's him."

"He is a spooky son of a bitch," Joe confirmed, "but magic? I'm not really sure—"

"He's the closest thing we've got," John put in. "Plus we can't leave him to the *Venifucus*. Regardless of what he can or can't do, we have to rescue him."

"The fact that they took him prisoner in the first place has to mean he poses some kind of threat to their plans," Steve said. "But your lady is right. He does have magical inclinations. I saw it for a fact back in our Army days."

"And I've got a talisman that allows me to see certain kinds of magic," Bob offered. Everybody looked at him, as he knew they would.

"Since when?" Steve wanted to know.

"Since Italy, apparently. I discovered this morning that when Father Vincenzo's cross touches my skin, it allows me to see those *Venifucus* tattoos. The Border Patrol agent had one on his left hand."

Bob pulled the chain out from under his shirt and showed the cross to the men in the car. They needed to know he had a means of identifying the bad guys before they went in, even if he still couldn't quite believe it himself.

They went on to discuss logistics while Bob moved the SUV back onto the main road. He wasn't quite sure where they were going just yet, but getting away from the caves seemed like a good idea. They couldn't stay inside the rocky structures while earthquakes were a very real possibility.

"Jezza's being held in the old mine. I did the recon myself early this morning," Joe reported. "They don't have a huge force with him. Just a couple of guys that I could see. The extraction should be pretty straight forward except that one of the men questioning him had to be a mage."

"Why do you say that?" Serena asked.

"Well, he wasn't a shifter. He looked human, but the others—all bobcats—deferred to him, and he was the one doing the interrogating. Jezza was fighting some kind of compulsion. At least that's what it looked like. And it seemed to be coming from the human guy."

Bob didn't like the sound of that. "That sure sounds like a mage to me. Serena, your people were involved with a human drug cartel, right? What was the attitude toward the humans your leaders worked with?"

"They made fun of them. Jack thought the human cartel boss was a weakling, but he was willing to work with him if it kept bringing in the money. Jack and Lizzy both liked their little comforts, but they liked the power it gave them even more."

"So the deferential treatment of a human doesn't sound like normal behavior for these bobcats?" Bob insisted, looking deeper into the possibilities.

Serena seemed to think about it. "No. I'd say not. Nobody respected the humans, but they were willing to put up with them for the money."

That clinched it then. The human Joe had seen was almost certainly a mage if the bobcats deferred to him. Bob didn't like it, but at least they knew a bit more about what they were up against.

They spent a few minutes discussing the specifics of the mine and planning their assault. Steve listened and put in a few words here and there, mostly leaving the planning to the on-site guys. Bob was glad his big brother didn't try to take over. He had worked long and hard to earn his brothers' respect and it was a good feeling to still have it. Even though Bob hadn't served in the military, his brothers had taught him well. Before too long, they had a workable plan.

"We need a place to hole up for a few hours," Bob said

when the planning session was winding down. He had almost reached the main road and they would have to make a decision soon about which way to turn.

"I think I know a place," Serena offered. "There's an old house out near the bluff not too far from the mine, but not visible from the mine road or entrance. Humans built it back in the 1920's, but a shifter family bought it about forty years ago. An old man and his wife. They were old even back then and last I heard, they were still there—too old to put up much of a fight when the Clan turned bad, and too stuck in their ways to move out. For the most part, the Clan left them alone. I know for certain Jack didn't like the old guy, but saw him as no threat. His name is Jeremiah and his mate is Betty. I think they'll put us up if we ask. If they're still there. If they've been run off, it's doubtful anybody would want to live there. It's not the most ideal location, but for our purposes, it'll keep us close to where we need to be, but not in too obvious a place."

"And even if they object, we can always talk them around," Joe said with only a small hint of an evil grin. Bob knew the soldiers could take the place by force—and would, if necessary.

"Let's try to talk to them first, if they're there." Bob tried to be the voice of reason.

The other men nodded, though the two wolves had grim expressions on their faces. They would do whatever they had to do, Bob knew. He set out, following Serena's directions, the other vehicle filled with Joe's men, following behind.

The old homestead was as Serena remembered it. Rundown and deceptively decrepit on the outside. She knew for a fact the old couple kept the inside of the place neat as a pin and in good repair. She had sought refuge here a time or two when things got too bad at home. Not often. No, she hadn't wanted to bring the wrath of Jack and Lizzy down on these nice people, but a few very memorable times, she had been taken in by Jeremiah and Betty, given a good meal and a place to rest for a few hours before she had to go back to the hell that was her home. They were good people.

The four of them approached in Bob's vehicle, leaving the rest of the guys in their truck, back up the lane, out of sight for the moment. Serena and Bob would go up to the door first and get the lay of the land. The old couple knew Serena. They would recognize Bob as a cat and an Alpha, even if he wasn't of their Clan. If Betty and Jeremiah were still there, they would at least listen to what Serena had to say—she hoped.

She didn't know what they would make of the group of wolves she had brought along. But times were desperate and she hoped they would help out of the goodness of their hearts. She wasn't really sure how they would react, but she was hoping they would be reasonable. They had always struck her as people who would have stood up to Jack, if they had been a little younger...and a little more dominant. Jeremiah was a beta through and through. He hadn't been born to lead, but he had taken care of his mate and done what he could for the Clan, while its leadership had still been on the right side of the law and the Lady. Once the drugs moved in, Jeremiah had made himself scarce, claiming to be too old to be involved with Clan politics anymore.

Bob took Serena's hand, offering comfort as they walked up the dusty pathway toward the house. They'd decided to try the direct approach first, in case the couple was still in residence. If they got no answer to their knock on the door, they would nose around a bit and see if anybody else was there. If they ran into trouble, Joe and John were their backup, as well as the truck full of soldiers just down the road.

As it turned out, nobody was home. The place was deserted, and there were no signs of recent occupation. All of Jeremiah and Betty's furniture was still there, including plates in the cupboard, and towels and sheets stacked neatly in the linen closet. It looked as though the couple had left the place closed up, like they'd gone on vacation or something, intending to return.

"Maybe they headed for safety," Serena thought out loud as they prowled through the house. Bob had jimmied the lock while Serena called softly for the older couple. When nobody answered her, they moved farther into the house.

From there, Joe had come in, doing a quick recon with Bob while Serena checked out the living room and kitchen. Bob had gone upstairs and Joe had gone into the basement. They met up again in the hallway on the ground floor a few minutes later.

"Looks safe enough," Joe kept looking around, on guard. "I'll call my guys in." He jogged out the front door, leaving Bob and Serena alone in the hallway.

He pulled her into his arms and she was glad to feel the safety of his embrace, even if it was only a temporary sort of safety. She was exhausted. Adrenaline only lasted so long and she had been running on it since yesterday. There was a fine tremor of fatigue running through her limbs as Bob stroked his hands over her arms.

"I saw a comfy-looking bed upstairs. I think you should spend a few hours in it. Preferably with me, but we might get sidetracked from sleep if I do that," he teased. She smiled up at him.

"I wouldn't mind." He seemed pleased with her open invitation.

"I'd like it too, but honey, you're exhausted. This might be our only chance for a real rest before we have to run again. I think we should make use of it as best we can." He kissed her sweetly, then pulled back. "Why don't you go upstairs and nap while we secure the place. I'll be up to join you shortly, I promise. We both need sleep if we're going to be at our peak for the op."

"Op?" She shook her head. "You're talking like one of those military guys." She liked it.

He had sounded not only comfortable but impressively adept when he had been talking strategy with the other men. Who knew her hottie was also a badass soldier? Every little thing she learned about him made her admire and love him more.

"Wait 'til you meet my brothers. You've heard how Steve talks. When he and Grif start reminiscing over their Army days, it's definitely something worth listening to." He smiled and leaned down to kiss her again as the front door opened.

"Don't mind us." Chico's voice held suppressed humor as he waltzed past them, some sort of electronic gizmos in his hand. Another guy was following him, more of the little gadgets in his arms. "We're just setting up a perimeter," Chico explained as he and his helper moved through the hall, toward the back door.

Serena realized they were putting the devices around the house. It was probably some sort of electronic surveillance system that would help keep the place secure while they were here. She stepped out of Bob's arms and headed for the staircase. She didn't think Jeremiah and his mate would mind them using their house as a resting place in this crisis. She sent a little prayer up to the Lady, hoping the older couple was safe wherever they were.

CHAPTER TWELVE

Bob helped Joe's guys secure the perimeter and talked over their plans one more time with John. The wolf Alpha wasn't as familiar with military lingo as Bob was. Strangely, Bob felt a sort of kinship with Joe and his team. Having grown up with two brothers who were almost legends in military circles, it was easy to fall into old patterns with the lieutenant and his subordinates. Somehow, that was reassuring.

They were up against evil forces and they had no choice but to stand and fight. In fact, they had to take the fight to the enemy, so to speak, venturing into enemy territory to rescue Jezza. With any luck, and perhaps a little divine intervention, they might be able to pull off the rescue without a major battle erupting. That would be best, of course. Jezza knew the most about the enemy at the moment. He had been with them for almost a full day and would have observed his captors' behaviors, numbers and words. He could be of great help in identifying the key players and strategizing the best way to bring about the group's downfall—if he was still conscious.

They didn't even know for sure that he was still alive. He had been when Joe had last seen him, during Joe's silent reconnaissance the night before. That was no guarantee that

Jezza was still among the living all these hours later. Bob knew they had to find out for sure. They were operating under the assumption that this was a rescue mission, but the moment Jezza's status was confirmed from alive to dead, everything would change.

They had planned for that contingency too. Joe was thorough and Bob was inclined to respect the man. He was proving himself to be a capable leader and he had his men's loyalty and respect. Bob knew such things were not given lightly among shifters, even with Pack creatures like wolves. Although they loved working, traveling and living as a group, Bob knew they didn't suffer fools gladly. At the first sign of ineptitude, they would've taken Joe out as leader and replaced him with someone better, stronger and more capable.

It didn't take long to set up camp, so to speak. The military guys were posting a watch and Chico's electronic net was up and running, making it easier to keep an eye on the perimeter remotely. Bob wanted to stand watch with the rest of the men, but Joe convinced him that he needed to grab at least a few hours of rest before their night mission began.

John was already asleep in the second small bedroom upstairs when Bob crept up to join Serena. The rest of the guys would sack out on the ground floor. The couch was up for grabs as were the two recliners in front of the television and even the sheepskin rug in front of the fireplace. Even as Bob left them, half the platoon was already napping in various spots around the house. Military men knew how to make the most of any opportunity to grab some rest. They knew they needed to be at their peak of performance when called upon, and sleep was a big part of maintaining optimum levels.

When Bob arrived at the slightly larger bedroom of the two on the top floor, he found Serena stretched out under a light quilt, breathing softly. His very own Sleeping Beauty.

He wanted like hell to kiss her awake and then just keep kissing her and loving her until they both found blissful oblivion, but he knew she really needed the rest. So did he.

They hadn't had the most comfortable of nights in the back of the SUV and he knew being on the run took a toll on both the nerves and the body.

He kicked off his shoes and climbed under the quilt with her. She rolled into him, seeking his warmth and he opened his arms to her, a smile on his face. There was nothing like the welcome of one's mate. How he had lived without her for so long, he would never understand. He thought maybe the only reason he'd survived was that he hadn't known exactly what he had been missing. Now that he'd found her, he would never let her go. Not in this life, or the next.

Serena woke slowly, aware of a feeling of safety and warmth…and a trail of kisses leading up her bare arm. She realized quickly that she was naked under the covers. She hadn't gone to bed that way, but apparently Bob had taken it upon himself to undress her while she slept. That she hadn't woken up during the disrobing was an interesting point. It indicated she trusted him so implicitly that none of her self-protective instincts had been aroused by his actions.

"You are so beautiful," Bob whispered in her ear when he made his way up that far.

His warm breath in her ear made her shiver. The rough skin of his hand stroking her arm sent tingles up her spine. She turned to face him, twisting around so that she was facing him, only to find he was naked too. She felt his warmth against her, the hard evidence of his arousal rubbing against her thigh. She wanted this. She wanted him. If they only had this short time together, she wanted to grab it with both hands and hang on for all she was worth.

"Do we have time for this?" She fought back the mindless desire that threatened to take over. She had to be at least a little practical about this situation. There was danger all around and this calm before the storm could end at any moment.

"We'll make time," Bob answered in a voice already gruff with passion. His mouth was only an inch from hers.

She closed the distance, unable to maintain a level head. Desire ruled the moment. Hunger drove them both. The bobcat within her wanted to feel the possession of its chosen mate. The human heart of her wanted to forget the troubles that faced them for a short time and revel in the love of her man.

She knew in her heart that he loved her. The bond between them was strong and had only gotten stronger as time went on. She had been half afraid that coming back to the Cascades would tear them apart, but it had done the opposite. It had made her love him more, if that was even possible.

His mouth was warm and welcoming, his tongue continuing to teach her new things about kissing. She was totally addicted to his kisses now, willing to follow wherever he led in all things passionate. She felt a rumbling against her chest and knew he was purring. A sure sign he was her true mate.

Just as she could make him purr in human form, he did the same to her. She felt the quiet rumble in her chest and knew he felt it when his lips curved upward against hers. He drew back and she could see the smile she had felt. It was knowing. Loving.

Bob's hand stroked over her hair. "I never knew how it could be between mates."

"Me neither." She was more than a little breathless.

"I'm glad you're a cat. Even if you're a cute, little cat."

She knew he was teasing and it charmed her. "I'm only little compared to you, big guy."

He nodded, still smiling. "As it should be."

"Sexist pig." She batted at his shoulder and he oinked at her. She loved this playful side of him. In fact, she loved every aspect of him she'd seen so far and looked forward to learning more about him as they aged. If they had the chance.

"Fluffy little kitten," he countered, petting her hair, then ratcheting up the intensity as he wrapped both hands around her waist and pulled her right up against him. *Oh yeah.*

She knew they didn't have a whole lot of time, despite what he'd said, but it didn't matter. She was ready, willing and able. Gung ho, in fact. Almost all he had to do was crook his little finger and she was wet for him, ready to go.

She gasped as his hard cock slid against her thighs. He kissed her again, taking the kiss deeper this time. Licking his way downward over the sensitive spots on her neck, he paused at her breasts, paying special attention to the hardened nipples, plucking, stroking and enticing her into an even higher level of excitement.

One of his hands played over one of her breasts while his mouth tugged hard enough on the other to make her gasp with pleasure. His other hand went between her legs and slid into the warmth hidden there, teasing the nub of her desire. She clutched at his shoulders when one of his fingers slid inside her. When he added another finger, her fingers morphed a bit, her fingernails sharpening just enough to leave scratches.

He growled as her hands went to his back and her thighs opened wide, showing him how ready she was for his possession. She didn't want to wait and thank the Goddess, he didn't have time to make her wait much longer.

Two fingers slid in and out, evoking even more of a response from her body. She was so ready for him she could have cried. She'd beg if she had to, but she knew his care for her showed in every motion of his body and talented hands. He was taking care of her. Making sure she was truly ready.

"Don't make me wait." She gasped, her arms clinging to his back, claws digging in just a little.

He seemed to hesitate, pulling back to look down into her eyes. "I wanted to take this slow."

"Next time," she whispered, straining upward to match her lips to his.

He growled as he positioned his hips between her accommodating thighs. Still, he held back, not quite making the contact she so desperately needed.

"I'm sorry we don't have more time." The regret in his

eyes touched her deeply. "I wanted to see you come again and again before I joined you. I want to give you so much, kitten. I wanted this to be perfect."

His words and gentle tone crept right into her heart and took up residence. He was showing his care in every motion, every thought, every word.

"*You're* perfect," she reached around to stroke his cheek, letting her sharp fingernails trail into his hair, away from his sensitive skin. "I love you, Bob. *That* is perfect."

The change in his expression echoed the love that flowed through her heart. "I love you so much." His voice trailed off as he moved into position, thrusting deeply in one strong move that made her squeak in surprise. Nothing hurt. In fact, everything was right with her world now that her lover was inside her once more.

It was still new, but it was also achingly familiar. Not the exact sequence of events, but the feelings of love. The emotional ties going from her heart to his and back again. She'd never felt closer to another being. She didn't think she ever would, and that was okay. This incredible connection was meant for Bob alone. Her mate. Her one true love.

Then he began to move. His gaze held hers as their bodies began to a slow groove...like dancing...naked...in bed. Yeah, her disjointed thoughts probably wouldn't make a lot of sense to anyone else, but she knew what she meant. She knew nothing had ever felt this good, this *perfect*, to use Bob's word.

His pace accelerated and her fingernails sharpened on his back. He seemed to like it and she knew the cat within him didn't mind. Mating between shifters often got animalistic. In fact, Bob's hands were digging into the bedding on either side of her head. She wanted to feel them on her skin and she wouldn't mind if he went clawed. In fact, the cat inside her craved it.

She ran her fingernails down his back and he growled, moving even faster. She was whimpering now, little mewls from her inner bobcat spurring him on as her passion rose higher and higher. She came with a little yowl she tried to suppress, scratching him, which only made him seem more determined to drive her wild. Another climax took her by surprise, followed by another. One long orgasm had her in its thrall for long, long moments as he finally came deep within her, growling and allowing his clawed hands to pull her close.

He crushed her to him while they both shook with the most amazing pleasure. She hadn't known her body was capable of such a thing. Maybe it was the desperate situation they were in. Maybe it was the threat that this could very well be their last time being together. Maybe it just was the way they were learning each other and the fact that she'd never had sex with her true mate before she met Bob. As they got to know each other better and made love over and over, maybe it would continue to get better.

So far, that had been the trend. Each and every time they'd been together, they'd gotten better at knowing what each other wanted and needed. This time the claws had come out early. She loved the feel of the little pinpricks of his sharp digits against her back. And she liked the way he responded to her scratching. Judging by what had just happened, he really liked it.

"I hope I didn't hurt you," she thought aloud. "I didn't mean to claw you." Maybe he hadn't liked it as much as she'd thought in the moment? As her head cleared, doubts came into her mind.

"Hurt me?" He gasped as he disengaged from her body and rolled to the side. Even as he separated them, he kept his hold on her sated body, keeping her close to his side. "Honey, you can hurt me like that any time you want. I loved your little claws. I want to feel them more often. Every day for the rest of our lives wouldn't be too often for me."

"You're sure?" She was worried she'd drawn blood, carefully inspecting her fingers. No blood. Thank the Goddess. "I didn't mean to get so carried away."

He leaned in and kissed her cheek, still breathing hard. "I loved it. I love you, kitten."

A knock on the door to the bedroom broke the blissful

silence.

"Time to roll," Joe called through the door. "That is, if you two can tear yourselves away from each other for a few minutes." They could hear him chuckling as he walked away.

"I'm going to kill that fucking wolf," Bob mumbled at her side, sending Serena into a fit of giggles. They were both wiped out by their amazing climax, but they also both knew it was time to get going.

Smells wafting from the kitchen drew Bob's attention the moment he opened the bedroom door. Somebody was cooking and from the quiet clank of dishes and the water rushing through the pipes of the old house, it sounded like the platoon had turned the old folks' kitchen into a makeshift mess hall.

"Smells yummy," Serena said, popping up beside him.

He could hear her stomach grumbling, even as his did. Food had been both scarce and cold the past couple of days and he was more than ready for a hot dish of whatever they were cooking up.

When they entered the kitchen, they found half the platoon eating off of flowery china from the kitchen cupboard. One of the men was frying fish on the stove while another was gutting more of them near the sink. Where they'd gotten the fresh fish, Bob didn't know, but it was likely there was a stream nearby. Apparently werewolves also made good fishermen.

"You guys certainly made yourselves at home," Serena commented with a raised eyebrow and a smile.

"A soldier needs fuel in his body and ammo in his weapon," Joe said unapologetically. "When this is all over, we'll thank the owners of this house properly. If they're still around."

"Do you think they're dead?" Serena looked worried.

"No sign of anything like that, ma'am," Joe was quick to reassure her. "Could be they just packed up and left when the trouble started. Or maybe they're on a conveniently timed vacation."

"Where did the fish come from?" Serena asked, seeming to want to change the subject.

"There's a pond out back full of 'em. Looks like the fella who lives here set it up for just that purpose." Joe stood up. "I'm going to do a final check outside. Sit down and have something to eat. We'll be moving out soon. The rest of my guys have already eaten. As soon as these guys are done, we're out of here."

"What's up?" Bob asked, not sure what had been discovered since he and Serena went to bed.

John walked into the crowded kitchen at that moment. "The Alpha will fill you in on what we found," Joe replied. I'll be back in five and we can discuss the plan of attack."

John sat down at the table opposite Bob. "There's a back tunnel into the mine."

"Where?" Bob was surprised.

"In the basement of this very house. Joe's guys explored it a bit. It leads to a disused side passage in the old mine."

"You're kidding." Bob was astounded. Was this some kind of trick or was the Goddess smiling on them to put them in exactly the right place at the right time? "Is it safe?"

"We think so. I took a look at the setup. Old Jerimiah is a neat bugger. He had an old map of the mine next to a set of slightly rusty keys and a can of oil down by the locked iron door in the basement. There are a series of heavy doors in the tunnel, each locked. I examined the locks. Looks like nobody has used any of them in years. We oiled the hinges and opened a few to explore. Heavy dust coats everything and hadn't been disturbed until we walked there. The tunnel structure seems sound enough. It's shored up with old timbers, but the engineering is thorough and the beams aren't in bad shape."

"So we have a backdoor into the mine and the keys to the kingdom?" Serena asked, sounding as amazed as Bob was himself.

"Looks that way," John answered.

171

"Do you think it's a trap?" Bob asked, thinking hard about this startling change in their circumstances.

"It could be, but I don't think so. Joe agrees, though he's cautious too. It all looks legit and we think it would've been hard to set all this up on the off-chance that we would be here, doing what we're doing." John ran one hand through his long hair. "I don't think the *Venifucus* expects resistance. They're probably counting on the bobcat leadership to keep everybody in line and they've got my people on the run. They probably think we're happy just to have escaped with our lives."

Joe came back in and sat at the only open spot at the small table. John, Joe, Serena and Bob were at the little table. A few of Joe's guys were perched on counters or leaning against appliances, eating. One was even sitting on the floor.

Plates were set down in front of Serena and Joe with sizzling fish and what had to have been canned green beans borrowed from the kitchen cabinets. The guy at the stove, shut off the burner and began to clean up, putting things away and passing the dirty pots to the guy at the sink. They worked like a well-oiled machine, as if they had done this before. Bob supposed they had. Soldiers lived and fought as a unit, and wolves were Pack animals by their very nature. They worked well in groups—better than cats in a lot of cases.

They ate as Joe sat and unfolded an old, dusty map, placing it in the center of the table. "This was in the basement, near the hidden door."

"Hidden?" Serena asked, eating daintily.

"Yeah, the door to the mine wasn't exactly easy to find. In fact, we didn't see it on our first sweep through the house. It was cleverly concealed behind a false panel. Waldo there knocked on the wall and heard it ring hollow," he gestured toward the man just finishing cleaning up the stove. Waldo turned, saluting them with a dish towel and gave a lopsided grin before turning back to his work.

Bob looked at the map as he ate, noting the markings for doors, passageways and one particularly ominous marking at the back of one of the larger branches off the main tunnel. That one might come in handy. He was familiar with old mine maps, having been involved with more than a few building projects in California where old gold rush mines were either on or near the existing property.

In such cases, the old maps were carefully studied to see if the old tunnels could be used in the new designs—some shifters liked to have underground dens or escape tunnels. If the building site was meant for humans, the danger posed by the old mine site was also weighed carefully. Redstone Construction wasn't in the business of building anywhere children of any species might get into trouble.

"Behind the false panel was a little vestibule of sorts," Joe went on with his informal briefing. "Old Jeremiah had built a small shelf where we found the map and that oil for the hinges. Looks like he had it all set up to use as an escape tunnel but didn't get the chance when the *Venifucus* moved into the mine."

"Suits our purposes to a T, though," John put in. "If this is viable, we can sneak up on them. They probably won't be expecting someone approaching from within the mine."

Bob was looking at the map, turning it toward himself to see if he could read some of the markings a little better. He tried to put his brothers' lessons to good use, thinking of the setup from the enemy's point of view.

"If they have any forces in reserve, they'll probably be either here or here." Bob pointed to a specific notation on the map. "This sign indicates larger caverns with airshafts."

Joe cocked his head and narrowed his gaze on the map. "What's this one mean?"

Bob smiled and he knew it was a little bit of an evil grin. "On the old gold rush maps I've seen in California, that's the symbol for a bottomless pit. There's probably a barricade of some sort in front of it. If we're lucky, it'll be one of those doors we have the key to. Open that and herd any enemies toward it…" He didn't have to finish the thought as Joe's mouth turned up in a grim smile. John looked a little more cautious about the idea of herding the enemy to their deaths, but he was still a predator and an Alpha protecting his Pack.

"I sent two men out to do recon," Joe said after a moment. "They should be back shortly. If things are still as they were when I went up there yesterday, I think the tunnel through the mine is our best way in. They've got the front entrance too well fortified."

Bob finished his meal and handed the empty plate off to the guy still manning the sink. The back door opened and the men who had finished eating went out while two more men came in. The recon team was back and reported what they'd seen. Sure enough, the front entrance to the mine was as heavily guarded as Joe had seen the day before.

Jezza was still in the front chamber, tied to a chair, set up like bait. There was even a spotlight set up to shine in his face—probably both to help interrogation and showcase their prisoner to anyone who might be watching.

One of the men had taken photos with his phone and Serena was able to identify two of the bobcat captors as guys who were definitely couriers for the drug trade. They spent about fifteen minutes revising their plan to utilize the sneak attack from within the mine and then it was time to move.

CHAPTER THIRTEEN

Serena went with the men because really, it was the safest place to be. Hiding on her own in the house or elsewhere wasn't safe if the bad guys spooked and ran. If she had to be here, she would rather take her chances with the soldiers than being on her own. Plus, if she got the chance, there were a couple of bobcats in particular she would love to claw…or shoot.

They'd given her a gun. Not a big one, but something she could definitely handle. Rocky had been teaching her how to shoot so she was familiar with the concept and Bob gave her a quick primer on the specific handgun he had given her. She felt better with the heavy weight of it in her hand and the spare clips in her pockets.

Bob hadn't liked having her along, but he had seen the sense in what she had to say. He was good like that. Willing to listen to her and give a little when what she said made sense. She valued that. None of the bobcat men she'd known had been even remotely willing to listen to a female.

The Cascade Clan of bobcats was made up of chauvinist pigs from what she'd seen. She had almost begun to think all shifters were that way, except she remembered her parents. They had been partners. Two halves of a whole. Her father certainly hadn't ordered her mother around like a slave, and he had valued his female cub. He hadn't treated Serena as a disappointment because she wasn't born male. He'd loved her.

She remembered the love especially.

But it took seeing the way the shifters on the Lords' mountain lived to remember it all and realize that there was something seriously wrong in the Cascade Clan. Seriously. Wrong.

"Are you okay, kitten?" Bob asked her in a quiet voice as the team of men prepared, checking gear and making last minute preparations in the basement.

They had cleaned the kitchen and the rest of the house to leave it in the condition in which it had been found. Nobody—except maybe the homeowners—would realize they had been there.

The Alpha wolf had sent a small team of his men around to the front of the mine to catch any bobcats that might try to escape that way. The front door team, as he called them, was also tasked with reporting movements to the tunnel team. They had tiny little radios that fit in their ear canals over which they communicated in some kind of code she couldn't quite decipher. It must be some kind of military lingo, she supposed.

"I'm good," she replied. The seriousness of their situation wasn't lost on her. They were walking into danger and everything could change in the time it took a bullet to hit its mark. She moved closer, stepping close to Bob and wrapping her arms around his waist. "I love you," she whispered, resting her head in the space where his shoulder met his neck. She breathed deeply of his reassuring scent and tried to hold the goodness of him inside her—just for a few moments.

He soothed her, stroking his hands over her back. She knew she had surprised him with her moment of sentimentality, but he was coping. He pulled her closer and his arms went around her back, enveloping her in his warmth.

"I love you too, my sweet mate. I'm so glad I found you,"

he whispered low enough that only she could hear him. She took his words into her heart and held them close.

A throat cleared behind her and she pulled away from Bob slightly, looking up. Turning her head, she met the sympathetic gaze of the werewolf Alpha. He seemed to understand her fear and his words were softly spoken when he told them it was time to go.

Bob gave her a final squeeze and then let her go. She stood there, watching while he checked his gear for a final time. He was armed, but he had left his outer shirt in the SUV. If he had to shift, he was ready. The rest of the men were similarly attired. She guessed this was the way shifter soldiers went into battle—ready in human form with human weapons and tools, but able to ditch them quickly and shift if the occasion called for it. That made a lot of sense.

"It'll be okay," the werewolf Alpha spoke quietly at her side while they both watched the soldiers. "We have the Great Spirit on our side."

She looked up at the wolf who was so clearly of Native American descent. A lot of shifters had some Native blood in them, but this guy was much closer to the source than most. His face could have been chiseled in granite and there was a nobility about him that spoke to her soul. She knew without a doubt that he was a good man. A good Alpha to his people.

"I'm glad our paths crossed, Alpha. I haven't known many wolves besides the Lords, but I'm sorry for the damage done to your Pack and I'll try to help in any way I can."

John favored her with a somewhat amused expression. "You and your mate have already been more friend to us than any of your Clan."

"They're not my Clan," she was quick to answer. "Not anymore, and never by choice. I suppose I'll be part of the Redstone Clan after this is all over—if they'll take a bobcat."

Bob paused and turned back to her, having heard the entire conversation. He bent down and kissed her on the crown of her head.

"What kind of talk is that? Of course they'll have you.

You're my mate, Serena. They're going to love you," he scoffed quietly as the first soldiers began moving silently down the tunnel.

"As it should be." The Alpha nodded once and moved into position. He was going to be part of the rear guard, with Bob and Serena.

And then there wasn't any more time for talking as they made their way into the tunnel. It was show time.

Serena thought the tunnel would be ickier than it was. Sure, there were a few cobwebs here and there that the soldiers hadn't disturbed, but her cat felt an inner sense of adventure she had seldom experienced. The bobcat that shared her soul was actually enjoying this. Serena's human half had to shake her head in bafflement. The cat was the daredevil side of her personality that loved a good hunt. The human had learned to be a lot more cautious.

Bob too, seemed to be enjoying this, as did the wolves. Give a predator a chance to stalk prey and they were right at home. If the soldiers had been in wolf form, she would bet all their tails would be wagging with excitement. The thought amused her and made her grin a bit as they passed through the second door, about fifty yards down the tunnel from where they had started in the basement.

They had locked and booby trapped the basement door after they were all through it to prevent any bad guys from getting in behind them without their knowledge. They would do the same for the rest of the doors as they went. The only way open to them now was forward.

Bob had tucked Father Vincenzo's cross under his shirt, against his skin. As long as it was in contact with his skin, he figured it would allow him to see any bad stuff that might be in the mine. Like the eerie red glow in the passageway ahead.

Shit.

He tapped out the pre-arranged signal that would only be audible within a few yards. Instantly, the wolves froze. Bob moved forward, to take point, using the hand signals his brothers had taught him to communicate to the wolves what he had in mind.

There was something weird about the corridor ahead. Something was glowing red and only he could see it. When he got to the front of the short line of men, he lifted the cross out away from his skin, muffling its effects in the fabric of his T-shirt. Sure enough, the red glow faded away. When he released the cross to once again lay against his skin, the glow returned.

Bob inched closer, trying to get a good look at what might be causing the phenomenon. When he rounded the slight bend in the narrow passageway, he cursed under his breath. Magical glyphs glowed on the walls of the tunnel, and angry red scar on the surface, forming a circle around the passageway. The walls, floor and ceiling held the evil symbols and Bob didn't know enough about magic to see a way around it.

A hand touched his elbow and he turned to see Joe at his side. Bob went back around the slight curve in the tunnel. The bend would muffle the sound of what he needed to say.

But before he could open his mouth, the ground trembled. A massive earthquake made the entire mountain sway. Bob looked for Serena before ducking for cover himself. He was relieved to see the werewolf Alpha had sheltered her under his own body. John was a good man and Bob would owe him one for looking after her—if they made it out of this alive.

When the shaking finally stopped, a fine layer of dirt and some rocks that had been in the ceiling and walls were now on the ground. A couple of rocks had hit the guys, but all were smart enough to cover their heads. The scent of blood was sharp in Bob's nose, but the wounds were minor. A few cuts and scrapes. Everybody was okay. For now.

Serena didn't let anyone hold her back once the ground stopped shaking. She moved right up next to Bob and put her hand in his. He could feel her trembling, but she didn't make a sound. His girl was a trooper.

Bob peeked around the bend and much to his surprise, the red glow was gone. He tried removing and replacing the cross against his skin and the results were the same both ways. No more glow.

"I was going to report a magical blockage ahead," he said in the lowest possible tones so that only Joe and Serena could hear him. "But I think the earthquake nullified the spell. There were glowing glyphs, but I can't see them anymore. I'm going to take a closer look. Keep everybody else back until I give the signal."

He squeezed Serena's hand once before letting go and moving around the bend again. Sure enough, the symbols were fading even as he watched. A part of the ceiling, right where the glyphs had been, had collapsed and the dirt and rocks scattered, taking the spell with them. The rest of the circle faded to nothing and then were no more. It was like their energy had been absorbed into the earth, the spell unsustainable without that big chunk of the ceiling.

The rest of the passageway looked sturdy enough. Just that area where the spell had been was gone, which led Bob to believe that perhaps the Goddess was giving them a helping hand. He knew damn well that nobody in their group had the skills necessary to negate that magical ring. Without the timely intervention of the earthquake, they'd have been truly stuck, and probably would have had to turn back.

He gave the hand signal and the rest of the group joined him on silent feet. They began moving steadily forward once more.

This side tunnel met up with a much wider, main passageway around the next bend. There were no more doors. No more keys. Just open tunnel from here on out. Bob figured it was a sure bet the *Venifucus* had scouted the part of the mine they were about to enter. He would have to be on the lookout for any more signs of spells. The mage had probably set up things that would warn him if anything moved in the tunnel system that wasn't supposed to be there. It made sense that the barrier that had come down in the quake had been something like that, though Bob was certainly no expert.

They joined the larger passageway and everyone went on even higher alert. They could run into enemy forces at any time now. Bob recalled the map they had studied. Between them and their goal—the main entrance that had been hollowed out to form a staging area for the rest of the mine—were two natural caverns. Somewhere between those two caverns was the passage that had been marked with the sign for a bottomless pit.

The line of men behind him reshuffled as Joe gave orders through hand signals. Bob stayed up front as the magic-detector. He didn't like being separated from Serena, even by a few yards, but he knew he had to be on the lookout for magical traps. Joe was at Bob's side, also on point now that the passageway was wide enough.

Bob glanced over the group and realized Joe had partnered Serena with John. The Alpha would take good care of her, Bob knew, if for no other reason than he loved his sister and his sister liked Serena. Of all the wolves, John perhaps, understood Serena the best. He knew what she had suffered in the past at the hands of her former Clan. Plus, Bob had sensed something from the other Alpha. There was a sense of kinship—a bond that was hard to put into words.

They approached the first cavern cautiously. If there were going to be larger groups of enemy troops, they would likely be in one or both of the caverns. Bob gave the signal to halt when a flash of glowing red met his gaze. More glyphs. He moved slowly, craning his head to get a better look. As before, the magical symbols ringed the cavern entrance with their evil light.

"What?" Joe asked quietly, coming up beside Bob.

In answer, Bob took the silver cross out of his shirt and gestured for Joe to touch it. He looked skeptical, but reached out carefully to put one finger on the small silver cross.

"Look," Bob advised, his gaze moving toward the glowing red glyphs surrounding the cavern entrance.

"Sweet Mother of All," Joe breathed as he saw the evil magic for the first time. That experiment confirmed to Bob that the cross could be used by others, not just him. It truly did allow the blind to see—those who were blind to magic could see its presence when touching the ancient silver talisman.

Joe let go after a moment and nodded to Bob. "What now?"

"It's probably empty," Bob answered, risking the brief conversation but keeping his voice as quiet as possible.

"Let's look," Joe answered already moving to one side.

They moved closer in unison, peering into the cavern, moving in tiny increments. If Bob's guess was right, the entrance had been warded to prevent anyone or anything from coming or going. If he was right, the cavern would be empty.

Sure enough, when he and Joe peered in from opposite sides of the opening, only dark emptiness met their gaze. The tiny amount of light that filtered down from air vents allowed them to see into the far recesses of the cavern and it was well and truly empty. So far, so good.

At that moment, the earth shook again, a little more violently this time. Once again, Bob looked first to make sure Serena was covered. Two of the soldiers had her between them, sheltering her under their hunched bodies. Bob bent over, protecting his head as best he could while the mountain rumbled its displeasure. He could almost feel its anger at being disturbed, and yet...

There was a feeling of deliberate purpose in the tremor as well. Bob had never been overly religious or magical in any way, but he felt something as a section of the cavern's entrance crumbled before him. A big rock narrowly missed hitting him and he stumbled back in surprise, his cat reflexes taking him out of the path of danger just in time to see the cavern entrance break up on one side, the evil glyphs winking out of existence as the wall of rock and earth they were bound to crumbled.

Hot damn. If he hadn't thought it before, he now *knew* the Lady was clearing the way for them.

The tremor ceased and Bob looked up to find that everyone seemed to be all right from this round of dust and rocks pelting them. Serena popped up and he went to her side. Joe reorganized his group and was at Bob's side a moment later.

"Same thing as before," Bob reported. "The tremor broke the spell. We can use the cavern. I think the Lady wants us to. It's like She is clearing our path."

John nodded, having joined them. "I feel it too. Koma Kulshan rumbles to the Great Spirit's design. She is angry, but helpful to those of us who seek to help Her."

"That's good because we need a place to stash Waldo. A big rock hit his ankle. He's not going to be able to move for a while." Joe looked back at the man who stood on one foot, holding his assault rifle in one hand and bracing his arms against the rock wall beside him with the other. The man who had been smiling as he flipped sizzling fish only an hour ago now looked pissed, and more than a little embarrassed.

"Damn. I missed that. I didn't think anyone was hurt," Bob admitted.

Joe shrugged. "Why do you think we call him Waldo? Dude is like a chameleon. Blends in whenever he wants. But he's too hurt to go on. We can leave him here in the cavern and I would suggest leaving your lady too. She'll be safe with him to guard her." Joe smiled at Serena, who was bristling a bit at Bob's side. "Or maybe she can guard him. Either way, I don't want to leave anyone on their own down here. It would be good to leave a team to guard our back trail."

Bob turned to Serena, ignoring the other men for a moment. "Much as I want you by my side, he does have a point." Bob reached out, tracing her soft cheek with the back of one finger. She met his gaze and he saw understanding begin to replace anger. Her gaze still held a healthy dose of fear, but she was gaining strength even as he watched. "Waldo can't go on as he is and someone needs to stay with him."

"It makes sense for me to stay," she finally admitted in a small voice. "Even I can defend a cave with only one entrance."

He held her gaze for a long moment. "You're one in a million, sweetheart." He leaned in and delivered a hard kiss, not caring who watched. This was his woman. His mate. The perfect match for him in every possible way. This latest situation only proved it. He was so proud of the way she had discovered her own strength. He drew back, looking deep into her eyes. "I love you with everything that's in me."

"Back at'cha, big guy," she replied, kissing him once more, lightly, before she stepped back, removing herself from his embrace.

He was kind of glad she had taken the first step away because right then, he wasn't sure he could've made himself move away first. He really did love her. This situation only reinforced how perfect they were for each other. He also had to believe that the Mother of All was looking out for them. He had to have that elusive thing Father Vincenzo had always counseled him to seek—faith.

Bob sent a quick prayer up to the Goddess as Waldo moved painfully toward him. He would have to pass Bob to reach the cavern entrance. Bob watched the other man draw closer, evaluating his injury with practiced eyes, but Waldo paused in front of him.

"I won't let anything happen to her."

Bob held the soldier's gaze. "See that you don't," he said quickly, trusting the soldier to do his duty and protect the innocent. Serena was vulnerable, but she was also strong. "And don't underestimate her. She has a backbone of pure steel. She'll help. You just need to give her a chance. Don't forget, she's a predator at heart too."

Bob knew Serena heard his words as he looked over Waldo's shoulder to meet her gaze. She smiled at him, the suspicious glint of tears in her eyes. Bob refocused on the man who stood painfully in front of him.

"Understood, Alpha."

The fact that Waldo had used the respectful title for him meant something among shifters. It meant the soldier had accepted the task given by someone of higher rank that he respected. He would do all in his power to fulfill the Alpha's expectations of him. It was a promise and a symbol of the hierarchy that made their society work, and even thrive.

Waldo nodded once more and moved on, his gait painful to watch as he entered the cavern. Serena lagged behind, waiting for Bob to meet her at the opening. He pulled her into his embrace for one last kiss.

"Free Jezza and then come back to me," she whispered, nearly breaking his heart. "Waldo and I will make sure nobody gets past us."

Bob looked over her shoulder and met the eyes of a giant wolf. Waldo had shifted into his animal form and Bob could see he was already getting around better on four feet than on two. He was also as dark as midnight. When his eyes closed, he just about disappeared from view. A chameleon indeed.

He kissed the top of her head and made himself release her. "Stick with the wolf and stay safe for me, kitten. I'll be back before you know it."

He let her go and moved to follow the rest of the soldiers. He was at the back of the group, but he would have to take his place on point as soon as they were out of sight of the cavern. Only he could see the magical traps, and everyone was moving cautiously until he got back into position.

Bob looked over his shoulder right before the passageway turned and saw Serena wave once before she disappeared into the cavern. He sent up another silent prayer to the Mother of All to keep Serena safe and rounded the bend, taking his place at the front of the expedition.

CHAPTER FOURTEEN

Bob called a halt when he saw broken timbers up ahead. The breaks were fresh. As if the old beams had fallen recently—perhaps in one of the earthquakes they had been experiencing. Was this more divine intervention? Bob could only shake his head in wonder. If he was right, the timbers had served as a barricade against the danger he had seen marked on the map.

He signaled for the rest of the team to wait while he went ahead and checked out the large, newly-opened passageway. About twenty feet in he saw it. A dark so deep even his superior night vision couldn't penetrate it. He dropped a pebble into it and heard the rock bounce off the walls for a long, long way downward until the sound just faded out. The shaft was deeper than he could easily gauge. A mantrap if he'd ever seen one.

Bob backtracked and cleared the timbers from the entrance, scooting them to the sides of the dirt walls. He and the guys with him would recognize the timbers on the ground, but it was likely nobody else would think anything of them. Judging by the newness of the breaks in the old wood, the fall was fresh. The enemy troops probably hadn't been able to get past the barrier and if there had been magical warding on the area, it was gone now.

It was easy to get turned around inside a cave system. Bob was betting on that—and the fact that the path had changed without enemy knowledge—to consider this a viable strategy if they ended up encountering a large force. Bob told the team what he had found and each of them looked suitably grim, but also intrigued by the new possible weapon in their arsenal. They would use anything they could to come out on the winning side of the battle ahead.

They continued down the main passageway, and Bob thankfully didn't see any more magical glyphs. What they did see was signs of occupation. Footprints on the dusty ground. Many of them. Skid marks where things had been dragged recently. And sounds started coming to them. The sounds of men talking in low voices and moving around quietly. The sound of metal. The sharp scents of oil and gunpowder.

Joe sent him a questioning look and Bob knew the lieutenant was asking whether there were any magical telltales. Bob shook his head in the negative and moved back from the point position. He had to leave the military decisions to the lieutenant and the men he had worked with for years. They were too good a unit to interfere with.

Bob fell back while the military guys sorted themselves out and found himself next to John the werewolf Alpha. The ground had been rumbling under them for a while now, but there hadn't been any more big earthquakes. It was as if the mountain was complaining, but not yet up to full tantrum strength yet. He only hoped they were out of the tunnels before it got to that point.

"You may not act like it, but you are a wise man," John surprised him by saying. "I like the way you lead, but also listen. If we survive this, I think my Pack would benefit from a closer association with your Clan. And there are things your Clan could gain from my Pack as well. Eyes on the border, for one."

Bob considered his words very carefully. Alliances like this weren't really decided on his level, though he usually did a lot of the background investigation. Ultimately though, it was Grif who made the deals. He was the Clan Alpha.

But Bob had seen the Pack in action and so far, he liked what he'd seen.

"If we get out of this alive, you'll have my support, Alpha."

John nodded, understanding the step they had just taken toward a more formal alliance. There wasn't time for anything else as the soldiers began to move. Joe signaled to them and Bob and John moved forward to go wherever the lieutenant would lead.

"My guys are taking the cavern. The three of us are going to see what Jezza's been up to."

They crept along the passageway, past the soldiers who had pre-positioned themselves at the mouth of the large cavern. Bob could hear enemy soldiers inside the larger space, but there weren't any stationed at the entrance. As he drew closer and saw the crumbled rock and bloodstains, he thought he understood why. Somebody had been standing there during the last tremor and gotten clobbered. The rest of them were standing clear for now, which was lucky for the assault team.

The three of them edged past the opening, keeping to the shadows. The cavern had low lighting, but it wasn't enough to reach out into the passageway and expose their presence.

Once past that hurdle, the path was relatively clear to the main entrance and the staging area that had been carved out of the mountain right there, at the entrance to the old mine. Bob went first, looking for signs of magic. He halted the moment he peeked around the last bend. The entire staging area chamber was lit by a hazy reddish glow. This wasn't the bright, fiery red of the glyphs, but a dark, almost brownish red. The color of old blood. Sickly. Putrid. Evil.

He took a cautious peek around the side of a crate that had been left just in front of the natural bend in the wall and realized the source of the glow wasn't a glyph. It was a man. A mage.

Holy shit.

If ever evil walked on two legs, that was it.

Bob ducked back behind the curve in the wall to catch his breath. He'd seen a lot in that little moment of tableau.

A guy who had to be Jezza was tied to a chair. Bloody. Bruised. His blood flowing into a little river that had been carved into the earth beneath his feet. A channel in the form of a circle went around the chair, Jezza's blood flowing freely into it as he was slowly drained from a hundred different shallow cuts all over his body. The chair acted as a conduit, allowing the blood to gather on the straight lines of its legs and back, flowing from there into the channel on the floor that glowed red with magical power.

The mage stood in front of the chair, doing something that seemed to pull a golden light out of Jezza's tortured body. Was the mage stealing Jezza's magical energy as well as his blood? Bob wasn't sure, but it definitely looked that way. Bob had listened to the priestess of his Clan enough to know such things could happen.

All he knew was that it had to be stopped. The evil mage couldn't have any more of Jezza's blood…or power. If he did…

Bob spoke one word that he knew would start an inescapable, but necessary cascade.

"Go."

Bob stood and walked into the staging area, facing the mage and drawing his attention. Behind him, he was counting on Joe to give the order for his guys to attack the cavern full of soldiers. Once engaged with the mage, Bob couldn't afford any distractions.

"Who the fuck are you?" the mage asked, annoyance in his tone. "Get the fuck out of here!" The mountain trembled, grumbling loudly.

"Can't," Bob said, moving closer. He didn't know what he could do against a mage, but he had to get the man to stop draining Jezza. The mountain continued to protest, shaking violently this time. The ground seemed to roll under their feet.

"Who the fuck do you think you are?"

The mage had a definite eastern accent—maybe New York or New Jersey—and seemed incapable of forming a sentence without the word fuck in it. Bob filed that information away for later. It might help trace the origins of the bastard—after Bob ripped him to shreds.

To that end, Bob took off his T-shirt as he walked toward the man across the large open expanse. The mountain quaked, the volcano rumbling in the distance as the mage funneled pure golden energy from Jezza, into himself, and then that warped, brown-red magic went into the ground at his feet—into the mountain. Making it angrier by the second.

Bob somehow knew what had to be done. The magic flow had to be stopped. Not only to save Jezza, but to quiet the mountain. The mage was using Jezza's power to augment his own, morphing the golden light of Jezza's magic into the rusty red color of the mage's before sending it into the mountain, waking the slumbering, volcanic giant.

*

Back in the cavern, Serena heard the rock scream to life as the quakes started again. She covered her ears and her head, noting that Waldo had morphed back to his human shape to protect her. When the world didn't stop shaking but the cavern seemed mostly intact, she looked up, sensing something. Something was…

A blast at the back of the cavern signaled the arrival of intense heat. And light. Golden red light and baking, blistering heat. Lava.

Sweet Mother of All.

"We've got to get out of here or we'll be baked alive," she shouted over the rumbling of rock.

The lava was flowing sluggishly, pushing upward from beneath them, toward what she had thought was another of the many vent shafts in the immense cavern. Only it wasn't a ventilation shaft. It was the lava tube that would lead to the very top of the mountain.

If the pressure from below built up enough, hot lava would fill this cavern on its way toward the sky.

Another crack and boom and suddenly a slab of rock separated them, near the entrance to the cavern, from the lava. Cool, solid rock stuck upward between them and the dangerously hot molten rock, shielding them from the worst of the heat. As if the mountain was trying to protect them, even as it was driven toward blowing its top.

Waldo was dressed in his soldier gear once more, the wolf having retreated to allow the soldier to take point for the moment. She was glad. She needed his advice right now, not his wagging tail.

"The rest of the group has made contact with the enemy," he reported, tapping his ear.

She knew he still wore the little device in his ear canal that apparently stayed there whether he was in wolf form or human. It allowed him to hear what the rest of his team were up to, via the short range radio it contained.

"The second cavern held about a dozen soldiers. They're being dealt with," he reported. "Your mate, the Alpha and the lieutenant are engaging a mage at the mine entrance."

"I don't think we can stay here." Serena looked at the glow of the lava reflecting off the cave walls. It was almost too hot to breathe.

Waldo seemed to consider. "Agreed. My ankle is bad though. I can't move too fast."

"That's okay. We'll go slow." She moved to his side, putting herself under his left arm, leaving his right arm free to hold and shoot his rifle, if necessary.

They made their way down the passageway. It was cooler here than in the cavern, but the temperature throughout the mine had changed dramatically over the past few minutes. The noise level was incredible. She heard the low rumble of lava moving behind solid walls and prayed the rock walls would hold until she and Waldo had passed.

And then she heard the sound of gunfire. Ahead of them, she heard men calling out and a few screams. Staccato blasts and the ping of bullets ricocheting off solid rock.

"Firefight ahead," Waldo said grimly. "Better hold up a minute and see if it dies down."

He guided her to a more or less defensible position near a secondary mineshaft that had broken timbers lining its walls. She could see a dull glow of red from somewhere below a small ledge. Lava was flowing down there somewhere and she suddenly realized that wasn't a ledge.

"This is the bottomless pit Bob saw marked on the map," she told Waldo. The other man didn't look too surprised, but a calculating light entered his gaze as they settled in to wait.

*

There were two guards near the mine entrance that turned around when they heard the mage speak, but so far, they weren't doing much to stop Bob's advance. They seemed confused. Like they weren't sure if he might be one of their guys. They didn't seem to seriously think anyone could have snuck up from behind—from within the mine itself. That hesitation cost them.

Gunfire erupted from the direction of the troop cavern and Joe popped up from behind a crate to plug two holes in the guard nearest him. The other guy fell shortly thereafter, getting off only one wild shot that ricocheted around the cavern for a bit before falling harmlessly to the dirt floor. All the while, Bob moved closer to the mage.

That was when the real fun began. The mage seemed to realize Bob was a threat a split second later and launched a fireball at him.

Bob sprang forward, calling on all his feline agility and strength. The fireball missed, falling in the spot where he'd been a moment before. But the mage was fast. He had another blast of magical power aimed at Bob before he could blink. And this one hit.

Or rather…it hit the cross hanging around Bob's neck. The magical cross that allowed him to see magic. Apparently it also shielded him from magic as well.

Not only did the cross stop the bolt of energy, it reflected it back toward the mage, making him stumble.

"What the fuck?" the mage raged, seemingly surprised and royally pissed off at the sudden turn of events.

Bob didn't let anything slow him down. He covered the big empty space on steady feet, even as the mountain continued to vibrate with suppressed anger. He was bare chested and planning a quick shift to his cougar form as soon as he saw an opening he could exploit. His pants and boots wouldn't hinder him too much. The boots would simply fall off when his feet turned into paws, and the pants would either follow suit or be easily wriggled out of shortly after his shift. He just had to time it exactly right.

"Let Jezza go," Bob said, buying time.

At the sound of his name, the jaguar roused, his head lolling toward Bob and his eyes opening a fraction. That he was still aware, even after everything that had been done to him both magically and mundanely, was really something. The guy must have reserves of strength Bob could only guess at.

"Why the fuck should I listen to you? You're only hired muscle. Go back and play with yourself like the rest of the assholes back there." The mage was stupider than he looked. It still hadn't occurred to him that Bob wasn't one of the soldiers from the cavern.

"You're an idiot," Bob said finally, halting a few yards from the mage. "Can't you understand what's going on? You're under attack. Those assholes, as you call them, aren't going to come to your aid. They're under fire from the guys I came in with. The guys who want you and your kind dead. The guys who fight on the side of the Light."

The moment he said it, the cross did something it had never done before. It began to glow. A shining, white-gold brilliance that was as pure as anything Bob had ever seen. The mage shielded his eyes and cringed backward as if the light burned. And maybe it did.

Bob could feel the goodness in the light. It was from *the* Light. Purity. Good. The Mother of All by whatever name you called Her. Bob had no fear of Her Light. He embraced the moment, allowing the Light to bathe him in its strength.

He took heart from it and knew he could defeat his enemies, as long as the Light was on his side.

*

Serena felt something change. Something in the air brought the tang of ozone, like after a lightning strike. The fresh scent of rain-soaked earth. All those images came to her as the noise of the firefight in the cavern died down a bit.

And then there were stealthy footsteps coming their way. She sensed Waldo tense on the other side of the wide mouth of the passageway. They had decided to each take one side so that anyone entering would face one or the other of them.

As it turned out, the man who entered was unshaven and unkempt. She smelled him coming before she saw him, but he was closer to Waldo's side of the passageway.

She recognized him. It was the Border Patrol agent. Parker. Definitely an enemy, slinking away from the cavern where the rest of Joe's platoon was fighting with the enemy soldiers.

Parker was human and couldn't see well in the dark. He had a little flashlight lighting the path in front of him, but it wasn't really adequate. The beam was weak and not large. Parker was the next best thing to blind in the dark tunnel. The predator in her wanted to lick its chops in satisfaction. This one might be an easy kill.

But it was Waldo's kill to make. While Serena's bobcat was comfortable thinking in terms of killing just about anything, Serena's human side really wasn't up to killing a human being. She knew the man was evil and that helped her rationalize the need to neutralize him, but she wasn't sure she would be able

194

to do it herself. Not like this. Maybe in the heat of battle or in self-defense, but not in this pre-meditated way. Thankfully, she wouldn't have to act this time. Waldo was already sneaking up on their prey. Serena would be there to back him up if things went bad, but she doubted an experienced warrior like Waldo would need her help at all.

The soldier sprang at the last possible moment, taking Agent Parker by the scruff of the neck and hoisting him over his head, throwing him into the pit with unerring accuracy. Serena didn't have to help after all. Injured as he was, Waldo had still managed the feat of strength all on his own and it was something she never would forget. The man was a force to be reckoned with.

Agent Parker flew into the bottomless pit, screaming on his way down. The sound of it was something she would never forget either, but thankfully, the screams faded fast and ended in a final screech of agony as he hit the river of lava far below. Serena shuddered, but at least the evil man had been given a quick, almost merciful, end.

She heard Waldo speaking in low tones to his colleagues via the little radio in his ear. The battle in the cavern was over, it sounded like, and they were going to send someone back to help him move a little quicker toward the mine entrance where they were regrouping.

"All the enemy forces we knew about have been accounted for, but keep your eyes open," Waldo told her in low, urgent tones. "There could be more of them."

She kept his warning in mind as they met up with Chico, who supported Waldo on the other side while they made their way slowly toward the main group. The rest of the men had split up—half had gone ahead to the mine entrance while the other half waited by the cavern for Waldo and Serena to catch up. They set off quickly once Chico, Waldo and Serena arrived, to regroup with the rest of their unit.

The men all but carried Waldo now that the majority of the enemy forces had been dealt with. Chico had told her what their lieutenant had reported back to them. The only enemy left was a mage and Bob was taking him on by himself. Serena wanted to run at that point, but the rest of the guys had nixed the idea. They took her safety very seriously and though they hastened their steps, they wouldn't allow her to run ahead.

Serena arrived at the mine entrance in time to see a ball of visible, evil red fire engulf Bob. Clearly, they were magical flames. She would have cried out, but John took her hand and pulled her back toward the dubious cover of some crates.

"Watch," John counseled. "The priest's talisman protects your mate."

And sure enough, the cross around Bob's neck seemed to block and reflect the magical fire, sending it back on its creator. Serena was astounded. She had never seen anything like it before in her life.

The mage seemed enraged and as he took a stumbling step back, toward the mine entrance, Serena caught sight of Jezza, strapped to a bloody chair. He looked half dead and his head lolled to one side. His eyes were cracked open and she met his gaze, knowing somehow that he was looking directly at her. A small smile played over his swollen and bloody features. Her heart went out to him.

Jezza had been so strong. So willing to put himself on the line to help her escape her bad situation. He had taken a lot of risks to help her, and it looked like it had all finally caught up to him. He was in really bad shape, but she vowed then and there, it was time for her to begin repaying the debt she owed him.

She shook off John's hold, realizing the Alpha decided to let her go. She would've had a fight on her hands otherwise, being a lot smaller and less muscular than the big werewolf. But he seemed to understand. He let her go and she felt a calm descend over her being.

She stood from behind the crate and moved into the light. She realized finally that the light was coming from the cross around Bob's neck and she knew it was there to help them. It was protective and healing. It was goodness itself.

She got her first good look at the man who had been lobbing the fireballs and her breath caught in recognition. She had seen him before. Many times, in fact. She even knew his name—Victor Ramos. He was one of the drug cartel leaders. The one who had made the bobcat Clan leadership dance to his tune.

Well, no more.

"Imagine that," she said, drawing Victor's attention away from Bob. "Ramos is a mage. Who knew?" Serena was secure in the belief that as long as the light stood between her and the mage, his evil could not reach her.

"You're that bobcat bitch that wouldn't bend," Victor said. "Where the fuck did you come from? Where the fuck did all these dickheads come from?"

Serena laughed, understanding finally that Victor wasn't the all-powerful boogeyman she'd imagined. He was a pitiful creature, too stupid to realize when he'd been defeated.

"We were sent by the Lady. She sends Her regards." The mountain rumbled, as if in agreement.

Victor seemed to get angrier.

"You shouldn't have tried to steal Koma Kulshan's power." John's voice came from Bob's other side. She peered over and realized the werewolf Alpha was standing with them, against the mage.

"The mountain isn't alive, you primitive animal," Victor sneered. "You're weak, you fucking werewolf asshole."

His language hadn't improved since she last saw him. She'd never spoken directly to Victor before, but she had witnessed him talking—cussing every other word—with her adoptive father any number of times.

"And you are mistaken. The mountain lives." The earth rumbled and shook slightly as if to emphasize John's words. "And you are the weakling."

Victor tried to let loose a bolt of concentrated power at them, but the cross reflected it back and in a split second, Bob had transformed into his cougar, and pounced. He took the drug dealer mage to the ground and ripped his throat out with one angry screech.

Serena was trembling with relief, but found her feet and ran to Jezza's side. He halted her before she could cross the bloody circle, his voice scratchy and raw.

"Don't touch me, sweetheart. There's something that has to be done before the spell will be completely broken."

She waited impatiently but it was John who answered her unspoken question. "We have to feed the mage's body to the fires of Koma Kulshan. Only then will his magic disperse completely and let our friend go.

The cougar looked up, but kept his unsheathed claws on the still body of the mage. He was dead, but the magic was still strong—probably linked to the volcano somehow. The earth still trembled.

"Blood and magic tie us both to the mountain now," Jezza clarified. Throw him to the flames and let the mountain have him. It might stop it from erupting, and release me. Or it could take me with him. Either way, it will end this. Thank you for coming to get me." Jezza's smile was sad.

"I'll see that it's done," John said, nodding solemnly to Jezza before turning to walk toward the mage and the cougar that guarded his body. The cougar transformed into Bob and she smiled at him before turning back to Jezza.

"I'll stay with you. John and my mate will send the body into the volcano's fire." She turned back to talk to Bob. "The bottomless pit is filling with lava. Take the body there and throw him in."

Bob was covered in blood, but the cross still shone silver against his bronzed skin. It had protected him and she prayed it would continue to do so. Bob smiled at her and she read something in his gaze that hadn't been there before this mission. In addition to the caring and love, there was also pride. Pride in her.

He was beginning to see her as an equal and she was starting to feel the same way. It was a novel idea to the bobcat that had been beaten so far down that she didn't think she'd ever feel comfortable in her own skin again. Not only had Bob helped her reclaim her *self*, but he'd encouraged her to grow into a woman who could face down a mage at her mate's side. A woman who would be his equal and his helper. A woman he—and she—could be proud of.

*

Bob and John bore witness as the mage Serena had called Victor was consumed by lava. He burst into flames and then was gone. What was even more interesting to Bob was the release of golden-hued magic that snaked its way back up the bottomless pit and made its way through the passageways of the mine. Bob followed its progress as he loped back toward the mine entrance, John at his side.

Sure enough, the magical energy went back to its source. It filled Jezza, lifting him from the chair and breaking the circle of blood that was dried in a flash of heat from the mountain and then turned to dust—absorbed into the dirt of the floor. All that remained of that evil ring was a slight furrow in the ground.

The bindings that had lashed Jezza to the chair were also turned to ash—as was the chair itself. It left only Jezza, standing on shaky legs for a harsh moment when the golden light infused his body, giving him the momentary strength to stand.

And then it faded and he slumped toward the floor. John moved to catch him even as Serena reached out to help steady him. Bob came up behind her, supporting her. His woman was proving to be a force of nature. A creature to be reckoned with. An amazing lady with hidden depths.

He looked forward to discovering every hidden facet of her personality over the years to come. He couldn't have asked for a more perfect mate and he was so damn proud of her for sticking this out and regaining the strength she should have had all along.

"You're amazing, Serena," he couldn't help saying.

She turned and smiled at him briefly. He knew he was a

mess. He probably still had Victor's blood all over himself, but there wasn't time to clean up. Not yet.

Joe ran over to them, a frown etched into the grooves on his face.

"Something's going on farther up the mountain," he reported, even as the earth began to shake again.

This wasn't over.

CHAPTER FIFTEEN

"The bobcat Alpha and his council went up there with the other mage," Jezza gasped, his strength at its lowest ebb. John was basically holding him up, his arm around Jezza's shoulders.

"Another mage?" Serena asked, her head whirling. She had thought they were done, but now they weren't? And there was another threat? She cursed under her breath.

"There's a fissure up there that leads right to the caldera. Best place to try to tap into the volcano," Jezza coughed, clearly in bad shape but willing to fight to get his message out.

"They're really trying it? To seize the power of a volcano?" Joe asked, his brows drawn down in concern.

"They really are," Jezza confirmed. "Thanks for freeing me, but the job isn't over yet. You have to stop them."

"But none of us have magic. How do we stop a mage?" Joe asked, still frowning.

One of Jezza's eyebrows rose and Serena could see the humor in his eyes. "How did you stop Victor?"

"More luck than wisdom," Bob admitted, also frowning. "I can see the magic, thanks to this talisman, and it seems to protect me, but..." he trailed off and Serena knew he was concerned about trying his luck against a mage for a second time.

"Well, somebody's got to face her. I tried but there were too many pawns in play." Jezza's eyes burned with anger at his own failure. Serena knew it was going to take a long time before a man like Jezza forgave himself for not being able to stop the bad guys from winning—even temporarily.

"We're here for you now, brother," Joe said in a strong, reassuring voice. "I'm only sorry we didn't know what you were up against sooner."

"You said somebody's got to face *her*?" Bob asked, picking up on something Serena had noticed as well. "The second mage is female?"

Jezza looked straight at Serena and she felt a frisson of premonition. She almost knew what he was going to say before the words came out of his mouth.

"You're not going to believe it. Hell, I didn't see it until she turned on me. I always knew she was a witch, but I didn't think it was literal. Somewhere back in her ancestry—and not too far back, I imagine—there had to be a mage." Jezza was sort of rambling as his eyes started to close, his blood loss catching up with him.

"Who? John asked. "Who is the second mage?"

But Serena didn't need him to say the name. She already knew.

"Lizzy. The woman who went out of her way to adopt me when she realized I was being raised by a human foster family. Lizzy is the mage. She's pulling the strings." Serena felt the knowledge click into place inside her mind. Somehow, she'd always known what Lizzy was capable of, but hadn't wanted to admit it.

Lizzy had played her role to the hilt, allowing Jack to take the lead. Lizzy outwardly gave every impression of being a good little bobcat wife, following everything the Alpha and her mate told her to do to the letter. In reality, Serena now realized, it was Lizzy who'd been giving the orders all along.

And finally, Serena knew what she had to do. If there was

going to be any peace in her future, she had to confront her past.

"Lizzy came to the Cascade Clan from somewhere back east," Serena said, thinking back. "They were always vague on the details. Jack was from here. Old Jerimiah was his uncle."

"She's a follower of the *Venifucus* and the main driver behind this entire operation," Jezza revealed. "She intends to use the power of the volcano to weaken the barrier between the worlds and pull Elspeth back into the mortal realm. And damn me, but she's really close to achieving her goal. I could feel the veil weakening when Victor had my power connected to the volcano. The mountain is resisting, but it needs a being with free will to direct its energy. I tried, failed and was captured. But one of you might succeed where I couldn't do it alone."

"I can speak to Koma Kulshan," the werewolf Alpha said with startling conviction. "If you can get me close enough and distract the mage, I can try to connect with the mountain."

Serena and Bob stared at John. She was wondering if he could back up his brave words, but he seemed confident and assured.

"Well, then." Bob's voice brightened with purpose. "Looks like we have the seeds of a plan. I'll go in first and work on distracting Lizzy while you do your thing with the volcano."

"And I'll try to free the Alpha and his council," Serena piped up. "They might have done evil things, but they don't deserve to die for Lizzy's insanity. All the Clan wanted was to make money. I can't believe any of them would buy into a *Venifucus* plot to bring about the end of the world as we know it. They were stupid and greedy, not evil."

"I don't think—" Bob began, but she cut him off gently, stepping close and looking deep into his eyes.

"I have to do this so we can have a future together—free of my past," she told him. His gaze narrowed and she could see that he wanted to come up with some plausible argument against her going into danger yet again, but he finally gave up. Bob reached down and kissed her once, lightly.

"I don't have to like putting you in the line of fire, kitten," he whispered.

"I know," she whispered back. "But thank you for letting me be who I want to become. I know it's hard for you, but I also know it's necessary." She felt that truth down to the soles of her feet.

"I'm sending our medic and Chico down the mountain with Jezza and Waldo," Joe added in a firm voice. "The rest of my guys and I will help up top in any way we can."

The mountain rumbled and a few rocks fell inside the old mine. It was clearly time to get this show on the road. They headed toward the exit, helping Jezza as they met with the small cluster of Joe's men who waited just outside the mine entrance.

"Serena," Jezza's voice made her pause as Joe handed him off to another soldier. "Jack is up there too. You should know…" his voice was getting weaker as his wounds began to catch up with him. "Most of the Clan has been in thrall. Under a spell. If Lizzy dies, it might free them. Tread lightly. I think none of them have been in control of their own destiny for years. They might not even realize what they've been doing all this time."

It was good to have Jezza confirm her thoughts. She nodded. "Thank you for helping me get out when you did, Jezza. You'll never know how much it meant." She had to say something, in case she never saw the jaguar shifter again.

"I know, sweetheart. I saw…" his voice trailed off as he turned away. The medic was treating him right then and there, not waiting for them to get to safety before staunching the continued flow of his blood.

Serena met the gaze of the medic, who up 'til now had been just another one of the soldiers. She didn't know his name, but she could easily interpret his expression. Jezza was in bad shape.

"We'll be here on the slope for a little while, ma'am," the

medic said as he continued working. "No sense moving him farther until we have him stabilized a bit. The guys will help and we'll take good care of him."

Serena saw how Waldo and Chico were already assisting, one holding equipment ready and the other cleaning off wounds on other parts of the jaguar shifter's body. Jezza was in good hands and as safe as they could make him for the moment. Of course, nobody would be safe until Lizzy was stopped.

Serena nodded her thanks and turned toward the slope of the mountain. Far above, they could see a glowing fissure in the rock that had been hidden until now. There was a dirt path that snaked along the outside of the mountain, leading right up to where they needed to go. She walked up to Bob and looked around, noting that Joe and the remainder of his men were already fanning out, heading up the mountain by various paths.

"Shall we?"

Bob and Serena took the trail up to the fissure in the rock. It was the easiest path, even if it wasn't the most direct. The werewolf Alpha, John, was their silent shadow, following close behind.

"I don't see any magic along here, but I expect there'll be quite a bit once we hit the fissure up there. Don't take any chances," Bob advised as they jogged up the path.

The mountain began to rumble again and the light coming from the crack near the top of the mountain intensified.

"I bet the area geologists are going nuts right about now," Serena observed as they made their way ever closer. "They have instrumentation buried all around here to read and record seismic events. The mountain hasn't been this active in hundreds of years." She knew the history of the area, as most residents did.

The air grew hotter as they ascended and the light coming from the fissure seemed to grow from red to orange. The mountain shook a few times while they were climbing and

Bob reached out to steady her.

"You don't have to do this, Serena." She knew he was pleading with her for his own peace of mind, but she also knew she had to confront Lizzy once and for all. This was Serena's time to make a firm break with her past and the opportunity might never come again—especially if they didn't manage to stop Lizzy's insane plans.

"Sorry, but I do. You'll see. Let's just get up there. I don't think we have a lot of time left." She didn't have words to explain the compulsion driving her now, but she knew she had to go up, into the glowing fissure.

Bob looked up and then back at her as something within the mountain roared. "I think you're right."

They didn't waste more time on words, heading straight for the fissure that was only a few yards away. Bob paused when they drew even with Joe, who was hiding in the shadow of a boulder off to one side of the entrance.

"There aren't any magical traps here," Bob reported somewhat tersely. "But I can see into the fissure a bit and the pathway into the mountain is marked with the remnants of glyphs. Most of them have shaken loose already and the glow of the string of symbols is fading. Follow where I walk and you should be okay."

He took Serena's hand and led her inside. John and Joe followed in their footsteps and she thought maybe a few of Joe's guys followed, but she didn't look back to see. Her full attention was on the wide crack in the mountain that went up more than sixty feet to form a high, narrow passageway that wound deep into the heart of the mountain. The heat intensified as they went deeper, but it was still manageable. At least for now.

Bob paused as they came to what appeared to be the final turning in the passage. Peering cautiously around the bend, she could see the bobcat Clan council lined up in a horseshoe configuration facing the center of the volcano, their backs to the passage she was in. There was a wide ledge at the end of the passage that overlooked a vast caldera far below. Swirling and bubbling lava filled the pit and seemed to grow angrier by the minute. At the center of the horseshoe of men was Lizzy, her hands stretched out toward the swirling pit below, in which red lava flowed lazily, bubbling occasionally as it became more active. The heat was nearly unbearable and the smell of sulfur almost choked her.

Lizzy had stirred the mountain to life so that the red crust of lava far below was turning to orange at a rapid pace. Things were—quite literally—heating up.

On closer inspection, Serena saw that the horseshoe formation was becoming ragged and Lizzy looked awful. Maybe when they severed Jezza's power from Vincent's spell, it had taken its toll up here on Lizzy. Serena could only hope that had been the case.

There were six bobcat elders in the horseshoe, the Alpha and Jack among them. Lizzy stood facing the caldera of the volcano and even Serena could see the air shimmering with power as whatever Lizzy was doing managed to weaken the veil between realms.

Bob stepped out of cover first. Serena was right behind him, as was John. Joe stayed hidden for the moment, keeping his forces in reserve.

"I really don't think you should be doing that," Serena called in as loud a voice as she could muster in order to be heard over the roaring of the mountain.

Lizzy turned around, startled, and her gaze fell on Serena. "You!"

Oh yeah, Lizzy was pissed. Too bad. So was Serena.

"Yeah, I'm home. Did you miss me?" Serena couldn't help the sarcasm but she almost regretted her rash response when Lizzy lobbed a magical fireball in her direction.

She was at Bob's side, so instead of being burned to cinders, the power rebounded back toward Lizzy, reflected from that handy cross around his neck. When this was all over, Serena was going to hunt down that old priest and give him a big hug and kiss on the cheek. That old man's kindness had saved them over and over this night.

Lizzy screamed in frustration and a little pain when her own fireball pushed her toward the edge of the pit. She scrambled for footing, finally righting herself, but whatever spell she'd been working on to make the air shimmer and wave had been interrupted. It hung in the air, but grew no stronger while Lizzy was otherwise engaged. Good. Now they just had to end her to make it all go away.

Easier said than done.

"You bring me a wolf pup and a..." Lizzy sneered at Bob, sniffing loudly. "Some kind of big cat, is it? With a magic trinket. You can't stop me!" she screamed. "Nobody can stop me." She turned back toward the pit and raised her hands once more. *Dammit.*

"Koma Kulshan will never answer to you, evil one," John called out, stepping forward, though he was careful not to go past Bob's line of defense. Lizzy ignored John—until he started chanting.

Serena felt the power in the native words and the cadence and rhythm of them. She didn't know what they meant, but she understood they acted as some kind of counter to whatever it was Lizzy was trying to accomplish with the mountain. As Serena watched, Lizzy's spell unraveled and fizzled, the woman making a guttural sound of anger and frustration before she turned back toward them.

"I told them Iceland was the better choice," she muttered, clearly so angry, she was more than a little unhinged. "But *no...*" she exaggerated the word. "Some stupid tiger had to mess everything up and then they gave me the honor, but I wasn't ready. I wasn't ready for any of this!"

She seemed sort of pathetic just then, but Serena looked around at the men who were clearly enthralled. Their blank gazes held no knowledge. Their scruffy appearance reminded Serena of everything bad about the Clan, even though it was clear now that there had been magic at work. Evil magic. In the form of Lizzy and those she served—most likely the *Venifucus.*

John continued to chant and the mountain began to quiet

by slow increments. It was still wild. The lava still flowing far beneath them in the caldera, but the jets of steam and gas had quieted down to bubbles instead of geysers. Whatever John was doing was having a good effect.

Lizzy seemed to realize it too, casting her desperate gaze about the massive chamber. She screamed and seemed to pull herself together. She wasn't a young woman, or particularly good looking, but now that it was out in the open, her power was palpable. Serena swallowed the fear response Lizzy so easily invoked and steeled her resolve. She had to stay strong. It looked like Lizzy was losing this battle, but she was still a force to be reckoned with and they had yet to truly defeat her.

Lizzy pointed to one of the bobcats standing in the semicircle and began issuing orders to her minions. "Kill the werewolf," she shouted, and the man—the Alpha of the bobcat Clan—turned to do her bidding. His eyes were blank, but he was still a strong shapeshifter. In fact, he was the biggest and strongest of the bobcats, used to fighting and leading. Though his beast was smaller than the wolf, in human form they were a good match. If they fought on two feet, he would be a challenge, even for the wolf Alpha.

"There's our opening," Serena whispered to Bob, who stood close by her side. The space where the Alpha had been, at the apex of the half circle allowed a straight path through to Lizzy.

John kept chanting even as Lieutenant Joe appeared to intercept the bobcat Alpha. Lizzy ordered more of the bobcats to join the fight and Joe signaled his men to come out of cover. Before long, one side of the cavern had erupted in battle, leaving an even clearer path to Lizzy.

Bob and Serena advanced on the woman—a single unit with a single purpose.

"I can't believe I didn't realize all these years what an evil bitch you are," Serena spoke, her goal to distract Lizzy enough so that Bob could take her down. "I mean, I knew you were a bitch, but I didn't realize you were in league with the *Venifucus*. How low do you have to sink to associate yourself with bottom feeders like them?"

"When I return Elspeth to this realm, I will sit at her right hand and rule over the earth at her side. I'll kill you last, Serena," Lizzy spat. "You've been a thorn in my paw since the day I first spotted you. Why they made me adopt you, I'll never know."

"They?" Now Serena was truly intrigued. "Who made you adopt me? I thought it was your idea."

Lizzy spat at her. "Me? Saddle myself with a brat? I don't think so. I wouldn't have done it if the High Priest hadn't ordered me to. He didn't want you running around on your own. Said with my influence you wouldn't dare interfere in our plans and yet look, here you are, interfering with my plans. You've always been a total pain in my ass, Serena. Well, no more."

Lizzy launched a bolt of power directly at Serena, but Bob and his cross were there, redirecting the energy back at Lizzy. She stumbled as the bolt rebounded, sending her closer to the edge of the pit. She didn't seem to realize how very close she was to falling into the roiling mass of super-heated lava.

"You've always been cruel, Liz. Consider this my termination of adoption. I don't want you in my life anymore. I never did."

Bob stepped closer to her as Lizzy prepared another volley, this one even bigger than the last. Perhaps she thought battering at Bob's shield might eventually break it? Serena thought that was a pretty weak strategy, but Lizzy kept forming her ball of power. It glowed red in her hands and continued to gain in size as Lizzy conjured it.

Doubt crept into Serena's mind, but Bob didn't hesitate. He prowled forward, closing the gap between himself and Lizzy. Serena could see the claws tipping his fingers as his body morphed into the fierce battle form that was the deadliest combination of animal and human. It wasn't easy to hold that form for any length of time, but Bob was an Alpha. He was stronger than most shifters and the way he prowled and stalked Lizzy in that most taxing and deadly of forms proved his strength beyond the shadow of a doubt.

He advanced and Lizzy let loose with the biggest strike yet. It bounced off Bob, like all the rest, rebounding on Lizzy and sending her straight over the edge of the pit this time. Her scream echoed through the rumbling cavern as she plummeted to her death.

Serena and Bob rushed to the ledge, watching her tumble. There was no way to save her. No chance for her to escape her fate. She splashed into the pool of molten rock and disappeared.

The lava and jets of fire boiled up around the place where her body had been for a long moment, before finally subsiding. When Serena looked up, Bob was back to his human form and John was on her other side.

"Koma Kulshan has taken her power into itself," John said over the continuing rumble of the mountain. "She is no more."

"Praise the Lady and Her Light," Bob intoned, reaching out to grasp Serena's hand. The connection between them was strong as they turned to face the ongoing battle.

Joe's guys had been fighting with the six bobcat elders, keeping them from helping Lizzy, but when Serena turned around to look, three of the elders were out cold. One was dead and the other two were just standing there, dazed.

Serena grit her teeth as she realized it was the bobcat Alpha and her adoptive father, Jack, who were still standing. They looked a little worse for wear, having taken more than a few hard hits from the soldiers, but they were still conscious, if a bit confused.

Serena marched right up to Jack and slapped him across the face. When he didn't respond, she subsided, but she had a few choice words to say to him. Dimly, she realized John had started chanting again and the volcano was beginning to simmer down behind them. But it didn't really matter to her. Jack was her focus now and Bob was right behind her, there if she needed him.

"You were supposed to protect me," she accused, pointing

her finger at Jack's chest. "You adopted me and then abused that sacred trust. You're a worm, Jack, and if I never see you again, it'll be too soon."

Jack's response was like nothing she could have predicted. He sank to his knees in front of her and hung his head.

"Forgive me." His voice broke on the words. "I saw what was happening, but I was powerless to prevent it. I didn't want her to adopt you, but she wouldn't be denied. She always did as she pleased and for the past few years, she made me do whatever she wanted regardless of my wishes. I've been weak and you paid the price. I'm sorry, Serena."

Stymied by the apology she had never expected, Serena didn't know what to say. She felt Bob's hands cup her shoulders and she just shook her head. She didn't have words to speak to the man who had beat her up so many times. Could she forgive him? She honestly didn't know. If she did, it would take time. A lot of time.

Serena turned to Bob and gave him a quick hug. "Let's get out of here."

Bob stroked her cheek and nodded, smiling briefly at her. He then looked up to find Lieutenant Joe standing right behind Jack.

"Let's get the bobcats out of here. I'll see if there's anything I can do to help John, but I think the crisis is past now. Unless some other mage shows up out of the blue, we should be done here."

The lieutenant nodded and helped Jack to his feet, treating him more gently now that the spell holding the bobcats had been broken by Lizzy's death. Serena watched as Joe's men took charge of the fallen bobcats and headed toward the passageway.

But before they could get there, an unexpected face appeared coming through the fissure. Jezza had arrived. He was supported by Chico on one side, but as soon as he entered the incredibly hot chamber, he was able to walk forward on his own.

As he walked closer, his injuries began to fade and he

seemed to gain strength with each step.

"How is that happening?" Serena asked aloud.

"The volcano is healing him. I think its power is still linked to him somehow," Bob answered. "I can see a line of energy flowing from the caldera straight into him." Bob seemed stunned and they turned to watch Jezza's progress as he moved toward John, on the rim of the sheer ledge.

If Jezza was going to turn bad, this would be the moment... But no. He simply stood at John's side, breathing in the hot, slightly sulfurous air, gaining strength before their eyes.

Then he stretched out his hands over the edge of the pit and spoke words Serena couldn't hear. She could see his lips moving, but only John was close enough to hear the words. Whatever it was Jezza said, it calmed the volcano. As they watched, the lava's glow went from bright orange to red, and a thick, rocky crust started forming at the edges of the pit, working toward the center as the mountain cooled its temper.

CHAPTER SIXTEEN

Bob had seen the evil magic surrounding Lizzy, thanks to the amazing powers of Father Vincenzo's gift. When all this was over, he'd have to take Serena to Italy and introduce her to him. He would also thank the man personally for the incredible gifts of protection and sight bestowed by the cross he'd given Bob. Without it, he shuddered to think what might have happened on this journey.

The cross allowed him to see the goodness of the Lady's Light shining all around Jezza right now—and to a slightly lesser extent, the werewolf Alpha. Both men were more than capable of calming the mountain and putting things to rights with the power Lizzy had been calling up from the depths of the earth.

Jezza, in particular, seemed more than equal to the challenge, and Bob could still see the tendrils of energy linking him to the mountain. It was a sight to behold for a man who had never been able to see magic the way a few very gifted members of his Clan could.

He had never worn the cross at home, so he had missed out on all the things he might have otherwise picked up on during their encounters with marked *Venifucus* agents. But at least he had taken Father Vincenzo's words to heart when he had gone on trips. Thank the Goddess, he had worn the cross on this particular trip. It had saved his life—and Serena's—more than once.

But seeing magic and being able to use it were two very different things. He could do no more to help the men who dealt with the residual energies Lizzy and her lot had stirred up. No, Bob's part in this task was done. Now he had to concentrate on the aftermath…and his mate.

He turned to Serena and pulled her into his arms for a moment, so thankful that she was whole and healthy. "I love you," he whispered over the low roar of the mountain. It didn't matter if she heard. He just needed to say it out loud.

She reached up and kissed his cheek, his jaw, anyplace she could reach. "I love you too," she breathed against his lips as she joined them in a tender kiss against the backdrop of the smoldering caldera.

But they couldn't stay there. It was unbearably hot, for one thing. Most other beings wouldn't have been able to stand here this long, but shifters had special abilities to withstand things—both magical and mundane—that humans did not. Still, they were pushing the limits of what a shifter could take, even with the cross's power helping to protect them.

When the kiss ended, Bob looked up to realize the soldiers and the bobcats were gone. They had already left through the fissure. It was time to follow them and leave the magic to the other guys.

Getting off the mountain took some time, but eventually they met up with the wolf soldiers on a road just below the old mine entrance. There was a cleared area there where the miners had parked vehicles and buildings had stood once upon a time. Now it was just a scrubby area free of trees for the most part. A good place to regroup.

Some of the soldiers had retrieved Bob's SUV and their own vehicle, plus one they had liberated from the old farmhouse's barn. They would need more seats to accommodate everyone.

Bob went straight to his truck and got bottles of chilled water out of the cooler, passing them around to anyone who wanted them. Serena followed his lead, unloading the compartments of junk food, sandwiches and munchies, passing them out among the soldiers, who shared with the bobcats.

Most of the bobcats were awake now and looking stunned. Bob noticed that Serena kept well clear of her former Clansmen and the soldiers were quite obviously running interference between her and the bobcats. The platoon was protective of her and their small acts of kindness earned Bob's wholehearted gratitude. These guys were solid and he would fight at their side any day of the week.

After they had finished passing out the food and water, Bob took a break, sitting in the comfy front seat of his SUV. Serena was at his side, her head tipped back, eyes closed, as she breathed deeply, finally allowing herself to take a break. She sipped at her water bottle and they just sat for a moment, trying to process everything that had just happened.

Bob knew this idle time couldn't last. He had a duty to inform his brothers what had happened, but for just one moment out of time, he was glad to be alive. He took that thought, savored it, and reached for Serena's hand, loving the feel of her warm grip against his fingers.

"I think it's time to call in," he said finally, opening his eyes to check the time. Scratch that thought. It was way past time to call in.

Reaching toward the controls, he placed the call to Steve, allowing the call to route through the speakers and mic in the car. The soldiers would hear—and so might the bobcats—but there were no secrets in what Bob was going to report to his big brother.

Steve answered on the first ring and Bob could tell from the way he answered that he had been worried.

"We're watching reports of a volcano going nuts," Steve told him. Bob could only laugh tiredly.

"Yeah, that's accurate. The *Venifucus* up here were trying to use the power of the volcano to weaken the veil between realms and bring back Elspeth. They failed. This time. But what I found even more interesting is that the sorceress mentioned Iceland specifically. She said a tiger had messed up their plans to use the volcano there and her leadership had given her the honor instead, only she wasn't really ready."

"Thank the Goddess for small favors," Steve said on the other end of the line. "I've spoken a little more with the tiger king. According to him, his own personal magic is bound to the volcano where he has his stronghold. He seems to think we're going to need something similar if we want to keep the *Venifucus* from trying again up there. We've been tossing around ideas about someone who might have that kind of magic, but it's sort of a tall order with a very specific and obscure skill set."

Bob smiled, though he knew his brother couldn't see his expression. "I think we've already got a good candidate. Maybe two of them. Turns out one of the mages here was draining Jezza's magic into the volcano. When I killed the mage, the magic went back to Jezza and from what I saw, the link is still active. He's up there in the caldera right now, calming things down. And the mountain healed him right before our eyes. The wolf Alpha was at his side, also communing with the mountain. Seems he has native roots and some of the elders in his Pack knew the lore about how they used to communicate with the mountain. John was chanting almost from the moment he entered the caldera chamber and it definitely had a calming effect."

"Well, hot damn," Steve marveled.

"Hot being the operative word," Serena added in an amused tone. Bob looked over at her and they shared a smile.

"Yeah, Steve, we're going to stay here for a little bit, catch our breath and then we'll be back on the road heading home. I'll keep you posted, but it looks like the really bad stuff has been averted for the time being. John will have to sort things out with the bobcat Alpha, but I expect the wolves to be the dominant Pack in the Cascades from now on. The bobcats have some major work to do to make amends and set their Clan to rights. John's a good man and a better Alpha. I think he'll be even-handed with the cats, given half a chance. I'll try to get the lay of the land on that before I leave, but as soon as we're rested and refueled, we're heading south."

"Can't be soon enough for us, brother. You've done some amazing work up there, but it's time you came home. Lindsey has been planning a welcome home-slash-mating reception since she found out you'd claimed your mate. When you get back, there's going to be a big party, but act surprised because according to Lindsey, I wasn't supposed to tell you. However, my mate gave me explicit instructions to warn your mate so she'd have a chance to prepare. According to my lovely Trisha, no woman likes to be caught unprepared when first meeting her mate's family."

"Tell Trisha I think I love her already," Serena piped up from the passenger seat. "And thank you for the advance warning. I definitely owe you both."

"No sweat little sister. Welcome to the family and thanks for what you did up there. I know it can't have been easy, but you were both in the right place at the right time with the right skills and courage to save the world a whole hell of a lot of trouble. If nobody else says it, take it from me, you two did something really good up there tonight. Thank you."

Bob held Serena's gaze and saw that she was a bit choked up at Steve's heartfelt words. He squeezed her hand and answered for them both.

"Just doing the right thing, Steve. That's all."

After a fully healed Jezza came off the mountain with John by his side, Bob finally took his sleepy mate somewhere private where they could rest. They'd all decided to use the old farmhouse once more, just for the night. It was big enough to house everyone and they would put the bobcats in the barn with a few guards, just to be safe.

It would take time to discover exactly how complicit the

individual bobcats might've been in Lizzy's activities. They were being given the benefit of the doubt—to a degree—but the wolves were going to be watching them carefully and questioning them at length before anything would be decided.

Bob was happy enough to leave all that to the wolf Alpha to sort out. It was his territory after all. Bob was just a visitor here.

When they arrived back at the house where the assault had been launched from only hours before, the wolf soldiers set up a watch schedule while Bob took Serena up to the bedroom they had used before. He wanted nothing more than to be alone with his mate.

The master bedroom had an attached bathroom and Serena made a beeline for it, throwing off her dusty clothes as she went. Bob followed along after her, pausing only long enough to lock the door to the hallway. He did not want to be disturbed for anything less than World War Three or the apocalypse. He'd had just about all the excitement of that kind he could take for one night. Now it was time to pursue a different, more intimate, kind of excitement.

Serena was naked by the time he closed the bathroom door and already had the water started. He saw the steam rise shortly after she stepped past the curtain and he hastened to join her.

"What took you so long?" she asked in a weary, yet playful voice when he stepped into the mercifully large shower behind her.

He couldn't answer past the need in every muscle as he took the soap from her hands and created a lather between his fingers. He then stroked those soapy fingers over every inch of her wet body, taking his time, savoring every touch, every inch of her soft, slippery skin.

He needed this. He needed the closeness. The cougar that shared his soul needed the reassurance that his mate was safe, and whole, and with him. Just touching her skin helped calm his inner beast and still the panic that had risen after the action was over and he began to realize just how much danger she had been in.

Even now, his shoulders shook when he realized what they'd escaped tonight on the mountain. What they'd averted. While he'd been in the situation, doing what needed to be done, he was cool and collected, but now? Now he was a desperate man, very aware of the chances they'd taken and the dire consequences that had been only narrowly avoided for both his mate and the world at large.

"It's so strange," she said quietly as they stood under the warm spray of the water together. He'd finished soaping her and now just held her back to his front, his arms around her waist, while the water sluiced over them, rinsing the soap from the front of her body. A moment of peace in a world that had gone completely crazy only hours before.

"What is, kitten?" Bob had been keyed up from the battle, but now that they were safe, the desire to protect his mate was replacing the basic need to fuck her brains out and prove to the cougar once again that she was theirs and would be forever. He could be gentle—especially with his mate, the life partner he was meant to protect with his last breath and cherish all his days.

"So much has happened in just a few hours," she said, her tone contemplative. "Everything has changed for the Cascade Clan. They've lost all their power and the drug trade is seriously hindered by the death of Victor Ramos. I suppose the wolves will take over the Range now. They seem like good people with an honest leader. It's for the best."

Bob turned her in his arms and let the water rinse her back as he used one finger under her chin to coax her head upward so he could meet her gaze. How he loved her. Now, perhaps more than ever. And it nearly stopped his breath to think of the danger he'd allowed her to face that night.

"Never again," he growled.

"What?" Her head tilted adorably to the side as she tried to follow his thinking, which had devolved to the caveman basics of protecting his mate.

He tried again. "I don't ever want you in that kind of

danger again, Serena. I can't take it. The cougar is going nuts thinking about how close we came to disaster tonight."

She lifted her hands to his shoulders, stroking his wet skin with gentle fingers. The cougar began to calm again inside his skin.

"It's okay. We're okay," she whispered, raising up on her tiptoes to place kisses along his jaw. "I promise you, Bob, I'm not an adrenaline junkie by any stretch of the imagination. Tonight was about all the excitement I need for the next century or two. I won't go seeking situations that make your cat crazy." She smiled and reached upward to kiss his lips, taking the kiss deeper with each passing second, her words placating the cougar, her touch, igniting the fire that hadn't been far from the surface in the man.

Both halves of his soul wanted her in every way. Right now, he was still caveman enough to want to take her body, claim it as his, knowing a woman like Serena would never give her body without her heart. The more reasoning part of his mind knew that and reveled in the fact that she loved him as much as he loved her.

They were true mates. Perfect partners. And they would be together for the rest of their very long lives if he had any say in the matter.

He took the kiss deeper, taking control and taking her fully into his arms. He lifted her up and spun her to the side of the stream of watery droplets coming from the showerhead.

The tiled wall was a little chilly against her back at first, but Bob's kiss drove any small discomfort straight out of her mind. She shivered with delight at the hard, fast need she felt rise in her to match his. She loved that she could drive her mate so close to the edge of control. Her inner cat wanted to yowl in pleasure as he joined their bodies with few preliminaries.

But she didn't need any preliminaries. Not this time. Bob and she were attuned to each other in almost every way. Her body felt the same raging need as his, her mind craved their complete union—body and soul. There was no need to wait. Not when two beings were so perfectly aligned.

Regardless, Bob slid home gently, tempering his strength with care for her comfort. How she loved her tender, powerful, warrior. He was everything she ever could have dreamed of in a mate and never dared hope for. He was her every wish come true—even the ones she didn't know she'd made. Somewhere in the heavens, a fairy godmother had waved her magic wand and given Serena the perfect man. The perfect mate.

Fanciful thoughts fled though, when Bob pushed deep, pressing her back against the wet, tiled wall, possessing her completely.

Oh, yeah. She definitely wanted more of *that.*

She clutched his shoulders and hung on for dear life as he began to move, slowly at first and then with the passion that threatened to overwhelm them both. His hips pistoned up into the open V of her thighs, connecting them, joining them, making them one. She trembled as he pushed her against the wall, crushing her body in a way that made her hotter than she'd ever been before.

Her head lolled and then dropped forward, to rest in the crook of his neck. Her mouth opened and she licked his salty skin, wet from the shower and his exertions. She drank the flavor of him down, ratcheting her desire higher. And then, as his thrusting took on a desperate tone, she bit his shoulder and heard him roar.

The copper of his blood touched her mouth. She'd broken skin, but had just enough presence of mind not to cause too much damage. Her inner bobcat had come out to play and caused a slight shift of her teeth and hands. She knew her claws were pressing against the skin of his back as he came hard within her body.

She wasn't far behind. All it took to push her over was his continued thrusts and the feel of his mouth against her neck. His sharp teeth scraped over her pulse and then lowered to the place where her neck joined her shoulder and he returned the mating bite. The very instant his teeth closed over the muscle there, her body spasmed in ecstasy, her cat yowled inside her, the sound drawn from her human throat somewhere between a scream and a roar.

Dear Goddess, her mate knew just how to please her.

Bob held her as she shook with intense waves of pleasure that started where they were joined and rippled through her entire body. He eased the hold of his bite and eventually raised his head to gaze into her eyes.

"You own me, Serena. Heart and soul," he whispered.

Drugged from the pleasure and the sexy, ragged tone of his voice, his words arrowed into her heart and echoed. She felt exactly the same and she wasn't afraid of it. No, her inner cat reveled in his claim of possession and her human half loved him with the same, deep intensity. How could that be scary? It was miraculous. A one-in-a-lifetime kind of occurrence. They had been blessed to find each other and she would never forget how lucky she was to have a man like Bob in her life.

"I love you too," she replied softly, reaching the few inches to kiss him with all the tenderness she was feeling. When she pulled back a moment later, she felt the need to reciprocate. "I'm yours, for life, and into the next realm, for all eternity."

Bob's smile was filled with joy and a little mischief. "It can't get much better than this," he joked. But then, after they'd dried off and headed to the big bed in the other room...it did.

EPILOGUE

By the next day, the mountain had settled into repose, but Jezza had stayed in the caldera chamber. Some of the wolf soldiers had brought him supplies and Joe had spent some time talking to the jaguar about what had happened. Joe gave Bob the basics of the story to report back to his Clan when they returned to Nevada and the bobcat leadership had been returned to their homes, still under guard.

John had spoken to Lewis by phone and the Pack was reported in good shape in the half-built development. Some of the werewolves had even hired on to work with the Redstone Construction crews while they were there, pitching in—with pay—to complete the homes they were living in temporarily, faster.

John left it up to each werewolf family to decide what they wanted to do. Their previous homes in the mountains were mostly destroyed or in need of major repair. Things were safer, though still unsettled. The wolves could choose to go home and rebuild, stay where they were, or come to the bobcat section of the mountain range and help with the clean up. John was very clear on one point—the bobcats would no longer be in sole possession of the northern part of the Cascade mountain range. Wolves would roam anywhere they wanted now that the core of evil had been routed out of the bobcat Clan.

The two older bobcats, Jeremiah and his mate, Betty, returned the next day and Bob and Serena made a point to tell them what had happened and how they had used their home in the emergency. Bob insisted on paying for the food the soldiers had foraged from the old couple's pantry and then some. Jeremiah tried to refuse at first, but it was clear the older couple didn't have a lot of money and could use the funds. Bob added a little extra without saying a word.

Jeremiah got an excited twinkle in his eye when Joe told him how useful his map and the keys had come in. The old bobcat spent an hour talking about how he'd always planned to use the mine as an escape route, if necessary, which was why he'd bought this particular house in the first place. Jeremiah was glad someone had finally gotten to use the secret access to the mine as he'd always intended.

Serena spent time with Betty and talked over a lot of the incidents that had taken place over the years. She was coming to terms with her past and finally was able to put most of it behind her. This adventure had helped her do that and while she doubted she would ever want to return to the Cascades, she was able to leave with a peaceful heart.

Bob drove them into Nevada a couple of days later. After leaving the wolves, they kept on the move, staying away from possible trouble. They kept checking in with Bob's brothers every six hours, as before.

The *Venifucus* attacks around the world had died down for the most part since they had defeated Lizzy and her crew in the caldera chamber, but now the shifter community worldwide was more aware of the ongoing threat. Everybody now knew the scope of the danger was bigger than anyone had guessed.

When the mages at Mount Baker had been defeated, the *Venifucus* besieging the Lords' mountain fell back. Apparently the siege had been solely to keep the Lords from sending anyone up to the volcano, which wasn't really that far from their territory. The consensus opinion was that the *Venifucus* would try something again, now that their many-tentacled plan had been exposed, but nobody knew exactly where they would strike next. The only good thing to come out of this was that almost everyone was now fully aware of the *Venifucus* threat. The world had changed drastically in just a few short days.

Serena had changed on a fundamental level as well. Finding her mate had made her stronger. While Bob completed her, he also gave her wings. He was the perfect man for her, willing to let her lean on him if necessary, but he also propped her up, helping her be more than she had ever been before.

She felt like he had changed as well from when they'd first met. He was happier, a lot calmer, more balanced and surer than he had been. The cougar she had first met by the little stream behind the cabin had been forever changed by finding his mate. She could see it, feel it, knew it in her heart of hearts.

They were both stronger for having discovered each other. And now he was taking her home to meet his family. She was nervous as hell, but she was also secure in the relationship that had been forged in fire and hardened by danger. She and Bob were a team now. They would grow old together, if the Mother of All willed it. The thought made her smile. She'd love to grow old alongside her handsome cougar.

The only doubts she still had were about how his family— a family filled with powerful cougar Alphas and very magical women—would accept a bobcat among them. The fact that two of the brothers weren't mated to shifters at all gave her hope, but bobcats and cougars weren't quite the same. They were both cats at heart, so they did have some things in common, but they weren't exactly the same. She was a little afraid that she'd have to fight for acceptance among the cougar Clan.

Bob said not to worry, but she couldn't help herself. Her last Clan had been a nightmare. The only experience she had with an accepting group of shifters had been at the Lords' mountain, but she knew that was an exceptional place with exceptional people.

They drove into a gorgeous housing development on the very outskirts of Las Vegas, bordered by desert and lots of wild land. Serena recognized it from the descriptions Bob had given her of his family's home. He'd told her that Redstone Construction had built this housing development a few years ago when they moved the headquarters of the company and the Clan to Las Vegas. It was specifically designed for shifters, though humans wouldn't realize it. Only members of the Redstone Clan lived within its confines.

Each of his brothers had built his own place, but the family home was at the center of the community and remained the home of the Alpha pair—the eldest brother, Grif, and his mate, Lindsey. That was their first stop. Bob said he wanted to introduce Serena to the Alpha first, which was only polite, and good protocol when bringing someone new into the Clan's territory. He wanted his brothers to meet her right away, he'd said. His exact words had been that he wanted to *show her off* to them, which was a kind way of putting it. He kept promising her that they were all going to love her as much as he did, but she had her doubts.

She tried to keep her worries to herself, but Bob must've picked up on her mood because he reached across to take her hand, squeezing lightly as they pulled up in front of a lovely, large house. She felt his excitement in the strength of his grip, but she was still anxious.

"We're here." He parked the SUV and shut off the engine. "Come on. You'll see. They're going to love you, I promise."

She sucked in a breath for courage. "If you say so."

He leaned over and kissed her quickly, then let go and climbed out of the SUV. He came around to her side, reaching for her hand again as they walked up to the big house.

The door flew open before they hit the doorstep and a young girl came out, running straight for Bob. He caught her as she launched herself into his arms and swung her around, kissing her cheek.

"Damn, Belinda, you've grown at least two inches since I left." He set her down and Serena realized the youngster was only a half foot shorter than she was and growing fast. "Sweetheart, I want you to meet Serena. She's my mate." Bob turned the younger woman to face Serena.

The girl reached out hesitantly and Serena moved forward to hug her. She understood Belinda's hesitation and her inner bobcat wanted to soothe the younger cat that seemed so unsure of itself. The bobcat wanted to mother the kitten it sensed still inside the girl. Serena had never felt such motherly instincts before, but she trusted her cat's instincts and it seemed to be the right thing to do when Belinda squeezed her tight, accepting her hug of reassurance and welcome.

"Bob's told me all about you, Belinda," Serena said as she let go of the girl. "I think we're going to be like sisters. You and I have a lot in common." Their common points were sad ones, but Serena wouldn't mention it now. In time, she would get to know the girl better and maybe they would be able to talk through some of the traumas in their pasts. This one member of the family, at least, Serena felt immediately comfortable with.

And then she looked up to realize the rest of the family had come out to greet them. Bob was being hugged by three men that had to be his older brothers. One by one, they thumped him on the back, tousled his hair and punched his shoulder, speaking words of welcome and praise for his work up north.

Two women came out from behind the guys and headed straight for Serena and Belinda. A pretty blonde stepped forward, her hand outstretched in welcome and a smile on her face.

"I'm Lindsey, Grif's wife. And you're Serena, right? Excuse the boys," she looked over at the men fondly, then back at Serena. "They've been eager to see their little brother back in one piece."

They shook hands and Serena smiled. "I'm glad he's in one piece too. I wasn't sure we were going to get out of there at all, at a few points along our journey."

Lindsey turned to the second woman and introduced her. "This is Trisha, Steve's wife."

Serena shook hands with the other woman, noting how Lindsey used the human term *wife* instead of the more accurate shifter term, *mate*. She remembered what Bob had told her about Lindsey being a shifter, but having come to it only recently when she had been changed by the Goddess's magic. And Trisha had been raised human, but had some kind of elemental power over water, according to Bob.

"Is it true you're a bobcat?" Belinda asked with a giant smile on her face.

"Yes. My cat form is a lot smaller than yours, I bet." Serena wanted to get that out in the open. She wouldn't be ashamed of who she was. Not with these people. If they didn't like her cat, then Bob had promised her they could go somewhere else, but he'd also been adamant in his belief that they would love her just the way she was. Serena had yet to know for sure.

"Not mine. I'm still small," Belinda answered with an easy grin. "I just think it's funny that my brother ended up with a bobcat mate since we call him Bobcat sometimes. It's like it was meant to be."

Serena was surprised by Belinda's statement. It seemed as if Bob had been right and they didn't mind what kind of shifter she was. Time would tell, but there might be hope yet for this place, and these people.

The women moved toward the group of men and Bob turned, grinning at her. He came over and took her hand, moving to introduce her to his brothers.

Grif was first, as the Alpha, and she lowered her gaze, showing submission, as the bobcat Alpha had always demanded. Grif surprised the heck out of her when he reached out and gave her a hug—the greeting of family, or established Clan. When he let her go from the quick embrace, he smiled at her.

"Thank you for everything you've done for my little brother and our side in this battle. From what I hear, you're one courageous little bobcat and I'm proud to welcome you to the family, Serena."

Stymied by such glowing praise, Serena didn't know what to say as the next brother came forward. The moment he spoke, she recognized his voice from the other end of those many phone calls from the road.

"Welcome to the Clan, Serena," Steve said simply, giving her a quick hug before moving back with a teasing wink.

"I'm Mag," said the third brother, stepping forward to give her a light squeeze. "Sorry my mate couldn't be here, but she's eager to meet you and will see you tonight." This was the brother who was mated to a vampiress. She almost hadn't quite believed it, but she guessed she had to start believing it now—and believing that maybe Bob had been right about the welcome she would receive from his family. It was all a little overwhelming. She felt tears start behind her eyes and did her best to fight them back. She didn't want to appear weak.

"It's so nice to meet you all," she said politely, doing her best to keep her voice even and strong, but she thought maybe Bob realized it was a big act. He put his arm around her waist and stood by her side.

"We want to hear all about your adventure," Belinda said eagerly and though Grif frowned at his little sister, he nodded.

"We're going to have to do a debrief," the Alpha said in serious tones, "but that can wait a bit. For now, we've got food in the kitchen and time for you to relax a bit from your trip. Serena only just got here, munchkin," Grif directed his words toward Belinda. "Give her a few minutes to get her bearings."

The women surrounded them again as they walked into the large house. It was a mansion really, by Serena's standards. She had never seen anything as big or as beautiful...or as welcoming.

Finally, she thought with a fond squeeze of Bob's hand, she might just have found a forever home. Not this house, per se, but among these people—her mate's family. And then she boiled it down to the crux of the matter. Wherever Bob was...that was home.

# # #

ABOUT THE AUTHOR

Bianca D'Arc has run a laboratory, climbed the corporate ladder in the shark-infested streets of lower Manhattan, studied and taught martial arts, and earned the right to put a whole bunch of letters after her name, but she's always enjoyed writing more than any of her other pursuits. She grew up and still lives on Long Island, where she keeps busy with an extensive garden, several aquariums full of very demanding fish, and writing her favorite genres of paranormal, fantasy and sci-fi romance.

Bianca loves to hear from readers and can be reached through Twitter (@BiancaDArc), Facebook (BiancaDArcAuthor) or through the various links on her website.

WELCOME TO THE D'ARC SIDE…
WWW.BIANCADARC.COM

OTHER BOOKS BY BIANCA D'ARC

Now Available

Brotherhood of Blood
One & Only
Rare Vintage
Phantom Desires
Sweeter Than Wine
Forever Valentine
Wolf Hills
Wolf Quest

Tales of the Were
Lords of the Were
Inferno

Tales of the Were – The Others
Rocky
Slade

Tales of the Were – Redstone Clan
Grif
Red
Magnus
Bobcat

String of Fate
Cat's Cradle
King's Throne

Guardians of the Dark
Half Past Dead
Once Bitten, Twice Dead
A Darker Shade of Dead
The Beast Within
Dead Alert

Gifts of the Ancients
Warrior's Heart

Dragon Knights
Maiden Flight
The Dragon Healer
Border Lair
Master at Arms
The Ice Dragon
Prince of Spies
Wings of Change
FireDrake
Dragon Storm
Keeper of the Flame

Resonance Mates
Hara's Legacy
Davin's Quest
Jaci's Experiment
Grady's Awakening
Harry's Sacrifice

Jit'Suku Chronicles
Arcana: King of Swords
Arcana: King of Cups
Arcana: King of Clubs
End of the Line
Sons of Amber: Ezekiel
Sons of Amber: Michael

StarLords: Hidden Talent

Print Anthologies
Ladies of the Lair
I Dream of Dragons Vol. 1
Brotherhood of Blood
Caught by Cupid

OTHER BOOKS BY BIANCA D'ARC

(continued)

Coming Soon

String of Fate #3
Jacob's Ladder
Summer 2014

Tales of the Were - Redstone Clan #5
Matt
Fall 2014

Jit'Suku Chronicles ~ Arcana #4
King of Stars
Winter 2014

KING'S THRONE

A woman living in secret, hiding her true nature...

Gina is a medical doctor in New York City. What nobody knows is that she's also tiger-shifter royalty, living in exile. Keeping her secret has kept her safe, but all that is about to change.

An injured soldier who heals in a way that makes him more than he ever was before...

Mitch is injured and out of the action. He wakes up in a strange place, with a beautiful woman. Normally, not a problem, but this woman is special. She's a white tiger and daughter of the lost tiger king. She's too good for the likes of him, but there's an undeniable spark of attraction drawing them closer and closer.

A love that will make the very earth tremble beneath their feet...

When evil challenges, Mitch will fight to keep Gina safe. A harrowing journey to the side of a living volcano brings secret knowledge and a power none of them ever expected. Will it be enough to prevail?

Only victory will keep his lady safe. And only victory will allow Gina to claim the man she truly loves.

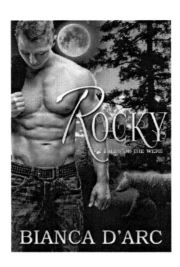

TALES OF THE WERE – THE OTHERS 1
ROCKY

On the run from her husband's killers, there is only one man who can help her now… her Rock.

Maggie is on the run from those who killed her husband nine months ago. She knows the only one who can help her is Rocco, a grizzly shifter she knew in her youth. She arrives on his doorstep in labor with twins. Magical, shapeshifting, bear cub twins destined to lead the next generation of werecreatures in North America.

Rocky cannot deny the attraction that has never waned for the small human woman who stole his heart a long time ago. Rocky absented himself from her life when she chose to marry his childhood friend, but the years haven't changed the way he feels for her.

And now there are two young lives to protect. Rocky will do everything in his power to end the threat to the small family and claim them for himself. He knows he is the perfect Alpha to teach the cubs as they grow into their power… if their mother will let him love her as he has always longed to do.

TALES OF THE WERE – THE OTHERS 2
SLADE

The fate of all shifters rests on his broad shoulders, but all he can think of is her.

Slade is a warrior and spy sent to Nevada to track a brutal murderer before the existence of all shifters is revealed to a world not ready to know.

Kate is a priestess serving the large community of shifters that have gathered around the Redstone cougars. When their matriarch is murdered and the scene polluted by dark magic, she knows she must help the enigmatic man sent to track the killer.

Together, Slade and Kate find not one but two evil mages that they alone can neutralize. Slade finds it hard to keep his hands off his sexy new partner, the cougars are out for blood, and the killers have an even more sinister plan in mind.

Can Kate keep her hands to herself when the most attractive man she's ever met makes her want to throw caution to the wind? And can Slade do his job when he's finally found a woman who can make him purr?

Warning: Contains a bit of sexy ménage action with two smokin' hot men..

TALES OF THE WERE – REDSTONE CLAN 1
GRIF

Griffon is the leader of one of the most influential shifter Clans in North America. He seeks solace in the mountains, away from the horrific events of the past months, for both himself and his young sister. The deaths of their older sister and mother have hit them both very hard.

Lindsey is human, but very aware of the werewolf Pack that lives near her grandfather's old cabin. She's come to right a wrong her grandfather committed against the Pack and salvage what's left of her family's honor—if the wolves will let her. Mostly, they seem intent on running her out of town on a rail.

But Grif, comes to her rescue more than once. He stands up for her against the wolf Pack and then helps her fix the old generator at the cabin. When she performs a ceremony she expects will end in her death, the shifter deity has other ideas. Thrown together by fate, neither of them can deny their deep attraction, but will an old enemy tear them apart?

Warning: Frisky cats get up to all sorts of naughtiness, including a frenzy-induced multi-partner situation that might be a little intense for some readers.

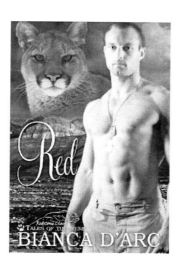

TALES OF THE WERE – REDSTONE CLAN 2
RED

A water nymph and a werecougar meet in a bar fight… No joke.

Steve Redstone agrees to keep an eye on his friend's little sister while she's partying in Las Vegas. He's happy to do the favor for an old Army buddy. What he doesn't expect is the wild woman who heats his blood and attracts too much attention from Others in the area.

Steve ends up defending her honor, breaking his cover and seducing the woman all within hours of meeting her, but he's helpless to resist her. She is his mate and that startling fact is going to open up a whole can of worms with her, her brother and the rest of the Redstone Clan.

TALES OF THE WERE – REDSTONE CLAN 3
MAGNUS

A tortured vampire, a lonely shifter, and a deadly power struggle of supernatural proportions. Can their forbidden love prevail?

Mag is the most reserved of the Redstone brothers, but he has good reason for his loner status. Two years ago, he met a woman who made his inner cougar purr. She was his mate. Too bad the lady had fangs...

Now Mag discovers Miranda being held captive by an evil mage. Mag frees her and takes her to his home, nursing her back to health and defying all to keep her with him.

When a vampire uprising threatens the stability of his Clan, Mag and Miranda are right in the middle of it, fighting against evil. More than just their necks are on the line when a group seeks overthrow the Master vampire of the area. But he and Miranda have powerful allies, and their renewed relationship has made them both stronger than either would ever be alone.

Will they prevail against all odds? Or will the daylight—and their two very different worlds—tear them apart again?

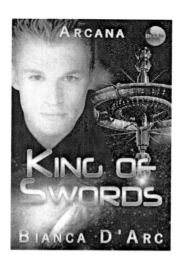

ARCANA, BOOK 1
KING OF SWORDS

David is a newly retired special ops soldier, looking to find his way in an unfamiliar civilian world. His first step is to visit an old friend, the owner of a bar called *The Rabbit Hole* on a distant space station. While there, he meets an intriguing woman who holds the keys to his future.

Adele has a special ability, handed down through her family. Adele can sometimes see the future. She doesn't know exactly why she's been drawn to the space station where her aunt deals cards in a bar that caters to station workers and ex-military. She only knows that she needs to be there. When she meets David, sparks of desire fly between them and she begins to suspect that he is part of the reason she traveled halfway across the galaxy.

Pirates gas the inhabitants of the station while Adele and David are safe inside a transport tube and it's up to them to repel the invaders. Passion flares while they wait for the right moment to overcome the alien threat and retake the station. But what good can one retired soldier and a civilian do against a ship full of alien pirates?

WWW.BIANCADARC.COM

CPSIA information can be obtained at www.ICGtesting.com
Printed in the USA
LVOW07s1446200714

395172LV00001B/131/P